as sure as the as stars

JENNIE K. DROLLINGER

and **TRICIA GOYER**

As Sure As The Stars 2026 by Jennie K. Drollinger and Tricia Goyer
Cover illustration 2026 by Roseanna White
Cover design 2026 by Roseanna White
Interior design & typesetting 2026 by Jamie Foley

Ebook: 979-8-9938057-0-2
Softcover: 979-8-9938057-1-9
Hardback: 979-8-9938057-2-6
Audiobook: 979-8-9938057-3-3

Published in the United States by Jennie K. Drollinger and Tricia Goyer

Printed in the United States of America

DEDICATION

Kelly
Boise, Idaho

IT'S NEARLY VALENTINE'S DAY,

arguably the worst day of the year. Red roses, heart-shaped balloons, boxes of chocolates wrapped in foil. All of it a cruel reminder that true love is a fantasy. Once, I believed in it. I tucked away pieces of hope like folded notes in my pocket. But hope doesn't keep you warm. Coffee does.

The wind nearly ripped the door from my hand as I stepped out of the car. Idaho weather clawed at my coat before I could slam the door shut. I shivered as a February gust bit straight through wool and bone.

Stepping into a puddle, I realized the parking lot was a slurry of gray snow and slush, and my shoes weren't right . . . again. Proof that life was cold, wet, unpredictable. And I was never prepared for any of it. Yet another happy, heart-filled holiday had come, and I told myself I didn't need any of the hoopla. I needed caffeine. I needed warmth. Not another manila envelope filled with legalese and regret.

How had my life become this? Regrets bound in legal jargon. Divorce attorney by trade. And a couple of years ago, divorce survivor by necessity. I wanted to help women not get trampled the way I had been. But I knew the truth that no amount of paperwork could fix: there's nothing in the law books that can heal a heart.

A second chance? Fantasy. And if my clients couldn't find one, maybe at least they wouldn't have to lose everything.

No one from my past could believe that the girl who was everyone's friend now knew the name of every judge in town and how to best present a case before each of them. It had always been this way, me not fitting in. Not as a teenager in Alaska. Not as the college girl who loved a boy so much she would've followed him to the ends of the earth. Except he left without me. And not now as the middle-aged woman who was inching toward fifty, the perennial third wheel to her best friend's perfect marriage.

Amy, bless her heart, still tried to make sure I felt included, thirty-two years after we graduated high school. It was kind. But sometimes reality had to be faced: true love was for some people, not others. My paycheck—and empty left hand—were proof enough.

Coffee. That was all I wanted. Nothing more.

I locked the car with a chirp, shoved my gloved hands into my coat pockets, and tucked my chin against the wind. I was here for caffeine, not comfort. Not connection. Certainly not nostalgia.

And yet my eyes betrayed me. They slid to the drive-thru car line without me even realizing I was looking, as if my subconscious were searching for something my heart didn't believe in.

And then I saw him. Second car from the drive-up window. Black SUV. The driver's side window partly rolled down. My heart lurched so fast it left the rest of me behind.

Jake?

His arm was stretched casually over the steering wheel—easy, relaxed, like he had nowhere to be. Dark hair. Sunglasses. Broad shoulders. That familiar tilt of his jaw.

I froze. Mouth dry. No. It couldn't be. Not here. Not now. But . . . it looked like him.

In a single breath, my pulse surged, fast and hot. My lungs forgot to work. And then came the flood. Tightly guarded memories cracking open like an old photo album shoved off a shelf. The Alaska sky above. My hand in his. Our bodies swaying gently to Madonna's "Crazy for You." A letter arriving with no return address but a simple promise that we'd see each other soon. Thirty-two years of "What happened?"

Jake Forester. My first love. The man who could undo me with a half-smile. I hadn't seen him in decades. And yet, one silhouette—just the possibility of him—and suddenly I was seventeen again. Riding shotgun, the windows down, his hand on the gearshift, and my heart floating as high as the clouds.

We used to dream with the windows rolled down and no map at all, like the world belonged to us. For a flicker of a moment, it was all back. The way he used to say my name, as if it meant something. That stupid, reckless belief that love could outrun real life and somehow win.

The first car pulled away. The SUV rolled forward. Morning sunlight hit the windshield just right—bright, blinding—turning the driver into nothing but silhouette and memory. My pulse betrayed me anyway. The shape of his shoulders. The angle of his arm hooked over the door.

No. It's not him. It can't be him.

He handed the barista a credit card, his head tilting in that familiar half-listening way. Something in my chest tugged, as if it recognized him before my brain would dare risk it.

The man turned toward me, lifting his sunglasses—but the glare caught again, breaking across the lenses, concealing instead of revealing. I saw just enough to doubt myself. Just enough to hope. Just enough to panic at the thought of hoping.

I straightened up, spine stiff, breath shallow.

Don't be ridiculous. People don't reappear at drive-thrus like scenes from the life you almost had. Jake Forester doesn't show up here. He doesn't show up anywhere.

A scoff scraped out of me, too soft to call laughter. Of course it wasn't him. Of course it wasn't.

And still—my hands trembled.

Last I'd heard, he had a wife, a wildly successful smoothie shop and health coaching business, and seven perfect, golden-lit children who probably ate kale chips by choice and got straight

A's in kindness. *La-di-freakin'-da.* A life that made people at high school reunions either adore you or secretly wish you'd trip over the catering table.

I turned away from the drive-up window, opened the coffee shop door, and stepped inside. The bell above the door jingled cheerfully, like it hadn't just witnessed my entire emotional relapse.

Warmth wrapped around me as I crossed the threshold, and the thick, saccharine scent of espresso and caramel hung in the air. I stepped into line behind a woman in yoga pants and a pink fleece. Her ponytail bounced when she walked, like her life had never derailed at all.

When my turn to order came, the barista caught my eye and smiled. "Same as yesterday?"

I nodded. "Same." But nothing felt the same. Not after that five-second nosedive into the past.

I stepped aside to wait, arms crossed tight over my chest. The espresso machine hissed behind the counter. Milk frothed. A lid snapped into place. It was all so ordinary. So painfully familiar. And yet, inside, something had shifted.

Perhaps it was seeing someone who resembled him. Or maybe it was just realizing how quickly the past could break through.

The barista called my name, and I reached for the paper cup. It was warm and familiar, and its white lid was already kissed with steam. I let the heat sink into my palms—something solid to hold while my insides wobbled.

Jake Forester was a chapter I'd closed. Or so I kept telling myself.

Outside, the wind scraped against the windows, relentless and raw, and work was waiting. Motions to file. Cases to argue. This was my life. How?

I lifted my chin and forced a smile as I handed the barista a twenty. "Keep the change," I said, pretending I had my life together. She beamed, and I let myself bask in the glow of her good mood.

Someone needed to have a great day. A great decade. A great life. I was trying. Failing, but trying.

What I wanted wasn't fireworks or movie-scene love. I wanted the quiet kind of love. The Tuesday-morning kind. The "I picked up milk and your favorite chocolate just because" kind.

I used to believe I'd marry young, settle into love like it was a soft blanket. Build a life with a man who didn't flinch when I fell apart. Someone who stayed. Did that even happen? Was it even possible?

In my dreams, there were kids we both adored. A house with a view. Nothing fancy, just space for backyard dinners and late-night strolls. Instead, I spent years trying to make someone love me. Chasing a flicker that always slipped away.

I breathed in. The warm swirl of espresso and caramel used to comfort me, but now it only reminded me how predictable I'd become. Same order. Same distractions. Same ache.

I sipped. The coffee burned the tip of my tongue. At least it proved I could still feel.

I turned toward the door, paper cup in hand, heart heavier than it looked on the outside. Maybe that's why I stopped here in the first place—because coffee shops hold hope in cardboard sleeves. Because for ten minutes, I could pretend I was just a girl with a latte and a quiet morning.

Then the vibration of a text message caught my attention. I pulled my phone from my coat pocket. A glance told me it was Amy, probably wanting to talk about our upcoming class reunion. *Not now. Not today.*

I usually liked receiving texts from Amy. She'd been my best friend since high school. The one who'd seen me in my blue eyeliner and jelly shoes phase and still chose to keep me around. But today, when her name lit up my screen, my stomach twisted. Because today was different.

Out in the parking lot, manila folders sat on the passenger seat of my car, thick with the weight of failed marriages. Case files. Other people's heartbreak. My own divorce? That ink had dried two years ago. The papers were long filed, the dust settled, the future rearranged.

I wasn't heartbroken anymore. Just . . . hollow in places. The love I'd once had for Troy had faded quietly, dissolving into something unremarkable—more distant echo than wound. Not tragic. Not dramatic. Just gone. To emphasize that, I went back to my maiden name.

The phone buzzed again. Thirty-two years since high school. Since I last believed in love. Since him.

No, Jake Forester was dead. Or, at least, dead to me. In my mind, he'd driven off the cliff at Point MacKenzie Bluff in that sleek black car of his, flames licking the night sky as he plummeted into the Knik Arm below. A tragic, cinematic ending. *Yes. Burn, baby, burn.*

Okay, maybe that was dramatic. But honestly? It was easier to imagine him dead than living a happily-ever-after with someone else—especially after my marriage turned out the way it did. Dead was clean. Final. No awkward run-ins at the grocery store. No late-night social scrolling and stumbling on photos of him teaching his adorable, smiling toddler to fish. No wondering if he ever thought of me, or if I'd been filed under "youthful mistake."

The phone buzzed again. Amy was nothing if not persistent.

I sighed, pushing open the door and stepping out into the brutal Idaho wind. I tried to send a voice text, but the wind swallowed my words, twisting them into nothing. Fine. I called.

The second Amy answered, I said, "Amy, I swear if this is about—"

"Oh, no, don't worry." Her voice rushed out too fast, like she was racing to get the words in before I hung up. "You've made it very clear that you don't want me to tell you about Jake."

"You've got that right."

"Yes . . . yeah . . . well, I won't tell you then." Was that disappointment I heard in her voice? Amy exhaled. "Nope, I won't say anything about Jake. Not one detail."

"Okay, what do you want then?"

"Just wanted to know if we can get together next week to talk about Alaska."

Yes, the class reunion.

"Uh, okay, yes. Sure." Hopefully, that would hold her back for a few days.

I yanked open my car door and slid inside, putting my phone into the cradle. The engine roared to life and, as if the universe had a twisted sense of humor, the '80s station blared "Danger Zone." Cute, universe. Real cute.

"I thought maybe we could make a vacation out of it. A real vacation. Maybe even reach out to a few old friends . . ."

I backed up and then slammed on the brakes. My coffee sloshed violently, scorching my wrist. I'd almost hit a soccer mom in a minivan. *Of course.*

From the passenger seat, piles of files filled with divorce papers went flying, scattering across the car like confetti from the saddest party ever.

"Frack," I muttered—because, apparently, I still censored myself like it was 1987 and my mom might be lurking around the corner.

I barely managed to shove my coffee into the cupholder before snapping at my phone again. "Well, which old friends are we talking about? Because you know where I stand."

Amy grew quiet, and suddenly, I knew.

"Ben's listening, isn't he?"

Another beat of silence. Amy cleared her throat. Then a hasty, "I have to go."

And just like that, the line went dead, and the song on the radio switched. "Love Will Lead You Back."

I let out a sharp laugh that tasted bitter on my tongue. "Not today, Taylor Dayne," I muttered, turning the dial. "Not today."

Jake
Boise, Idaho

THE WIND RATTLED AGAINST THE

SUV like it had something to prove. Jake drummed his fingers on the steering wheel, jaw tight, trying to ignore the pulsating knot just behind his right temple. A tension headache, or maybe just life trying to crush him into submission.

His phone buzzed from the passenger seat on top of a stack of folders he'd tried (and failed) to organize earlier this morning. The screen lit up with a new call. He glanced at the name.

Cameron - DO NOT IGNORE

Cam. Of course.

His business partner could sell protein powder to a monk and still miss the point of a conversation. Brilliant with numbers, zero with nuance, and the emotional finesse of a used tire. Jake blew a slow breath through his nose and let the call buzz itself out. He did not have the bandwidth for Cam. Not after yesterday.

Yesterday had been the gut-punch: a process server on his porch and, an hour later, a friend-of-a-friend attorney on speaker, rattling off phrases like "seized assets," "temporary injunction," and "you've got twenty-one days to respond." Worse, she warned him that his wife's team was already attorney shopping, booking "quick consults" with every top family lawyer within a fifty-mile radius just to conflict them out. If he didn't retain someone fast, the best options would be politely "unavailable," and the clock would keep ticking down.

The phone lit again. Cam again.

Jake let it go dark. He opened his notes instead—names of three firms he hadn't called yet, and a fourth circled twice. Time was the enemy now. Not feelings, not history. Twenty-one days. Find counsel before his wife locked the door from the outside. Then he'd deal with Cam, with the accounts, with everything else that was crumbling. One call at a time.

Buzz. A text lit up the screen.

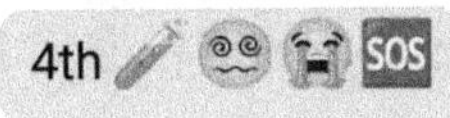

Rae

Jake snorted despite himself. His daughter was a master at digital manipulation. The emoji count alone was enough to warrant suspicion, but he typed back quickly anyway.

Dying, huh? What period is the test you're trying to miss?

Rad-Dad

The reply came almost instantly.

4th

Rae

Jake grinned, despite the mess that was currently his life.

OK, I'll check you out at lunch. You can take the test tomorrow.

Rad-Dad

A flood of heart hands and rainbow emojis burst across the screen. He shook his head and tucked the phone into the console, his grin softening into something quieter, more reverent. If he did one thing right in his life, it was her. Rae. Well, all his kids.

Buzz. Another message.

Call me when you can. It's about Mom.

Emily G.

Jake's smile faltered. His sister never texted cryptic messages. If it was about Mom . . . he already knew. They'd known the cancer was back, but they hadn't expected the doctor to use the words *aggressive* and *no guarantees*.

The line inched forward, but Jake didn't notice. His gaze had shifted to the parking lot. A woman was standing next to an Audi. He squinted. Shoulder-length hair tucked under a knit beanie. Gray coat. Arms crossed like she was bracing herself against more than just the chill. She tilted her head toward the drive-thru, just slightly, and—

His heart hiccuped.

Could it be? He blinked, leaned forward just a little, just enough to catch the profile again. No. It couldn't be. Not here.

But it looked like Kelly. *His* Kelly.

Before he could convince himself otherwise, a horn blared behind him—long, impatient, jarring.

He jolted. The barista at the window held out his coffee with a confused, slightly annoyed expression, paper cup poised like a white flag of surrender.

Jake rolled down the window. He handed her his credit card and waited. The wind slapped him in the face, icy and immediate. He reached for the card and his drink, muttered a distracted, "Thanks," and rolled the window back up.

But his eyes moved back to the parking lot. The woman next to the Audi was gone. He exhaled, breath fogging the inside of the windshield.

"Get a grip," he muttered to himself, pulling forward and into the parking lot. But his grip was already slipping—on his business, on his family, on his sense of stability.

And now? Now the ghost of Kelly Richardson might be slipping through town in a gray coat and a memory, sending his heart scrambling like he was still eighteen.

He set the coffee in the cupholder and let his hands rest on the steering wheel, just for a moment.

Jake Forester—nearly divorced, emotionally underwater, and former personal trainer turned health coach—had not signed up for this today.

And yet, here he was. Sitting in a Starbucks parking lot. With a coffee that tasted like nostalgia and a life he didn't recognize anymore. For the slightest flicker of a breath, he let himself imagine that it really had been her. Kelly. And if it was? God help him.

Kelly
Eagle River, Alaska
October 1985

I felt like a neon sign in a world of flannel. Standing in the hallway at Eagle River High, I could smell the floor wax and something sharper. Teenage nerves, maybe, or just the cold clinging to everyone's coats.

My jean miniskirt hugged my hips just right, and my off-the-shoulder sweatshirt showed enough collarbone to feel like a small act of rebellion. I'd spent almost an hour curling my bangs into a perfect wave, shellacking them into place, and stacking my hot-pink jelly bracelets on my wrist like armor.

But now? Now, I just felt ridiculous.

No one else looked like me. These girls wore parkas and hiking boots, their hair still damp from the morning frost. I tightened the strap of my sparkly purse and took a breath, letting the sweet, familiar smell of strawberry lip gloss steady me.

Moving from sunny Arizona to this backwoods, frozen edge of Alaska with my parents and seven younger siblings was something I never could have imagined. Worse, it was almost two months after everyone else had started, because my dad had a job change at the most inconvenient time.

I missed the mall and streetlights that didn't flicker. I missed the sound of skateboards rattling over pavement instead of wood-splitting machines whining in the distance. Living off a generator at the edge of town wasn't the teenage dream I'd pictured for my junior year. But today, I could pretend.

I'd pretend I fit in. Pretend I wasn't just the new girl whose dad was the new administrator, after the first one had a medical emergency and had to retire early. The new girl whose family stuck out everywhere we went.

My skin prickled beneath my oversized Esprit sweatshirt. I smoothed my hands over my skirt, feeling the scratchy denim. All I wanted was one good thing. Just one spark. Someone to talk to, a friend. Maybe even a boy who'd make me feel seen instead of invisible.

As if the universe decided to throw me a line, I heard footsteps—light, quick. I turned around, and a girl with the kindest eyes and a wild halo of brown curls bounced up next to me. She smelled like wintergreen gum and something sweet, like she'd just come from baking my favorite chocolate chip cookies that I'd learned to make in Home Ec back at my old high school.

"Locker 147?" she asked, tilting her head so her curls swung. "That's right next to me. I'm Amy."

I nodded, feeling the knot in my throat loosen just a little. "I'm Kelly. It's my first day . . . on a Friday. I know, lame."

Amy's cheeks were flushed pink from the cold, and she eyed me up and down. Then she smiled. "Are those jelly shoes?"

I looked down, heat rising up my neck. The shoes sparkled clear and glittery. So Arizona, so not Alaska. "Yeah. Too much?"

"Too perfect." Her grin was so genuine I almost believed her. "If Madonna and Cyndi Lauper had a baby, it'd be you. I mean that in the best way."

A laugh bubbled out of me, echoing off the rows of lockers. The tension in my shoulders melted, replaced by something fizzy and hopeful. "You're the first nice person I've met today."

And, for a second, the hallway didn't feel quite so cold.

"Give it time. Most people here are just thawing out."

The hallway lights buzzed overhead. They were a harsh yellow that made everything feel both too sharp and a little unreal. Yet Amy's voice curled around me like a blanket. It warmed me against the chill that seemed to seep through my sweatshirt. I liked her smile and the way she didn't seem to care that my shoes looked like they belonged on another planet.

"So . . ." I ventured, lowering my voice, "do cute guys exist in Alaska? Or is it just moose and bushmen?" I lifted one eyebrow. "I heard the neighbor talking to my mom. She said they come out once a year for Fur Rondy in Anchorage. Bushmen everywhere looking for a wife."

Amy's eyes sparkled with mischief. "Both," she whispered. "But I've got you covered. There's a school dance tonight. Come with me."

My heart stuttered in my chest. "A dance? Like, tonight tonight?" My voice sounded small, even to me. I pictured my parents' battered Suburban idling in the school parking lot and the smell of old coffee and French fries forever clinging to the upholstery. I pictured my siblings fighting over the radio, my mom humming off-key. A dance felt like another universe.

Amy nodded, curls bouncing. "Ben—my not-so-secret crush—is going to be there. And he'll be hanging out with his best friend, Jake. Tall. Quiet. Ridiculously good hair. You'll love him."

A dance. My palms went clammy, my stomach twisting with something that was equal parts dread and hope. I could almost hear the thump of a bass line, the swirl of perfume and sweat. My skin buzzed with nerves, but underneath it all, there was a flicker of excitement.

"Okay," I said, my voice barely above a whisper. "I'll go."

Amy grinned like she'd just won something. "Meet me here

after seventh period, and we'll make a plan for later. I'll make sure you don't chicken out."

Her hand brushed my arm—light, reassuring. It grounded me. The bell rang. Lockers slammed, voices rose and fell, the rush of bodies and possibility swirling around me. I could taste the metallic tang of nerves on my tongue, feel the thud of hope in my chest.

For the first time since moving to Alaska last week, I felt a tiny, stubborn bloom of belonging. Maybe just tonight, I could be someone new. Maybe just tonight, I could say yes.

Kelly
Boise, Idaho

I SHOULD HAVE KNOWN AMY WAS

up to something. She didn't call yesterday or the day before, which is very unlike her. And that silence? That was louder than any voicemail or double-text.

When Amy doesn't call, it means one thing: she and Ben are plotting. Whispering behind cupped hands like we're still in high school. Of course, I'm the clueless one who doesn't realize her locker's been filled with shaving cream until second period. Only now, the pranks involve real lives and real heartbreak. And the occasional attempt to resurrect ghosts of boyfriends past.

Amy and Ben had been trying to plan our high school reunion for months. MONTHS. They claimed anyone—even from other years—could come and it was "just a casual get-together reunion," as if the words "casual" and "reunion" even belonged in the same sentence. But I knew better. I'd made every excuse under the sun not to get involved. Too much work. Too little time. Boise traffic. But really? They both knew.

There was just one "old friend" I couldn't bring myself to reconnect with. One name that turned my stomach into a tumble dryer. *Jake Forester.*

Seeing that guy in the drive-thru, or someone who looked exactly like him—same jawline, same too-cool-for-real-life sunglasses—had hit me harder than I wanted to admit. I hadn't expected the flood of emotions. The way my lungs had forgotten how to work. The way my pulse had ricocheted through me.

It had taken everything in me not to text Amy that night. Not to ask, "Hey, do you know if Jake's in town?" Not to care.

But, of course, I cared. And Amy? She knew it.

My speaker chirped to life on the dresser, and "Good Time Good Life" by Erin Bowman burst into the room—bright, fizzy, all pep and confetti. The cheerfulness felt almost rude against the knot in my chest. I turned it down and let the beat thrum under my ribs like a dare.

Next, I wedged myself between a rolling rack of blazers and a stack of boxes still labeled *Master Closet (Maybe?)*, hunting for a pair of heels that weren't scuffed, pinched, or from the Bush administration. The song tried to sell me sunshine. I was busy trying to find my footing.

My place was charming, sure, but "cozy" was real-estate speak for barely enough room to breathe, especially when your wardrobe took up more square footage than your kitchen. Every closet was packed to the gills—clothes, shoes, handbags—all crammed in like passengers on an overbooked flight. I opened a closet door and a cascade of scarves and belts practically attacked me.

"Good morning to me," I muttered, batting away a stray sequin. Getting dressed in this house was a contact sport.

I finally settled on a black sheath dress that still mostly fit, a pair of hoop earrings I hadn't seen since Obama's first term, and the pink pumps that matched almost nothing but got the job done.

I wrestled my way into my pumps, one hand bracing against the hall wall while my heel caught on a moving box labeled *Kitchen Stuff I Might Never Unpack*. There were still too many of those. Boxes I hadn't opened, a new life I hadn't fully stepped into.

Today I had three client meetings, a mediation case, and zero emotional bandwidth for surprise Jake content.

But let's be honest, I hadn't stopped thinking about him. I tried to push him out of my mind while sidestepping a tower of unopened boxes, all of them labeled *Shoes.* I grabbed my case files, tossed them into my oversized leather tote, and stepped into the kitchen/laundry, where the scent of lavender dryer sheets and unspoken grief still lingered from my most recent emotional spiral.

Apparently, I do laundry when I'm sad. Some women run to the grocery store for Ben & Jerry's. I toss in a load of towels and pretend the smell of fabric softener can wipe away heartache. Folding things feels productive, even when my life isn't.

The galley kitchen was a wreck of unopened mail, half-washed dishes, and a rogue pair of reading glasses. I grabbed my coffee from the maker and poured it into the to-go cup like I had every ounce of my life under control. I didn't. Not even close. One sip later, and I burned my tongue. Naturally.

Outside the tall window, Boise was already showing off, sun sparkling like a diamond ring on a first date, mountains gleaming like they'd been watercolored into the skyline. I pressed speed dial, juggling my coffee, my bag, and my last sliver of patience.

Janie, my paralegal, answered.

"Tell Mr. Gaines we're not moving forward with mediation until he coughs up every last tax return from the past five years," I barked, twisting the lid on my travel mug until it clicked.

On the other end, Janie's voice came in tinny and way too calm for this hour. "Kelly, he says his finances are irrelevant to the alimony discussion."

I stopped mid-stride, one heel-click away from the door, and turned slowly toward the fridge. "Irrelevant?" I repeated, deadpan. My eyes locked on the Sedona postcard, faded at the corners but still defiant in its optimism.

Next to it, that photo. *Me.* Hair wild from desert wind, eyes squinting in a way that wasn't just sunlight. That woman still believed boldness could change everything. I'd nearly forgotten what she looked like.

Janie sighed on the line. "I told him that's not how this works, but he's not budging. He says we're being—his word, not mine—*combative.*"

I exhaled through my nose. "Okay, then tell him he shouldn't have been messing around with his tennis instructor."

There was a pause. Then a quiet, choked-off chuckle from Janie. "You want me to say that verbatim?"

I opened the door. "Yes. Verbatim. Actions have consequences. Shocking, I know. Never mind, I'm happy to tell him myself."

Janie snorted. "Living the dream, aren't we?" She hung up before I had time to respond.

Outside, the creaky porch steps groaned under my heels as I clattered toward the car. Sunlight warmed my back. For a brief second, I let myself breathe.

Another buzz. My phone screen lit up.

Def Leppard's Coming to Boise! Get Your Tix Now!

I froze mid-step, coffee halfway to my lips. My heart did that annoying thing it does when nostalgia punches you in the face.

"Oh, boys," I murmured, clicking on the graphic. There they were. My adolescent rock gods, in all their denim glory. "I'd be there if I could," I whispered, half to the screen, half to the seventeen-year-old me who would have sold a kidney for front row seats.

The band glared back like they knew. Like they were silently judging me for swapping out concerts for courtrooms.

"Don't look at me like that," I muttered. "A girl doesn't make partner by chasing encore sets and reliving high school heartbreaks."

I reached out and gently touched the screen. "I promise I still love you." Then I continued to my car.

The neighborhood was cute. Older. Tree-lined. It was a neighborhood where couples jogged together in matching windbreakers, waving at neighbors whose names they actually remembered. I hated how much I wanted to belong here.

With a sigh, I slid behind the wheel of my aging Audi. The front passenger seat was still littered with receipts, reusable totes, and the Sephora bag I'd forgotten to take into the house from the day before. Nothing says "coping" like overpriced concealer and a new lipstick I'll probably never wear. Fortunately, the stores had dared to close before I could cause any real damage, so I'd resorted to laundry instead.

The engine sputtered, coughed once, and then roared to life. I exhaled, relief pouring through me like a wave of grace. Then the radio kicked in.

"This is the good life . . ." a chipper pop voice sang, as if she'd never known heartbreak or IRS audits. I jabbed the buttons until something familiar clicked through. Duran Duran. "Come Undone."

Perfect.

I pulled onto the main road and straight into the one thing more persistent than Amy—Boise traffic.

"Come on," I groaned, tapping the steering wheel with increasing agitation. "Court in ten minutes. Can we please move?"

No one did. My phone rang.

"Hello?" I snapped, willing the traffic to budge.

"This is Elise from Mitchell & Hartman," the voice on the other end said too cheerfully. "I'm calling to set up a time for mediation."

"Not going to happen," I spouted. "We need clarification on Mr. Gaines's tax history." I rolled my eyes, even though I was aware she couldn't witness my dramatic flair. "Tell Mr. Gaines that until he turns over all five years of financial records, mediation is off the table. And also tell him—" I paused, dabbing at my lap with a stained napkin—"if he didn't want his affair with a tennis instructor on the record, he probably shouldn't have written her name on a joint credit card statement."

I hung up. And laughed. One of those dry, tight-throated laughs that carries a tiny trace of bitterness. It wasn't just the case. It was the irony. The lies. The entitled husband ducking responsibility like it was optional. It hit too close to home. Too much like Troy—charming in public, careless in private, and always two steps ahead when it came to covering his tracks.

No wonder I was tired. I pressed back against the seat and

looked up, past the grime on my windshield, past the power lines crisscrossing the Boise sky. "Could this day get any worse?"

Apparently, God has a sense of humor—and impeccable timing.

"And now, by popular request . . . 'Saving All My Love for You' by Whitney Houston."

The voice of the radio DJ was smooth and chipper, utterly unaware that he'd just punched a hole straight through my chest. The opening notes trickled through the speakers. Soft, haunting. Familiar. Too familiar. That song. That *stupid, beautiful* song.

Jake's black car. A summer night. My bare feet on the dash. His voice singing off-key. We'd played this song on repeat that summer, like the world would stop spinning if we dared to press skip.

I exhaled, slow and bitter, and glanced up again—this time at the car's ceiling.

"That was rhetorical," I muttered, flipping the radio off with a little more force than necessary.

The silence hit harder than the music ever could. *God.* Had I just been talking to God? He was there, I knew, but sometimes I didn't understand how He fit in this new life I felt squished into. I loved Him, but the hurt was too much at times. Did God answer some girls' prayers and not others? How many times had I prayed I'd find Jake? Or he'd find me? And later, that I'd find a way for Troy to love me? None of those things had come true.

Now, my faith seemed as unsteady as my quickened steps in wobbly heels. If I drew close to God, I'd have to face the fact that He'd heard every one of my desperate pleas and answered with a *No.*

Wiping away a stray tear, I turned past the courthouse and into the parking garage. My heart hadn't quite stopped racing. The song lingered in the air like a perfume I hadn't worn in years but somehow still remembered.

I dared to whisper a prayer that I wasn't the only one

running late. I parked the car and then rushed through the front doors of the courthouse. My heels clicked against the tile like they were trying to call attention to my tardiness.

Mrs. Davis sat alone on the bench, arms crossed over her chest, shoulders curled inward. She looked like a woman who still baked banana bread for neighbors and sent handwritten birthday cards to nieces and nephews she rarely saw. One who once believed in fairy tales—who thought love would always be enough. But now, with her dreams unraveling thread by thread, she wasn't holding on to a storybook ending anymore. From our conversations, I knew she was holding on to God. Quietly. Desperately. Like a lifeline. Like the only real thing left when everything else had floated away.

Across from her, Mr. Davis scrolled his phone like this was just another errand to check off. His suit was sharp. His tie straight. His face blank.

His lawyer—Reed, I think—stood when I approached.

"I'm so sorry," I began, breathless. "Traffic was—"

"The judge rescheduled," he said. Calm. Cold. "You missed your window."

"What? I'm only six minutes late."

He gave me a look I'd seen before—pity dressed as professionalism.

"I don't know what's going on in your personal life," he said, tone measured, "but I'd suggest you pull it together. For your client's sake. And mine. They both want this over and done with."

My jaw dropped, but I couldn't argue. Instead, I turned to my client.

Mrs. Davis said nothing. She didn't look up. She just kept staring at the tile floor, as if it might rearrange itself into a different ending.

Then Mr. Davis's phone rang. "Hey, baby," he said smoothly, stepping away from us without even a glance. "No, not done yet. The judge pushed it. Go ahead and book the church anyway."

I closed my eyes for a beat. Counted to three. Opened them again.

I sat down beside Mrs. Davis, folders sliding off my lap. I quickly picked them up and tucked them back inside my bag. "I'm so sorry."

She nodded once, lips pressed tight. But then she spoke—soft, almost inaudible.

"It's not true, you know." She blinked fast. "I don't want this 'over and done with.' I want my husband back."

We both looked at him, still whispering sweet nothings to someone else on the phone. And I felt it then. A sharp, quiet ache. Because I knew exactly what it was like to want someone who'd already moved on. To sit in the wreckage of something you built, while the other person started over without even looking back.

I rested my hand gently on hers. She didn't pull away. And at that moment, I wasn't her lawyer. I was just another woman with a bruised heart, trying to make sense of someone else's leaving. First Jake, then Troy.

I used to imagine Jake coming back. I used to want him to show up at my door in the kind of reunion that only exists in movies. I wanted him to say he never stopped trying to find me. That he never stopped loving me.

I don't imagine that anymore.

Usually.

Except today.

Because last night, Amy hadn't called. Which meant she was *definitely* scheming. Which meant . . . Jake Forester was probably on her radar. And I didn't know whether to brace for heartbreak or run for cover.

Amy
Boise, Idaho

Amy stood at the stove in Ben's ratty Broncos hoodie, scrambling eggs with a wooden spoon, her phone face down on a pile of reunion to-do lists. "Class of '88—Back to the '80s Casual Catch-Up," her foot. They'd been herding cats for months, and there was still one cat keeping her at arm's length.

Ben's cell buzzed again on the island. He didn't even look.

He just sighed, thumbed it, and wandered into the living room with a weary, "Hey, man," like he'd answered this exact call four times today already. Which he had.

Amy killed the burner and leaned in the doorway, spoon poised in midair, listening to the half of the conversation she could hear.

"Okay. Breathe," Ben said, pacing the rug in socks, one hand scrubbing his jaw. He had a coach voice—calm, immovable, pitched low like he was in a huddle. He nodded at whatever poured through the speaker, then pinched the bridge of his nose. "One thing at a time. Let's worry about who's staying at the condo with Nicole later. Right now? Sleep. And—no, seriously—food."

Noticing her interest, Ben switched to speaker mode.

On speaker, Jake sounded like a ghost of himself—thin voice, words clipped and tumbling. Amy's heart pinched. Divorce took everything and then asked for more. Ben glanced over and gave her the tiniest prayer-hands.

"They served me yesterday," Jake said, breathless, as if he were talking while running up stairs. "I've got twenty-one days to respond. And her team's already booking consultations all over town—just to tie everyone up. I can't even get a callback."

Twenty-one days? Amy's fingers tightened on the wooden spoon. The skillet ticked itself cool on the stove. The house gave a soft settling creak.

Ben didn't rush in. He dropped onto the arm of the couch, elbows on his knees, and let the silence breathe. He and Amy had been married long enough that whole conversations fit inside a look. When he glanced her way, she could read the plan in the lift of his brow. She gave the slightest nod.

"Okay," Ben said at last, voice even. "So you need counsel fast. Someone you can trust. Do you know anyone?"

A beat. Paper rustled on Jake's end. "No. I don't even know where to start."

Ben hummed, considering, as if the idea were arriving for the first time. "You could call Kelly."

A sharp inhale crackled through the speaker. "Kelly . . . like Kelly from high school? Why would I call her?"

Ben kept his tone easy. "She works at a law office in town, and she knows the landscape. She can point you in the right direction—what to do first, who's legit, who to avoid. And she won't let you spin." He let that sit, then softened the landing. "Ask her for a referral. One call."

On the line, Jake went quiet. Amy could hear him thinking.

"I don't want to blindside her," Jake said finally.

"Good," Ben replied. "I won't give you her number unless she says yes. Let me check with Amy, and if Kelly's open to it, I'll connect you. You keep breathing. You make a list of who you've called. We'll move the ball one yard at a time."

Ben didn't oversell it. He didn't push. He just left the door open, letting Jake decide whether to walk through. Amy smiled, impressed all over again by the way her husband could make a rescue feel like a choice.

They wrapped up the call with a plan and a joke only boys who'd once shared a locker room would find funny. Ben hung up, rolled his shoulders like he was shaking off a game, and wandered into the kitchen. Then he snagged a clump of scrambled eggs straight from the pan. Ben yelped when it burned his fingers, then popped it into his mouth anyway.

"So?" Amy asked.

"He's at a hard simmer," Ben said around a mouthful.

"Classic." Amy set the spoon in the rest. "But we won't play switchboard. If Kelly's in, they talk. If she's not, we draw a line and hold it."

"Agreed." He nodded toward her phone.

She unlocked it. Kelly's contact photo on her phone was a photo from a recent trip. The desert wind was in her hair. Sunlight narrowed her eyes. It was the look she got when she was equal parts brave and breakable.

Before reaching out, Amy pulled a sticky note from the pad and wrote fast, in all caps, the way she did when she needed to keep her own heart in line.

CHECK IN FIRST (NO AMBUSH).
ASK IF OK TO SHARE NUMBER.
NO MEMORY LANE.
BOUNDARIES: NOT HER CASE. FRIEND ONLY.
REMIND HER SHE CAN SAY NO.

Ben leaned over her shoulder, read, and tapped the last line. "That one twice."

"Twice," she echoed, underlining it. She set the note where she couldn't ignore it, right beside the reunion spreadsheet and a grocery list that just said coffee, basil, and cheese.

"Hey," Ben said softly. She looked up. He was watching her with that expression that still made her feel seventeen. He hooked a finger in the pocket of the hoodie, tugged her closer, and kissed her forehead. "We're good at this. You're good at this."

"At meddling?" she teased, smiling despite herself.

"At loving people without making their decisions for them," he said. "Big difference."

She let that settle in her chest.

"All right." Amy exhaled and shook out her hands like she was stepping to a free-throw line. "I'll prime the pump."

Ben did a microscopic fist pump and immediately tried to make it look like stretching. She rolled her eyes and tapped Kelly's name.

The ring trilled once, twice. Amy cleared her throat nervously, and when Kelly picked up, she was ready.

"Hey, you. Guess who Ben just talked to?"

Kelly
Eagle River, Alaska
October 1985

THE SCHOOL GYM PULSED WITH

bass-heavy music and the unmistakable scent of Aqua Net, rubber soles, and over-salted popcorn. Not to mention the guys' colognes—whiffs of Obsession, Drakkar Noir, and Polo all over the gym.

Streamers sagged from the basketball hoops, and a glittering disco ball spun from the rafters, trying its best to hypnotize someone—anyone—into having a good time. It almost worked. Add in the faint tang of teenage sweat and waxed floors, and it was exactly what you'd expect from a small-town high school dance.

For the first time since moving to Alaska last week, I tried to pretend I didn't hate it. I still didn't love it, but things were better—or at least, less terrible. I'd met Amy today, and she somehow made this place feel a little less lonely.

Now, I found myself shifting from foot to foot, scanning the crowd and looking for Ben's friend Jake. I watched the doors every time they opened, pretending not to care, even as my heart rattled in my chest. The thing was, I had no idea what he looked like. Tall, nice hair—that's all Amy had said. For some reason, I hoped he *was* cute. Maybe I'd like him, and he'd like me back.

Maybe then I wouldn't feel as if my life was over. I mean, it was mostly over since I'd been cast to the far edge of the world, the place where the local stores sold Carhartt jackets instead of *Vogue*.

For a moment, under the spinning lights and the smell of popcorn and hairspray, I hoped I might be okay right here. I nibbled at my fingernail, watching Ben and Amy dance.

They were totally into each other, and they acted as if they were the only ones in this place. Ben snuck Amy a kiss when he thought no one was looking. Of course, I caught it.

As I stood there, I wasn't even worried that the dance was five songs in and no one had even approached to ask my name. Strangely, I was waiting for Ben's mystery friend. And I wondered if, maybe—just maybe—I could have something like Amy and Ben had too.

✦ ✦ ✦

Jake
Boise, Idaho

Morning light filtered through the blinds in long, narrow stripes. They cut across the hardwood like bars. Not harsh, but confining. Dust hung in the air, spinning slowly through golden sunbeams.

Jake lay on his back, staring at the ceiling as if it might finally offer answers. With his right hand, he slid his wedding band rhythmically between his thumb and forefinger. Up. Down. Up. Down. A habit that felt like muscle memory. Or penance. Or both.

He hadn't slept well. Again. Too much thinking. Not enough forgetting.

Beside him, a barrier of throw pillows divided the bed like a demilitarized zone. Nicole's side remained perfectly made—edges tucked, blankets smooth.

She hadn't stayed here in their mansion in a while, but she

hadn't taken her things either. And that in-between space? It was beginning to feel more punishing than a clean break.

Across the room, his old guitar leaned in the corner, half-forgotten. Dust rested along the fretboard. One string hung loose, arched like a question mark. It hadn't been played in months. Not since Nicole had stopped sitting across from him with her wine glass, mouthing the lyrics like she used to when she still looked at him like he mattered.

He used to play every night—after dinner, before the house dimmed down and the noise dissolved into bedtime routines. Now, the sight of the instrument made his chest ache. Like touching it would confirm that too much had changed. Like playing would break whatever fragile thread was still holding his family together.

He exhaled, realizing the bedroom was too still. Even the ticking clock on the wall felt accusatory. His phone buzzed on the nightstand, and the screen lit up.

> Great convo. Amy will let you know what Kelly says.
>
> Ben

Jake stared at the message. The words sat there, blinking in the blue-white glow. He didn't have time to ponder what Kelly would think. A soft knock—more of a warning than a request—sounded at the door. It swung open before he could respond.

Chris, his fifteen-year-old son and resident teenage critic, leaned against the frame, one eyebrow cocked, with his backpack slung over one shoulder, as if he belonged in a music video, not in Algebra II.

"Dad. Seriously?"

Jake sat up slowly, bracing himself on the edge of the bed. "What?"

Chris gestured broadly to the still-pristine half of the bed. "Mom hasn't been here in, what, months? And you're still sleeping like she's just in the bathroom?"

Jake scratched the back of his neck, suddenly aware of how cold the room felt despite the setting on the thermostat. "Old habits die hard."

He reached for the Henley tossed over the foot of the bed and pulled it on. His hair was tousled, but he didn't bother smoothing it. If there was one thing divorce did, it lowered your standards for presentation before 8 a.m.

"Time for school already?"

Chris gave him a look that said *Duh* in three different languages.

Right on cue, chaos erupted. A thundering of feet. Squeals. Shouts. And suddenly, the bedroom was wall-to-wall kids.

Rae, seventeen and too effortlessly beautiful for his peace of mind, stood behind Chris, arms crossed and phone in hand. Sadie, twelve and fiercely observant, leaned in the doorway with a knowing smirk. But the younger four? They launched themselves like cannonballs.

"Get up! Get up!" Becca shouted as she flung her eight-year-old self onto the mattress.

Tyler, ten, clambered across Jake's legs, nearly taking a pillow hostage in the process. "You promised we'd get donuts today!"

"I did?" Jake laughed, catching Lily and Leo—the six-year-old twins—as they catapulted into his arms like caffeinated squirrels. "Well, that doesn't sound like something a responsible father would say."

Lily grinned, showing a missing front tooth. "You said it in your sleep!"

"Convenient," he muttered, but he couldn't stop smiling.

He forced himself to shake off the lingering morning weight. The grief, the ring, the empty space on the other side of the bed. Instead, he leaned into the dogpile of children with full, exaggerated tickles. Laughter erupted like confetti.

"I'm up! I'm up! You maniacs win!"

"Victory!" shouted Tyler as he leaped off the bed in triumph.

Jake tossed his keys at Chris. "You're driving."

Chris caught them midair, eyes narrowing. "You're not seriously coming like that, are you?"

Jake looked down at his sweatpants and mismatched socks. "What, this? This is vintage fatherhood. I'm trending."

"No one says 'trending,' Dad."

"I knew that." He stepped toward the hallway, arms raised in mock swagger. "Alexa, play '80s hits."

"Playing: 'Oh Sheila' by Ready for the World."

The beat kicked in, and so did Jake's half-awake, entirely embarrassing dad dance. He spun once, snapped twice, and moonwalked down the hall with the twins mimicking every move.

Rae rolled her eyes.

Chris groaned. "Can you at least crouch when we get there?"

They twirled past the laundry basket, slid sock-footed down the hallway, and landed in a dramatic pose by the front door. Sadie dipped like it was choreographed. It wasn't.

"All right, Broadway stars," Jake said, breathless and grinning. "Grab your shoes. We've got places to be and teachers to impress."

Ten minutes, seven backpacks, and one lost shoe later, they were miraculously packed into the SUV—half buckled, fully chaotic, and perfectly on schedule to be late.

"Donut stop?" Tyler asked from the back seat, already peeling a sticker off the seat belt.

Jake didn't hesitate. "If Dad dances in the hallway before 8 a.m., donuts are officially on the table. Let's go."

The car erupted in cheers. Rae groaned like she was morally opposed to joy, but Jake caught the twitch of a smile on her face as she turned toward the window. They were off. Chris behind the wheel, the '80s station playing something about broken hearts and neon lights. And after a quick stop at the corner gas station, the warm, sticky scent of chocolate glaze filled the cabin.

Wednesday. Forester style.

Three blocks later, the traffic thickened, and Chris gripped the steering wheel like he was guiding a 747 through a thunderstorm. His knuckles turned white, eyes flicking nervously between mirrors and brake lights. For a kid with nerves of steel, it was ironic—especially when he'd nearly passed out last week when Jake made him try parallel parking.

Jake sat in the passenger seat, trying to project calm while sipping lukewarm coffee from his #1 Dad travel mug—still proudly sporting faded glitter from Lily's first-grade Father's Day masterpiece. Honestly, letting a fifteen-year-old drive his siblings through morning rush hour should earn a man something better than a coffee mug. Sainthood, maybe. Or at least a prepaid therapy punch card.

From the speakers, A-ha's "Take On Me" played low and steady. That synth-pop beat hit just the right nostalgic nerve. Somewhere in the back of Jake's mind, his 1986 self—with feathered hair and questionable fashion—was jamming on an imaginary keyboard.

Then Rae, ever the mood disruptor, wrinkled her nose. "Dad, when was the last time you showered?"

Chris didn't skip a beat. "That's what I keep asking him."

Jake arched a brow. "Are you two always this invested in my hygiene, or is this a new sibling bonding phase?"

"Just sayin'," Rae muttered, turning back to her phone, clearly plotting a scented intervention.

Jake leaned forward. "Eyes on the road, buster," he said as Chris edged a little too confidently through a yellow light.

Chris obeyed, letting out a sigh that translated to: *I tolerate you, but barely.*

Jake turned slightly toward Rae. "English report. Is it done?"

She suddenly found the hem of her hoodie incredibly interesting. "Almost . . ."

Which, in Rae-speak, meant not even close.

From the third-row peanut gallery, Sadie chimed in, voice brimming with righteous tattling. "She hasn't started it. She spent all night whispering to Chase."

"Excuse me?!" Rae spun in her seat. "You were spying on me?"

Sadie gave a shrug, her ponytail bouncing smugly. Then, in a sugary tone that dripped with mockery, she added, "I wish you were here too, Chase . . ."

Cue groaning and fake gagging from the back. Becca, Tyler, Lily, and Leo were all thoroughly entertained.

"DAD!" Rae practically yelled.

Jake held back a laugh. "Okay, okay. Everybody chill." He gave Rae a side glance. "How long's this Chase thing been going on?"

She sank into her seat like she wanted to be swallowed whole. "A couple of weeks," she mumbled. Then she lifted her chin. "But you'd like him. He listens to underground bands. And he thinks it's cool that I don't wear makeup or try to dress up. He says I'm . . . real."

Jake sighed. They were officially in the *boys-who-like-you-for-your-soul* era. The phase that required him to look supportive while secretly planning background checks.

"You know the rule," he said. "School comes first. And as long as this Chase kid keeps his hands to himself, I won't call in the Marines."

"Really, Dad?" Rae blinked. "Thanks."

Jake nodded, catching her eyes in the rearview mirror. "But the report's getting done tonight. Deal?"

"Deal."

For a moment, the car was quiet—peaceful, even—as the playlist shifted.

Then "Down Under" by Men at Work came on, and Jake grinned.

Chris reached for the dial.

Without looking, Jake said, "Red light."

Chris's eyes widened. He slammed on the brakes. The SUV jolted, and the back seat erupted like they were on a roller coaster.

"And don't touch my radio," Jake added, casually sipping his coffee.

Chris muttered something under his breath, but didn't reach again.

Victory. Sweet, minor, fatherly victory.

CHAPTER 5

Kelly
Eagle River, Alaska
October 1985

MAYBE IT WAS THE STREAMERS,

the cheap punch, or the faint hope that tonight might change something. Or maybe it was just loneliness dressed up as optimism. Either way, I kept looking toward the doors.

The gym buzzed with restless energy: the slap of sneakers on varnished wood, the scrape of folding chairs, the squeal of a balloon dragged across someone's jacket. Every twenty seconds, the DJ's mic squeaked as he muttered to himself, and the disco ball threw jittery shards of light across the basketball backboard like scattered stars.

A gust of cold October air slipped in through the double doors. A boy stepped through—hands in pockets, jacket collar lifted like he'd raced inside from the wind.

Brown hair pushed back in imperfect swoops. 501 jeans. A soft T-shirt under a Members Only jacket that looked broken-in instead of borrowed. He didn't walk like he was performing. He walked like the world wasn't something to conquer, just something to move through.

The other teens kept dancing, laughing, shouting—but the sound grew muffled, like someone lowered the needle on the night and let the world fade to background static.

His gaze moved across the gym—past the balloon arch, past

Amy and Ben, once again tangled up in their own universe—until his eyes found mine.

My pulse skidded. My palms went warm against the cold plastic cup.

Jake didn't look away. Didn't pretend he hadn't caught me staring. There was this tiny shift in his expression—like recognition that shouldn't be possible, like a secret neither of us had agreed to yet.

Then he started walking. A straight line, sure steps, sneakers whispering over waxed wood.

I pretended the punch cup needed adjusting. The cup squeaked, betraying me.

He stopped in front of me, close enough that I caught the scent of cold air on cotton, something clean like bar soap, and maybe the crisp edge of changing leaves still clinging to him.

"Hey, are you Kelly?" he asked. Not loud, not cocky—just warm. Like we were mid-conversation instead of total strangers.

"Yes, and you must be Jake." My voice tried to sound casual. My heart refused to cooperate.

He nodded a response and his gaze flicked down. "Your shoes are cool."

I laughed, breathless. "They're totally impractical."

"That's probably why they're cool."

The bass from the speakers thudded through my ribs. Someone somewhere popped a balloon and everyone jumped. Jake didn't even blink.

Bryan Adams's "Heaven" floated in, slow and dreamy, coated in record crackle and gym echo. A low hum buzzed in the lights above us. Basketball nets swayed slightly from the air vent kicking on.

He shifted his weight, and for a second, the cool confidence cracked just enough to be human. "Do you . . . wanna dance?"

My eyebrows jumped. "Right now?"

His grin tilted. It was half hopeful, half nervous. "Well, yeah. Unless you wanna wait until the janitor locks the place."

I set the cup down, fingertips damp from condensation. His hands found mine. They were warm and steady.

We stepped into the slow-moving crowd. His hand slid to my waist. My head found his shoulder like instinct, like gravity. The scent of his jacket wrapped around me. The floor vibrated faintly with bass, like the whole gym was breathing.

We didn't talk.

Guys and girls swayed around us. The disco ball spun, tossing silver specks across Jake's hair and my sleeves until we were dotted in tiny galaxies.

And for that song—just one high-school-gym slow dance under flickering lights—it felt like the world paused.

One heartbeat. One boy I suddenly couldn't look away from. One moment that hummed with possibility.

Something cracked open in my chest—quiet and bright and terrifying in all the best ways. I didn't know Jake. Not yet. But it felt like stepping into the doorway of something that would matter.

Maybe this frozen edge of the world wasn't exile. Maybe this night was the beginning.

Maybe he was the beginning of something wonderful.

✦ ✦ ✦

Amy
Boise, Idaho

Amy nudged the skillet back onto low heat, the scrambled eggs still warm from when she'd paused to take Jake's call with Ben.

Amy tucked the phone between her shoulder and ear as she picked up the wooden spoon. She finished explaining the situation to Kelly and then said, "I promised I'd check in before Ben shared your number with Jake."

Kelly exhaled on the other end, her voice small but steady. "Is this real? Like really real? I'm just sort of shocked. Hearing his name after all this time and . . . everything that happened. You know how hard it's been for me to have ended up alone.

And now Jake's marriage is falling apart, too? I feel bad for him. The guy who had it all together?"

"That's the thing," Amy murmured, stirring the eggs without looking at them. "Like I told you, he *doesn't* have it all together. Hasn't for a long time. He told Ben his wife's been in their condo across town for months. He's overwhelmed."

Kelly sniffed, then cleared her throat. "I don't know about this, Ames."

There was a quiet tap as Amy set the spoon down. "Just like I said before—I'm not asking you to jump into anything legal. Just . . . if you'd be willing to point him in the right direction."

Amy ignored the eggs as she waited for Kelly to respond.

"Ooooh!" Kelly moaned in frustration.

Another pause stretched between them.

"Your marriage ended, Kelly," Amy finally said, the wooden spoon in her hand again, "but at least you knew what to do. Jake's floundering. All we want to know is if you'll talk to him. Give him some good advice. I'm sure you'd love to help, right?"

Amy winced even as the words came out. It wasn't the most tactful thing to say to your best friend. But she was talking to Kelly. Even when her world was unraveling thread by thread, Kelly still wanted someone else's day to be a little brighter. Often it was a stranger—someone with a ponytail and espresso-stained apron who got to feel seen—because Kelly, even in heartbreak, couldn't help but give.

There was another long pause on the other end of the phone. Amy waited. She knew Kelly was thinking, weighing the pros and cons. Amy knew not to rush, but to wait.

Amy leaned against the counter, eyes flicking to Ben in the living room. He gave her the praying hands again—his silent plea to work her magic with Kelly. Amy couldn't help but smile.

Sometimes, it still hit her out of nowhere, how lucky she was. That she got to be married to Ben, her high school crush, the boy who once held her hand at youth group and told her she had the best laugh he'd ever heard. Now, they had a mortgage, matching travel mugs, and a shared Amazon Prime account. And yet . . . there were still moments, like this one, when she saw him across the room and felt seventeen again. Giddy. Stupidly grateful.

Of course, her friends were at the other extreme. Kelly had been divorced from her cheating husband for two years already. However, Kelly was hurting more than she'd let on.

And Jake . . . Jake was spiraling. But somehow, right here in the middle of all of it, they were here for each other. Just like they had been in high school. Or at least that's what Amy hoped would happen. They needed each other now, just as they had back then.

"Kelly?" she prompted.

Kelly finally sighed. "I knew it was over nearly as soon as we said, 'I do.' With Troy, I mean." Her voice was thick, as if she were speaking through smoke. "I kept hoping he'd finally . . . I don't know . . . choose me."

Amy pressed her lips together. Her heart cracked in sympathy. "You always deserved to be chosen. You've always been pretty special. I've known that from the moment I met you."

"Of course," Kelly muttered. "Everyone remembers the high school girl in jelly shoes—in the Alaskan snow, thank you very much—who was everyone's friend."

Amy smiled, flipping a piece of egg that had stuck to the edge of the pan. "Hey, that girl had great hair and better taste in lip gloss than the rest of us combined."

Kelly snorted. "Until my gloss turned neon in the gym lighting."

A laugh burst from Amy. "Okay, I admit, it was pretty funny to see pink glowing lips bounce around in the dark gym as you danced. Okay, yes, glowing-lips disco moment. Legendary."

She braced her hip against the kitchen counter, phone cradled between cheek and shoulder, her hand still hovering over breakfast, like she hadn't quite decided whether to feed Ben or her anxiety first.

"I just always pictured Jake having the perfect life, you know," Kelly said, turning back to the conversation at hand.

Amy softened her tone again. "I'm not saying jump back into the past. But you know Jake. You know what he needs to hear."

"He needs a lawyer," Kelly said flatly.

"He needs a friend," Amy said gently. "Someone who won't freak out when he spirals."

Kelly let out a long breath. "If I agree, it's only a call, right? That's it. No advice, no legal counsel, and no wandering down memory lane."

Amy reached for Ben's plate and scooped eggs onto it—her peace offering/bribery strategy. "Exactly. Boundaries stay intact. Promise."

Kelly cleared her throat as if she weren't being fooled. "Amy?"

"I swear. No memory lane. You can keep this entirely on your current highway of broken dreams."

Ben leaned around the corner. "Can she just say yes already?"

Amy waved him away, mouthing, "Eggs first, panic later."

Ben did the tiniest of happy dances in place.

"Look," Amy said, softening again. "Remember how steady you were for us back then? The four of us, after we all graduated, had big dreams."

"I dreamed of the mall and a steady paycheck," Kelly said dryly.

Amy chuckled. "You also dreamed of being seen. Jake saw you."

Kelly's voice dropped. "That's what scares me."

Amy swallowed hard. Her best friend was brave and brilliant—and terrified. And Amy got it. Because if things had gone a little differently, she might have ended up being the one reeling and wounded instead of tucked safely into a life with Ben.

"Okay," Kelly said at last. "He can call my work number. But if he even hints at using my name to help with his custody argument, I'm hanging up."

Amy grinned. "Great! Got it. You're the best friend/slash/boundary setter I know." And then, with a quick goodbye, she hung up.

Ben pumped his fists in victory. "Let's go!"

Amy shot him a look. "Eggs first, gloating second." Then she couldn't help but giggle. "Sort of eager, aren't you?"

Ben gave her an unapologetic shrug. "I've heard more about his feelings in the last three days than I did in all four years of high school. I'm going hiking tomorrow—just me and nature. I'm turning my phone *off*. I need him to call someone else."

Amy raised an eyebrow. "I hope we're doing the right thing."

Ben stole a forkful of eggs like a man who'd earned them with emotional labor. "Kelly's solid. She's smarter than all of us. She'll point him where he needs to go."

✦ ✦ ✦

Jake
Boise, Idaho

Chris pulled the SUV into the school drop-off lane with all the confidence of a teenage boy driving a tank through a minefield. Which, in fairness, wasn't far from the truth. The giant yellow STUDENT DRIVER magnet clung to the back windshield like a badge of shame, and Jake—well, Jake just braced himself.

The second the tires stopped moving, the doors flew open and the kids exited like clowns bursting from a circus car. Chris left the keys in the ignition and jumped out. Rae was gone before Jake could even turn around. Sadie and Becca darted into the flow of ponytails and oversized backpacks, blending into the chaos. Tyler launched into a sprint, as if school were a competitive sport.

Only Lily and Leo hesitated next to the vehicle. Still holding hands, still wearing their mismatched socks and lopsided smiles. Still his little ones.

Jake got out of the passenger side, ignoring the eyes he could feel on his back. He stretched his arms. It was part show, part genuine stiffness. Then he bent down to kiss the twins.

Chris was already halfway across the parking lot when Jake called after him, full dad-mode. "I'll be here after school to pick you up, buddy!"

Chris didn't turn around. Didn't nod. Nothing.

Jake raised his voice slightly. "You hear me, Chris? I'll be right *here*. Okay?"

A single thumbs-up floated up like a white flag of teenage

tolerance. Jake smirked, even as it tugged at something a little too close to the ribs. He turned to the two stragglers.

"Don't worry, Daddy," Lily said, ever the old soul wrapped in a tiny body. "He's just exercising his need for independence."

Jake blinked. "Where'd you learn that?"

"Annie's mom."

Leo chimed in, serious as a philosopher in self-fastening shoes. "She's a therespist."

Jake chuckled. "You mean therapist, bud."

They both giggled. He kissed their foreheads, pulling them into a brief hug that smelled like shampoo, Lunchables, and the unmistakable plastic of cartoon backpacks.

"All right, goofballs. Run along. I'll see you after school."

As they scampered off, Jake took a moment to lean back against the SUV. The sun was doing that thing where it pretended spring was closer than it was, warming his shoulders just enough to make him forget his stiff neck from a night of tossing and turning.

And that's when he saw them. The Moms.

Carol. Suzie. Beth.

Their sunglasses were perched too high, and their smiles were a beat too delayed. He could feel the triangulation from across the parking lot. Moms in their forties—just enough lip gloss, just enough yoga class, and a scent of judgment masked as concern.

He waved because he was raised to be polite. Because he still believed, stupidly, that maybe people didn't always mean the worst.

Suzie got there first. "Jake! How are you?"

He smiled at her. He hoped it read, *I'm fine* without offering evidence. "Doing well, Suzie. You?"

Carol didn't even wait for pleasantries.

"We heard about Nicole. Is there anything we can do to help?"

Jake straightened. "Nah, I'm good."

"You know," Carol added with the subtlety of a freight train, "my sister's always had her eye on you. I could set something up."

Jake's jaw flexed. He kept his tone light, easy. "Thanks, Carol, but I'm not dating anyone."

Beth leaned in, like a reporter sniffing out a scandal. "Hoping she'll come back?"

That one landed. Softly, but deep.

He didn't answer. Instead, he offered a smile so strained it felt like holding his breath, took a step back, and nodded. "Have a good day, ladies."

"It's so strange. I thought they were happy," Suzie's voice floated faintly as he walked away.

He heard Beth answer. "Some people just don't know how to make a marriage work."

He didn't look back as he got into the SUV. Didn't let the smirk drop until the door was shut. Didn't let the ache show until the car was in drive.

But in the rearview mirror, through the kids' fingerprints and smudged glass, he saw it. The three of them, now huddled together, heads shaking. Jake groaned. That mock-sympathy was way worse than outright meanness.

Jake gripped the steering wheel. On the radio, "Take On Me" had been replaced by "Time After Time."

Of course it had. Jake turned the volume down and let the silence say everything he couldn't.

✦ ✦ ✦

Kelly
Eagle River, Alaska
January 1986

The gym lights glowed softer than usual, as if dimming them could disguise the fact that we were still standing under basketball hoops and championship banners. Streamers in neon pink and electric blue hung in tired swags from the rafters. A disco ball borrowed from someone's uncle spun overhead, throwing fractured light across the waxed floor.

I stood near the bleachers with Amy, nursing a styrofoam cup of orange punch that tasted like melted popsicles. My fingers squeaked against the rim as I squeezed too tightly.

I told myself I wasn't watching the double doors. But I was.

And when Jake finally walked in—jeans, white button-down,

sleeves shoved to his elbows like he hadn't tried too hard—it felt like the floor steadied beneath me. The other guys, the ones I'd been smiling at and making conversation with all night, blurred into static.

My dad always said, "Make friends, Kelly. Be agreeable. Don't give anyone a reason to doubt us here." And I had. I'd laughed when I was supposed to, danced when I didn't feel like it. But none of them was Jake.

And lately, Jake hadn't been mine either.

He nodded at a few people, casual, like it cost him nothing. Not at me. My stomach tightened. Maybe I didn't fit anymore. Perhaps all my efforts—being the "friendly" administrator's daughter—seemed insincere to him. Maybe it pushed him away.

The DJ switched tracks, sliding from Whitney Houston into something moodier. A ballad. My pulse jumped when Jake found me near the bleachers. For a moment, it was just us again, like the dozens of times we'd driven out to the lake, stretched across the hood of his car, and shared secrets under the stars.

"I want to show you something," he whispered, voice so low it felt meant only for me.

I blinked as he pressed something into my palm. Cold metal, heavy. I looked down. His class ring.

My breath caught. "What's this for?"

He shrugged, suddenly all nervous. "I don't wear it anymore."

My heart tripped. "Jake, huh? You don't wear it?"

His smile didn't reach his eyes. "I just thought maybe . . . never mind."

The song ended, and the spell broke. He pulled the ring back, closing his fist around it like it hurt to hold. The moment cracked between us, fragile as glass.

"Uh," he said, too quick, shoving it into his pocket. "Why don't I get us something to drink?"

Before I could say anything, he was gone, weaving through the crowd toward the refreshment table.

I stood frozen, the ghost of the ring still pressed against my palm.

That was when one of the football guys, Troy, swaggered

over. His grin was all confidence. His cologne, a wall of musk. "Wanna dance?"

I shook my head. "I'm good."

But then I spotted my dad. Arms crossed at the edge of the gym. Watching. That familiar weight sank in: *Be agreeable. Be kind. Don't give anyone a reason to question our place here.*

Troy smirked. "Looks like you're changing your mind. C'mon. Just one song."

I felt my dad's gaze like a hand on the back of my neck. Against everything in me, I nodded. "Okay, you're right. Sure."

Troy pulled me in too close. My shoulders locked.

"Relax," he said, his breath too warm near my ear. "Broken Wings" swelled from the speakers.

I wasn't listening. My eyes searched the room for Jake.

And then I found him. Just a few feet away, two frosty root beer floats in his hands, hope written all over his face.

Until he saw me. Saw Troy's hand slide lower than it should. Saw my smile, even though he couldn't tell it was forced.

Jake's jaw ticked tight. Without a word, he turned, walking away with both floats still in hand. And just like that, the night fractured for good.

The stars outside pressed against the gym windows, trying to break through the haze of fluorescent light and the scent of teenage sweat. But they couldn't. Not that night.

Jake
Boise, Idaho

JAKE HADN'T PLANNED TO FALL

apart before nine a.m., but the universe rarely consulted him about timing.

The car's Bluetooth picked up the call just as he pulled out of the school zone. His mother's voice crackled through the speakers. It was soft, worn around the edges, but still unmistakably hers.

"They increased my pain meds," she said, no greeting, just honesty. "They're making me comfortable. But, Jake, I think it's almost time."

He gripped the steering wheel tighter. "How long?"

"They say three months. Maybe six if the Lord is generous." She paused, as if steadying herself. "I just want to see you happy before I go. Will you come soon?"

Jake blinked hard, staring straight ahead at the road unraveling before him. "Soon, Mom. Just hold on a little longer, okay?"

He ended the call, but her voice stayed with him—echoing, settling into the cracks he tried so hard to hide.

The radio came back on, mid-chorus. Bryan Adams. *"Somebody like you . . ."* The song he used to sing in the back of his dad's station wagon, air guitar and all.

He reached a red light and let his foot rest on the brake. Closed his eyes. Breathed.

But with that breath came the memory, just a few months old.

It had been late. Jake had lit every candle they owned, their kitchen flickering like it was waiting for something sacred. The guitar rested across his knees. He didn't play often anymore, but he'd written her something—a song that tried to bridge the growing space between them.

"I'm sorry," he'd said the moment Nicole walked through the door. "About the fights. I know I've been distracted. I know I haven't listened. But I'm here. I want us back."

He strummed the first chord, tentative. Hopeful.

Nicole didn't sit. Didn't smile. Just crossed her arms, then her heart.

"I talked to a few attorneys tonight," she said. No drama. No hesitation.

She fiddled with the strap of her purse like she always did when she was anxious to leave. "I just don't want you to be surprised when divorce papers are served." Then Nicole reached into her purse as if she had said her piece and was ready to go. "This doesn't have to be harder than it already is."

She hadn't even given him a chance to ask questions or make a plea. It had already been decided.

The memory hit like a punch to the lungs. Jake slammed his hand against the steering wheel, the thud echoing through the empty car. His heart thudded louder.

The light turned green, but he didn't move.

Then, just ahead, he saw it. A flash of red neon in the strip mall window: Donuts—Hot Now.

He hadn't been to that place in years, not since he was twenty-one and flat broke, living off caffeine, grace, and prayer. But the raspberry-filled donuts had been something holy.

He pulled into the lot. Ordered two.

When he slid back into the SUV, the scent of sugar and dough filled the air. He didn't eat. Not yet. He just sat. Let the warmth of the bag press against his chest. Let the memory of simpler mornings wash over him.

On the dashboard, a concert flyer flapped against the

windshield. DEF LEPPARD. Saturday night. One of those events he kept saying he'd go to "next time."

Jake stared at it like it might give him direction. Or at least a distraction. "Any advice, guys?" he muttered, half-smiling. The poster, unsurprisingly, didn't respond.

He let out a breath, long and shaky. "Yeah, well, if anyone can get me out of this mess . . . it's a glam rock band from 1987."

He pulled out the first donut and took a bite. It was warm. Sweet. Sticky with jam. Precisely as he remembered. And for the first time in weeks, something inside him didn't ache quite so much.

Kelly
Boise, Idaho

I knocked on the door even though it was already open. It felt polite. Controlled. The kind of move that says I'm a team player, even when I'm two hours of sleep and one espresso short of actually feeling like one.

"You wanted to see me, Mr. Alden?"

He looked up from a stack of contracts as if they were trying to confess something salacious. "Ah, Ms. Richardson. Yes. Well done on the Gaines case. Not only did he agree to mediation, he's already offered a settlement bigger than anything Mrs. Gaines dared hope for."

He gave a low whistle. "Not many people stand up to that man. But you did. And it paid off. You've made quite the impression among the partners. Please, come in and sit down."

I crossed the room with a confident stride. I hoped my demeanor read, *I'm back—even if the ghost of the old me is still dragging a suitcase somewhere behind.*

I shook his hand and took a seat, folding one leg over the other with the precision of a woman who has memorized her power moves and her coffee order. I was glad the tennis instructor leverage had worked with Mr. Gaines.

"Thank you, Mr. Alden."

He leaned back in his chair, lacing his fingers across his chest. "I must say, we were a little worried about you after the divorce. That extended leave in Sedona . . . How long has it been now?"

Six months. Long enough to change my hair, my number, and my definition of who I thought I was.

But I just smiled, as if it were all very casual. "About six months."

Back then, I wandered into downtown Sedona one morning, half-lost in my own head and trying to remember how to exist without my phone glued to my palm. I passed a bookstore, a crystal shop, and two tie-dye-clad street musicians arguing about parking. Then I saw her.

An elderly woman in a wheelchair, struggling to navigate the cracked sidewalk and the unrelenting Arizona sun. She looked out of place. Perhaps she was someone who came for a vacation and decided to stay. Or someone waiting for something important to happen. But what?

She wasn't waving or calling out for help. Just . . . sitting. As if she knew someone would come.

I paused. Something about her made me stop in my tracks. Maybe it was the scarf tied around her shoulders, too delicate for the desert. Or maybe it was her eyes. They were eyes that had seen too much and were still waiting for a reason to stay hopeful.

"Hi there," I said, stepping closer, lowering my sunglasses. "Can I help you get to some shade?"

She nodded, and her voice was paper-thin but sure. "That would be nice, dear."

I wheeled her over to a patch of shade near a juice bar. She declined the water I offered and said she was fine. But just before I turned to leave, she reached out and gently rested her hand on my wrist.

"Some things don't make sense until much, much later," she said. "But when they do . . . you'll see that it was always love."

Then she winked. She actually winked.

Back in the office, Mr. Alden didn't notice the shift in my expression as I reminisced. Or if he did, he wisely chose not to comment.

"Well," he said, sliding a folder across the desk, "you're clearly back in form. We'd like you to take the Wellington Estate case. It's high-profile, significant assets, and some tension around medical directives. Handle it with care."

I took the folder. The name on the tab meant nothing to me yet, but I felt the weight of it. Felt the shift that always came before something important.

"And Kelly?" he added, right as I stood.

I glanced up.

"Go easy on them when they assume you're just there to take notes—your kill count is getting impressive."

I smirked. "No promises."

Mr. Alden sat back, threading his fingers across his belly in that way he always did before delivering some sort of career prophecy.

"I know the battle with your ex was long and difficult," he said gently, "but you've come out the other side an even more productive member of this team than we could've imagined."

I nodded, keeping my smile polite and my chin lifted. Like "long and difficult" even began to cover it—may as well call the Titanic a "slightly damp situation." No need to tell him that my coping mechanisms involved alphabetizing my spice rack, shopping for lip gloss, doing laundry, and learning Portuguese on Duolingo before bed.

"Mr. Langford and I are particularly intrigued," he added.

"Intrigued," I repeated with a hint of a smirk. "That's a word you don't hear every day in legal briefs."

He chuckled. "Perhaps you should go to Sedona more often."

Now that made me pause. I let the name swirl in my head like wind over red rock.

"It is my favorite place to think," I said. And that wasn't a lie.

Alden's eyes twinkled like he was in on some secret. "Well, whatever's working for you, keep it up. I think there might be a corner office up here with your name on it."

Corner office. Funny how quickly those two words used to

thrill me. Now? I wasn't sure if they lit a fire in my chest or made me want to run back to red rocks and soft silence.

Still, I smiled and replied like the future wasn't holding its breath. "That would be . . . intriguing."

Jake
Boise, Idaho

Jake wasn't ready to go see his mom yet, but there was someone else he liked to stop in to see every few weeks.

Outside the hospice center, he sat in the parking lot a few minutes longer. He could've gone anywhere—back to the office, to his big house that seemed empty even though it was only minus one person, to the gym he hadn't set foot in since Christmas. But instead, he was here.

He reached for the bouquet on the passenger seat. White tulips.

Jake took a breath, deep enough to hurt a little, then stepped out of the car and into a slow and steady drizzle.

Inside, the place smelled like lemon disinfectant and overcooked peas. He nodded at the nurse behind the front desk and signed in, hands damp around the flowers.

Room 207. Second floor. The same.

He took the stairs. Needed to feel something underfoot. At the top of the landing, something made him pause.

Wheelchair wheels squeaked against linoleum. He looked up—and there she was. Same frail frame. Same faded scarf. Same quiet knowing in her eyes.

She was being pushed by a nurse, slow and steady. As they passed, her head tilted just slightly toward him—just enough to notice. Her eyes met his. And for a second, the sterile hallway melted away. Recognition. It hit him low in the chest. She knew him. Or maybe she didn't. The nurse turned the corner.

Shaking it off, Jake followed down the hallway and watched

as they went into Room 207. After the nurse left, he gently knocked on the door, forcing his heart back into rhythm.

"Hey, Ma," he said softly, slipping inside. "I brought tulips."

She turned her head on the pillow, eyes fluttering open. Her smile—worn but bright—was all the answer he needed.

"You always bring me what I need," she whispered.

He sat down beside her, handed her the bouquet like a peace offering for a world he couldn't control. Her fingers curled weakly around the stems.

They didn't talk much. Just sat. Her breath was shallow. His thoughts were louder than they needed to be. He wasn't ready for this.

Not the goodbyes. So many at once. Not the grief. Not the empty space he already felt opening inside him like a slow-splitting fault line.

Footsteps approaching pulled him from it. Ben stood in the doorway, rain still in his hair, a nervous smile on his face.

"Hey," he said, voice low. "Mind if I come in?" He grinned at the inside joke.

Jake stood. "Not at all."

Ben crossed the room and gave the older woman a gentle kiss on the cheek. She smiled, and for a flicker, the years faded. Jake watched the exchange with a mix of gratitude and guilt.

Ben straightened, nodding toward the tulips. "That was smart."

"So, is Ma doing okay?" Jake asked.

Ben's jaw worked. "They say she's comfortable. A few months. Maybe years. It's hard to tell." He winked. "And she's always liked you calling her Ma."

"I wouldn't know what else to call her. Maureen doesn't fit. She insisted, you know. She fed me leftovers and listened to me play my guitar."

"Yeah, leaving nothing for me to eat when I got home from football practice."

Jake just smiled and shrugged.

"I'm glad you stopped by. She asks about you, you know," Ben said. "Wanted to see you more often."

"Doesn't everyone?" Jake's throat grew thick. "Well, almost everyone. I'd love to head out of town to see my mom. Since I can't, I thought yours would do." He paused. "I just . . . I'm waiting until the divorce is finalized. One kind of loss at a time, right?"

Ben nodded. "Makes sense."

There was a pause. Jake shifted his weight and placed his hand over Maureen's. Her eyes were fixed on the muted television as if she were watching it. Was she listening? Did she understand?

Then Ben settled into the chair next to his mother's bed. "You know, I was thinking about Kelly the other day. Thought you might want to know—"

"Not the time," Jake said, too sharply.

Ben froze.

"Not the place," Jake added, softer.

Ben lifted his hands. "Yeah. I respect that, dude."

Jake glanced out the window, where the rain had started to lift, light filtering through gray.

Ben stroked his chin, making eye contact. "But maybe . . . I don't know . . . maybe there's a rainbow after the storm." His eyebrows lifted, hopeful.

Jake scoffed. "Seriously? Did you get that off a calendar?"

Ben grinned. "Hallmark. Or maybe an '80s power ballad. Hard to say."

Jake shook his head, but the corner of his mouth twitched. He wanted to believe in rainbows. He just wasn't sure they still happened for guys like him.

Kelly
Boise, Idaho

THE FEBRUARY RAIN HAD STARTED

right after I'd gotten home. At least it wasn't snow. I twirled pasta from the pot to a plate and caught my reflection in the glass of the frame propped by the toaster—me with my three kids, all sunburns and squinting smiles. Lauren, the oldest, in the middle, bossing the boys as usual. Braxton at twenty-two, pretending not to grin. Alex at eighteen, trying so hard to look serious, and failing. The photo steadied me, just as it always did. It was a reminder that I'd built something that lasted, even if not everything had.

My phone buzzed on the counter. FaceTime. Lauren.

I swiped, and her kitchen sprang to life on my screen—pasta boiling, a dog ricocheting off cabinets, three kids streaking past like comets, and a cartoon theme song battling the vent fan.

She didn't even say hello. "You cannot text me 'good news' from work and then disappear for three hours," she scolded, breathless. "Spill."

I hesitated, warmth blooming in my chest like someone had cracked the kitchen window and let spring in. "Not exactly a promotion. My boss mentioned partnership—just floated the idea."

Lauren squealed loudly. Pots clanged behind her. A child whooshed past with a dish towel cape. "Partnership? Mom!

That's huge. Please tell me you didn't downplay it in your classic humble-pie style."

"I might have mumbled something about 'that would be . . . intriguing,'" I admitted, twirling a strand of hair until it threatened to knot. It was my lifelong nervous tic. My fork traced circles through the pasta I suddenly wasn't hungry for. "Mostly because the idea terrifies me."

"That's why you'll crush it," she said, voice going sure and steady the way mine used to when she was little and afraid of the dark. "You do scary things and make them look graceful. That's your brand."

I huffed a laugh. "Graceful is generous. I feel more . . . wobbly gazelle."

"Fine," she said, grinning, "a wobbly gazelle in a power suit who bills at $450 an hour. Own it. You've climbed every rung with your hands full and your heart bruised, and you're still here."

Rain tapped the window like applause. I let the words land, let them settle into the quiet place under my ribs that still wanted permission to want more. "Okay," I said softly. "Maybe I'll stop mumbling and start saying it out loud."

Behind Lauren, the back door opened. Mike stepped in, cheeks pink from the cold, and kissed her on the cheek. Her kids shrieked "Daddy!" and tackled him in a pile of limbs and oversized socks. The dog added a victory lap.

"Braxton and Alex will be glad to hear it," Lauren said, breathless with her own chaos. "You'll finally get out of that place and move into a decent house again."

I rolled my eyes, even as I smiled. "Has it ever occurred to you and your brothers that maybe I like it here?"

"Mom." She gave me the look she had learned from me and improved upon. "That building is a hundred years old. It's one asbestos lawsuit away from being condemned."

"It is not," I said automatically, setting my wine down just as a loud plop hit the table. Another drop pattered on the wood. Without flinching, I slid a mixing bowl under the ceiling leak and adjusted it until the rhythm found the center. "It's cute and—" another plop "—charming."

She raised an eyebrow. "The only reason you moved in there is because you conceded too much to Dad."

"That's not true." The words came out too fast.

Lauren's silence said everything she didn't.

I huffed, softer. "Okay, it's partly true. But I've made back enough money. I could move out anytime." I twirled pasta, trying for a casual look. "I just don't want to."

On her end, she started plating dinner, her kids orbiting like small, determined planets. "Oh yeah? Then why are half your boxes still unopened in the guest room?"

I didn't have an answer. The camera caught my face anyway, and I watched the truth flicker there. Sometimes staying put feels safer than starting over.

"All I'm asking is," Lauren's voice was gentler now, "isn't this what you've been working toward? Making partner will help you start over, for real this time. No more limbo. No more crumbling bungalow. A fresh chapter."

Something thick rose in my throat. I stared at the slow ripple of red wine in my glass and nodded. "Say goodnight to the kids for me, honey."

"I will. Love you."

"Love you too."

We hung up. The kitchen fell back into its small sounds. The clock's soft tick, the rain keeping time with the bowl on the table, the hum of the old fridge that never quite stops.

My gaze drifted down the short hall to the guest room. Even from here, I could see the edge of a box I'd labeled in black marker months ago: *Fragile—Open First*. I'd never opened it. The tape still held, neat as a promise.

I took a bite of pasta that had gone lukewarm, listened to the rain, and told myself that maybe "not yet" wasn't the same thing as "never."

I leaned against the counter, staring at the rain-slick street outside. A couple hurried past, heads bent under a shared umbrella. Their shapes blurred through the glass, dissolving into the night as if they'd never been there at all.

I told myself I was glad Amy hadn't pressed and insisted we

talk more about Jake when she called the other day. That silence was a kind of gift. But the restless ache beneath my ribs told another story.

I could still hear my daughter Lauren's voice in my head. *No more limbo. A fresh chapter.*

My gaze drifted again to the guest room door. I stood, my limbs heavy and slow, unsure if this was bravery or foolishness. The hardwood was cold beneath my bare feet, and the air inside the guest room felt thinner, dustier, as if time had pressed down on it while I wasn't looking.

Boxes, ten at least, maybe more. Some were labeled in my handwriting, others not at all. I picked one up, arms straining slightly with the weight of memory, and carried it into the living room. A black trash bag waited like a quiet dare. I added the box to the pile, then grabbed my wine again. One last sip.

With the edge of a chipped fingernail, I pulled at the brittle packing tape. It peeled back with a slow tearing sound. Inside was my wedding album. Ivory leather, still pristine, our initials embossed in gold.

The scent of old paper and pressed petals rose to meet me. I stared at the cover for a heartbeat too long, then opened it. There we were. Smiling. Posed. Perfect. Lies printed in glossy 8x10. Me and Troy.

My throat burned, but I didn't cry. Not anymore. Instead, I picked up the album—firmly, with both hands—and dropped it into the trash bag. It landed with a muffled thud, as if something were breaking quietly.

I didn't stop there. The save-the-dates. The monogrammed napkins. The corsage, still wrapped in crinkled tissue. All of it followed, one by one. No hesitation.

When the box was empty, I sat back and drew in a deep breath. A first after being underwater too long.

Outside, the rain softened, but inside—something had shifted. Not loudly. Not in some grand, cinematic way. Just a gentle unfurling in my chest, the beginning of something that felt a little like freedom.

I moved toward the guest room and paused in the doorway.

Cardboard boxes lined the far wall, some still sealed with packing tape. Sharpie labels scrawled by a past version of myself read, *Office Stuff, Winter Clothes,* and *Photos – Fragile.*

I swallowed hard. Then I spotted it. One box was shoved farther back than the rest. My eyes snagged on the words scrawled across the lid in black marker—my own handwriting, slanted and hurried.

EAGLE RIVER.

The sight of it sent a jolt straight through me. My stomach clenched. I almost pushed it aside, telling myself I wasn't ready. However, the truth was that no amount of time could make me ready.

Bracing myself, I dragged the box closer and pried open the flaps. Dust swirled in the lamplight, the faint, musty scent of old paper and woodsmoke clinging to the contents within.

On top was a yearbook, its once-bright cover now dulled at the corners. My breath caught as I flipped it open. Hearts were doodled in ink all over the inside cover, along with words scrawled with a dramatic certainty only teenagers could manage:

This yearbook belongs to the future Mrs. Jake Forester.

A groan slipped from my throat before I could stop it. I rolled my eyes so hard they almost hurt and snapped the book shut— only to hear the faint slap of something falling.

A bundle of letters spilled into my lap, tied with a length of faded twine. At the center, fragile and crumbling but unmistakable, was a sprig of dried forget-me-nots. My chest tightened. Their petals were brittle, edges curling in on themselves, but they still held the memory of color, of meaning.

A Polaroid slid free, face down on the floor.

I reached for it with shaking fingers.

The photo was grainy, slightly overexposed, but the image was clear enough to undo me: Jake and me, shoulder to shoulder, his letterman jacket around my shoulders, both of us smiling too wide, eyes too bright. Amy's handwriting was scratched across the white border: *Summer '87 – State Fair.*

I stared at it, heart hammering in my chest, the room around me blurring. I could almost smell the fair again—the buttered popcorn, diesel from the rides, Amy's perfume mingling with cotton candy in the night air. I could hear Jake's laugh, deep and boyish, and could feel the rough wool of his jacket brushing my chin.

The Polaroid trembled in my hand as the memory rushed forward, pulling me back to that night I'd never forget—back to when the world felt small enough to fit between the Tilt-A-Whirl and the Ferris wheel. Jake Forester's name was written into every corner of my heart.

One photo, one bundle of letters, one sprig of flowers—and I was no longer in this bungalow surrounded by boxes and wine and broken promises.

I was back there. With him.

I blinked hard, forcing the fairground lights and Jake's teenage grin back into the shadows of memory. The Polaroid shook once more between my fingers before I tucked it carefully back into the yearbook. Closing the cover, I dropped it into the trash bag with a dull thump.

The bag was already overflowing—old napkins, wilted corsages, the ivory wedding album sinking beneath it all. It looked like a history lesson no one asked to take.

I sighed, dragging myself to my feet. My head felt heavy from wine and ghosts. Shoes. That was next. Something simple, something ordinary. I bent, pulling them from under the edge of the couch and slipping them on. The laces scraped dryly against themselves as I pulled them tight, tying neat knots.

Beside me, the bag shifted. The yearbook slid sideways, catching against the edge, its spine bending just enough for the bundle of letters and Polaroid to tumble free. With a quiet rustle, the whole thing slipped into another half-closed box. For some reason, I left them where they were. *Next time.*

I straightened, tugged the second knot into place, and grabbed the bag. The plastic crinkled loudly in my grip, its weight heavier than it should have been, the past resisting its burial.

I tied it shut, the knot biting into the black plastic, and hauled it out the door. The cool night air brushed against my face, carrying the faint scent of rain. Behind me, in the quiet bungalow, the yearbook lay hidden, its secrets tucked safely back into the shadows. Yet my mind was back there again.

Kelly
Eagle River, Alaska
April 1986

I balanced my books against my chest and spun the dial on my locker. The metal groaned as it swung open, and inside, my heart felt as cold and solid as that locker.

I don't belong here.
Who am I fooling?
Maybe I'm the fool.

I'd been so excited about prom when it was first announced. *A Night to Remember.* I couldn't have picked out a more perfect theme if I'd tried. I'd hoped that would be the night when Jake would officially ask me to be his girlfriend. Yet as the days passed and no invitation from Jake came, my heart started to crack . . . just like a frozen river did when spring arrived. Yet the river of emotions that filled me was more longing than hope.

Inside my locker, my secret world waited in the posters I'd stuck to the door: Madonna, all lace gloves and rebellion. Cyndi Lauper, her hair a neon scream. Heartthrobs torn from *Seventeen*, smirking like they knew secrets I hadn't even told my best friend. Stickers—stars, rainbows, and the kind that smelled faintly of fake fruit—were stuck to the posters on the metal. Usually, they cheered me. Today, they only looked tired.

I pressed one sticker back into place, my finger smoothing over its curling edge. That's when I felt a tap on my shoulder. Light, almost hesitant. I turned. And there he was. Jake.

The hallway noise blurred for a moment. The sound of lockers slamming and sneakers squeaking faded into the background. My pulse quickened, stumbled, and then leapt into my throat. The rest of the world dimmed, as if all the fluorescents overhead had flickered out, and the only thing left was him.

Then, in an instant, a burst of light exploded in my face.

I flinched, spots scattering across my vision like a TV screen gone to static.

When my eyes cleared, Jake was lowering a Polaroid camera.

"What?" he said, casual, as though my heart wasn't currently sprinting laps. "A guy can't take a picture of a Betty when he sees one?"

The word—Betty—slid under my skin. I knew he meant I was a babe, but I wish he'd just come out and tell me how he felt. My cheeks flushed. I rolled my eyes to cover it, but inside, something flipped.

The photo slid out with a mechanical sigh. He waved it, waiting for the image to bloom. Our gazes caught, neither of us looking away. My heart did somersaults, and I was sure I'd never been happier than at this moment.

"Kelly?" His voice was softer, careful. "Can I ask you something?"

"Yeah?"

The bell shrieked. The hallway filled with sneakers squealing against waxed tile, lockers banging shut, voices tripping over each other.

Jake leaned closer, his shoulder brushing mine. "About prom—"

"Kelly!" A guy's voice from behind me caused me to flinch, and suddenly I wished that the linoleum floor would open up and swallow me.

Jake's smile turned downward, and his eyebrows arched in.

I attempted to ignore the tall, handsome basketball player. I prayed that if I didn't look his way, he'd just keep walking and wouldn't bring to light what I'd done. After weeks of anxiously waiting for Jake to ask me to prom, I'd jokingly asked Troy Henderson during math class if he'd give me a ride. I was surprised when he agreed.

Troy, varsity jacket hanging open, swaggered past. The sharp bite of Drakkar Noir trailed after him. "I'll pick you up at five tomorrow, okay?" He didn't even slow down, yet his words hit Jake like a slap. Or at least that's what it looked like when Jake's face instantly turned red and angry.

"Perfect. Thanks, Troy." The words left my mouth before I could stop them, tinny and hollow.

Jake's brow furrowed deep. "You're not going with him, are you?"

"No." My arms tightened around my books, the corners pressing sharply into my ribs. "He's just giving me a ride. Nobody asked me . . ." I glanced up at him, the hope in me embarrassingly plain.

Jake's eyes narrowed. "I thought Troy was going with Cindy."

"He was," I said quietly. "Until she caught him cheating. Dumped him last week."

Jake shook his head, disgust plain. "Figures. And now what—he just swoops in and you're . . . what? His next in line?"

"That's not what this is." My voice caught, but I forced it out. "I wasn't serious when I asked him for a ride. But then he said yes, and suddenly . . ." I swallowed. "Suddenly, the other girls started talking to me. Like I wasn't invisible anymore."

His jaw tightened, fists flexing at his sides. "You don't need Troy Henderson to make you visible."

The words hung between us, heavy, sharp. Immediately, I questioned if I'd said too much. I'd shared a lot with Jake, but nothing like this. I felt both dumb and desperate. Could I make it any plainer? I needed Jake to know how I really felt. Deep down, I believed it would make a difference. This was my chance to lay all my cards on the table.

I looked down, tracing the worn edge of a book with my thumb. "Maybe I wanted to know what it felt like, just once. To be wanted. Even if it's fake."

Jake let out a rough laugh, the kind that sounded more like pain. "Fake's all you'll get with him. You deserve—" He stopped himself, cutting the words short.

I lifted my eyes, heart racing. "Deserve what?"

His gaze locked on mine, unflinching, raw. "Better. You deserve better. Better than him. Better than . . ." He swallowed, his throat working hard. "Better than what I can give you."

For a second, the hallway shrank down to just us. Two people standing too close, hearts tripping over each other.

I shook my head, and I was about to explain how that wasn't true. Instead, the bell announced that first period would start in three minutes.

As if the bell had just woken him up from a trance, Jake broke the stare. He cleared his throat. "Anyway. Save me a dance?"

Relief and ache tangled together in my heart, and I promised myself we'd finish this conversation later. "I'd love to."

Something flickered in his face. He hesitated, like he wanted to say something. Then his lips parted. He offered a smile, but it didn't reach his eyes.

"Save me a dance," he repeated before turning and walking away.

I wanted to follow him, beg him to say the rest, but I'd be in trouble if I was late to class again. Especially since only a few days ago, the principal had caught me and Amy at the shopping center down the street during school hours. Just our luck that Mrs. Weaver had been picking up pizza for teacher appreciation during the exact class Amy and I skipped to hunt for sales at Jay Jacobs.

All afternoon, I couldn't shake Jake's pained expression. I'd even called Amy that evening while curling my bangs. "Will you come with me tomorrow? Help me find him?" I asked, my voice thin as smoke.

"Find Jake?" she teased. "What for?"

"I need to apologize. I can't let it stay like this."

Amy's laugh tinkled through the phone. "I'll do it—on one condition."

"What?"

"That I get to be maid of honor at your wedding."

"As if," I muttered, but the truth was, the idea made my chest ache in a way I didn't want to admit. "Just . . . promise me you'll help me."

"I'll be your wingwoman," she said, suddenly serious. "Always."

Her words steadied me, but only a little.

The next night, I'd gone through the motions of getting ready, curling my hair, smoothing lip gloss across lips that didn't feel like smiling. Troy had looked sharp when he pulled up. His hair was slick, tux crisp. But when Mom begged for pictures on the porch, I refused. I didn't want any record of this.

When we arrived, the gym barely resembled a gym. Streamers draped from the rafters, sagging like they'd been holding their breath too long. A disco ball spun, scattering broken stars across satin dresses and rented tuxes. Duran Duran's "Rio" pounded through the speakers, every beat shaking the floor, rattling my ribs.

Amy looped her hand through mine as we stepped back in from the bathroom. "Okay," she whispered, her lips close to my ear. "You want me to help you find him?"

"Yes." My voice was firm, though my stomach quaked. "I have to talk to him."

"Then let's do it."

I smoothed the bodice of my dress, strapless and sparkling blue under the lights, like something stolen from a dream. For a moment, I felt almost beautiful. Girls I hardly knew stopped me to compliment the dress, to ask if Troy and I were really going together. Their voices carried envy, curiosity, even friendliness. A week ago, they hadn't looked at me twice.

But their sudden attention slid off me. I wanted only one thing: Jake.

Then Troy appeared, blocking my path. "Dance with me." His voice was confident, practiced, as though no girl ever told him no.

"I can't right now," I started, my eyes already darting around the gym.

And then I saw him. Jake.

He stood on the far side of the room, his gaze locked on me like no one else existed. Heat shot through me, sparking every nerve, rooting me in place. I was ready to move toward him, to close the space between us—

But he turned. Jake walked straight to Bridgette. Her teased hair reached for the rafters, sprayed in the kind of style that could survive a windstorm. Her prom dress was less gown, more rebellion—black satin with a sweetheart neckline, strapless, and snug at the bodice before spilling into layers of tulle that swished around her thighs. Sequins caught the disco lights, flashing silver with every move. Fingerless lace gloves climbed to her elbows, and a rhinestone choker glittered at her throat. She looked like she'd stepped straight out of an MTV video—daring the whole school to watch.

Without hesitation, he grabbed her hand and spun her into him. The sight knocked the breath from my lungs. Fine. Two could play.

"Yes, Troy," I said, my voice pitched too high, too bright.

His hand clamped at my waist, heavy, sure. We swayed into the crowd, but all I saw was Jake—his mouth on Bridgette's, her arms coiled around his neck. The kiss was messy, theatrical, meant for an audience.

Me.

A bitter taste filled my mouth, sharp as battery acid.

Amy's voice cut through the noise. "Kelly, no! You told me—"

I ignored her. My smile was sharp, brittle. "Want to get out of here?" I asked Troy, my voice steadier than I felt.

He grinned, smug and satisfied.

But before the gym doors closed behind me, I twisted back. Jake's eyes found mine. Even with Bridgette tangled around him, his kiss faltered. Regret—raw and fleeting—flashed there.

Too late.

Outside, the night hit me full in the face. The cold clung to my bare shoulders, sharper than any heartbreak ballad.

The North Star held steady overhead, stubborn and confident. The rest of the sky sprawled in disarray, constellations broken, scattered. It felt personal, like the universe was mocking me.

Troy's arm slid around me, his voice low at my ear, words I didn't catch.

A tear slipped free as I walked toward his car, regret echoing with every step.

Jake
Boise, Idaho

JAKE PAUSED AT THE DOORWAY,

his hand resting on the frame. The soft glow of Becca's bedside lamp cast the room in gold, shadows stretching long across the carpet. She was already curled up beneath her quilt, a book open in her lap, the faint scent of dryer sheets clinging to her pillowcase. Forget-me-nots sat in a rinsed-out jelly jar on her nightstand, their petals fragile and blue against the stark white of the wall.

"Hey, sweetie." His voice softened as he stepped in. "You need water or anything?"

Becca glanced up from her book, her hair spilling across her cheek. "I already got one."

"Okay. Sweet dreams. Love you." He leaned down, brushing his lips across her forehead. Her skin was warm, the way only kids were at bedtime, steeped in the day's sun and play.

"Dad?"

He turned back, catching the way her eyes flickered, her small fingers tracing the corner of her quilt. "Yeah?"

Her voice cracked slightly, almost lost in the hush of the room. "Why are you letting Mom leave?"

The question landed heavily. Jake exhaled, sinking onto the edge of her bed. The mattress dipped under his weight, the springs groaning in protest. He rubbed a hand over his jaw, buying himself a second. "Because, honey, when one person wants out of a marriage, there's not much the other person can do to stop them."

She pressed her lips together, eyes shimmering. "What if I promise to help out more? I've been keeping my room cleaner since Mom left and—"

Jake shook his head quickly, gently. "It has nothing to do with you or your siblings, baby. Mommy loves you all so much. She just . . ." He swallowed, the taste of old bitterness sharp on his tongue. "She just doesn't love me anymore."

"I miss her." Becca wiped at her cheek, but a tear still slid down, catching the light. The sound of it—her quiet sniff, the way she tried to be brave—cut through him sharper than any fight with Nicole ever had.

"I know, kiddo," he murmured, pressing a hand to her blanket-covered knee. "That's why you're going to visit her this weekend."

He forced a smile, hoping she'd mirror it, but her face stayed stubbornly still. His own chest ached, heavy as stone.

Looking for a distraction, his eyes landed on the forget-me-nots. "What are these, Becca?"

She brightened just a fraction. "I found them at school. Remember when you told me the story about the knight?"

Jake's throat tightened. He nodded slowly, fingers brushing the cool rim of the glass jar. He bent down and kissed her forehead again. She plucked one flower from the bunch and handed it to him, her small hand brushing his calloused fingers.

He twisted the stem between his thumb and forefinger, petals trembling with the movement.

"Yeah," he whispered. "I remember. Now get some sleep, kiddo. Love you."

Her eyes fluttered shut as he slipped out, the flower still pinched between his fingers. The faint sweetness of it rose toward him. It was fragile, fleeting, and impossible to ignore.

He stood in the hallway, letting his eyes adjust to the softer dark. The night-light by the bathroom cast a small moon on the carpet. Somewhere down the hall, a baseboard heater clicked and settled. From the boys' room came the slow, uneven chorus of sleep breathing. And from the twins' room, a soft shuffle as someone turned over and hugged a stuffed animal closer.

Jake looked at the tiny blue flower pinched between his fingers and felt how absurdly light it was. It was like holding a wish.

In the kitchen, the dishwasher hummed a low, steady note. Two lunchboxes sat open on the counter, peanut-butter knives rinsed but not put away, a constellation of crumbs glittering under the pendants.

Jake found a rinsed espresso cup, filled it halfway, and set the forget-me-not inside. The flower tipped drunkenly toward the light. He straightened it with a careful fingertip, then leaned his palms on the cool edge of the sink until the ache behind his ribs receded enough to breathe through.

The story came back to him. There was the knight, the river, and the plea to remember. He'd told it a hundred times at bedtime because the kids loved the part where the armor clanked and the current was too strong. He plucked the flower out of the cup and held it again.

Jake swallowed. There were some currents you couldn't fight. Becca's question lived in his chest now—yet another layer of hurt. He could answer the legal half, but he couldn't fix his daughter's longing.

He took the guitar from where he'd left it by the breakfast nook table after fixing the string after dinner. Then Jake sank onto the bottom stair. He tucked the flower beneath the low E at the headstock, where he sometimes kept a spare pick. Then Jake let his thumb find the shape of that stubborn melody. The house was quiet, and the first note felt like a secret released. Words skimmed across the surface. It was nothing fancy, nothing that would ever see a stage.

> *If you need the road, I'll watch the rearview*
> *If you need the dark, I'll leave a light*
> *If you need the river, I'll stand on the shoreline*
> *Saying your name to the night.*

His phone buzzed against the counter, interrupting the words that drifted through his mind. He got up and reached for it, thumb hovering, then flipped it over.

Sorry dude. Got busy at a job and forgot to send. Kelly will take your call. Call me.

Ben

For a beat, the room spun. The past and present overlapped like two radio stations bleeding into each other. Jake set the phone face down again and moved the forget-me-not from the guitar back into the little cup by the sink. One look at those blue petals, bold against the white tile, and the memory hit him like it had been waiting. Then he picked up the phone to call Ben.

✦ ✦ ✦

Jake
Boise, Idaho

The silence in the family room swelled, pressing against the edges of the ESPN commentary that spilled out of the television. His conversation with Ben replayed over and over in his head. Jake reached for a throw pillow, pulling it against his chest like an anchor. He sank deeper into the couch. The game played on. Scores flashed across the bottom of the screen. The announcers' bright voices clashed with the dull ache under his ribs.

Kelly Richardson. After all these years.

His eyes went to the photo frame on the end table. He picked it up, the cool glass smooth beneath his fingers. The picture was of his kids, grinning with sticky fingers at a backyard cookout. Amy and Ben smiled in the background. Everyone had been caught mid-laughter. A good day. The kind that went too fast.

Lamplight cut across the glass, making their smiles gleam brighter than he remembered. But as Jake stared, the edges blurred. He couldn't stop seeing the person who wasn't in the frame. The person who had drifted, the one who had chosen distance.

He set the frame down carefully, as if it might shatter with the weight of what it represented. Then he grabbed his phone.

Ben's most recent text glowed at the top of the screen: a single line, a string of digits. Kelly's work number.

The frame and the number. The present and the past. He just stared.

After a few minutes, Jake leaned back, running a hand through his hair. His chest felt tight, achy. The digits blurred for a second as his eyes burned. Thirty-two years. Thirty-two years since he'd heard Kelly's laugh without reservation. Thirty-two years since he'd brushed popcorn out of his hair after a basement pillow fight and since he'd tucked a strand of her hair behind her ear, feeling the ground tilt beneath him.

The phone was warm in his hand now.

If he called her tomorrow, nothing would be the same. If he didn't, he'd never know.

The muffled roar of a crowd came from the TV, and he clicked it off. Her number was there. Real. Present. Kelly Richardson wasn't a memory anymore. She was one tap away. And Jake wasn't sure if he was ready to open that door. Or if it had already swung wide without him.

Later, upstairs, Jake dragged himself into his bedroom. He took off his shoes and started the autopilot of bedtime: lamp, watch, and ring tray. Then he stopped, and a thought caught him by the collar. He crossed to the closet, shifted a row of shoe boxes, and reached high for the cardboard rectangle he hadn't touched in years. Dust bloomed when he pulled it down. He blew gently against the lid.

Inside were his old yearbooks, edges silvered with wear. There were band flyers and ticket stubs. A handful of Polaroids curled at the corners. He thumbed through them until he found the one he was looking for. Kelly at seventeen, neon bright in a hot pink top and acid-wash skirt. Her hair was half up in a scrunchie. She wore a sideways grin, as if she knew precisely how trouble started and ended. He felt the tug in his chest before the memory fully formed.

Kelly
Eagle River, Alaska
September 1986

THE AUTUMN SKY STRETCHED

endlessly above me, a black canvas pricked with stars so bright I could almost reach up and touch them. Cassiopeia, the Big Dipper—constellations I'd memorized as a kid. They shone down like old friends, constant and unwavering. Then, for a while, I doubted that. I was sure I'd taken a wrong turn somewhere and ended up on a one-way road to disappointment.

Jake Forester approached the car, his sneakers crunching against the gravel. He had a guitar slung casually over one shoulder, like it belonged there. Like he belonged there. With me.

He took a second to open the car door and put the guitar on the seat. Then Jake slid onto the hood next to me, mirroring my posture. One arm tucked behind his head, the other resting close enough that our fingers nearly touched.

I lay sprawled across the hood of Jake's black GT Escort, the metal cool against my back. My stomach quivered, but not from the cold. I was afraid to speak, afraid my voice would shake and give me away. Jake would think I was cold, and I was. But then he'd suggest we sit by the fire, which would be totally awkward since that's where our two friends were making out. So, instead, I stayed silent, staring at the stars as if my life depended on it.

The scent of pine mingled with the smoky tang of the bonfire crackling a few yards away. Over there, Amy and Ben sat curled up together, his arm draped around her shoulders. Their faces had been pressed together for so long that I half expected them to break some kind of record. *Come up for air, guys. Seriously.*

They were so wrapped up in each other that it made my chest ache. Or maybe it was Jake's closeness that did that. I watched them from the corner of my eye—the way their shadows flickered in the firelight, their whispers lost in the rustling of leaves.

Whitney Houston's "Saving All My Love for You" crackled through the car's radio, the soft melody curling around me, pulling me into something that felt too big to name. It felt like love. But we were too young for that, weren't we?

The night breeze picked up, carrying the crisp scent of pine and a faint hint of fish from the lake. It also held the last whispers of fall. The wind teased at my bangs—styled to absolute perfection with Aqua Net—before tugging at the loose strands of my hair. I imagined it lifting the scent of strawberry lip gloss and drugstore hairspray toward Jake and wondered if he liked it.

I took a deep breath and let the air settle in my lungs. I pressed a hand over my heart, feeling its steady rhythm beneath my palm. I wanted to believe I was as sure and steady as the stars above. But tonight, I wasn't so sure.

Amy's laugh rang out—light and breathless—before Ben silenced it with another kiss, and I looked away, my gaze drifting back to the sky. The stars blinked down at me like they held secrets I wasn't ready to hear.

My friends, Ben and Amy, had found their North Stars in each other. As for me and Jake? I hoped that our story might just be beginning.

The fire crackled again, sending up tiny embers that danced against the dark sky. The scent of burning wood wrapped around me like a worn-in flannel. Beside me, Jake shifted. The hood of the car gave a small, agreeable groan under his weight. The space between us felt impossibly small and impossibly wide at the same time.

"Have they come up for air yet?" I nodded toward the bonfire where Ben and Amy were still wrapped in their own universe.

"Nope." Jake's grin flickered in the firelight.

I sighed, shaking my head. "Someone should tell them the human brain can't survive without oxygen."

He laughed. It was soft and low. "Their SAT scores are going to suffer for sure."

I tipped my head back. The sky still felt close enough to touch. "Look," I said, pointing. "See that one?" I traced an invisible line through the dark.

He followed my hand.

"That one's Polaris. The North Star. It's the only star in the sky that doesn't move. Everything else wheels around it. That's why ships can navigate by it." I glanced at him, suddenly aware of how earnest I sounded. "It always leads them home."

"Good to know." He said it without a trace of teasing, eyes still on the point of light like it had just told him a secret. The fire popped. And somewhere in the distance, laughter drifted across the lake—thin, faraway—as if the rest of the world had pulled back to give us space.

✦ ✦ ✦

Kelly
Boise, Idaho

My mind wasn't on my work. Yet at the same time, it seemed as if all my senses were heightened with the realization that Jake had my number and might call.

I sat at my desk, door cracked open, the quiet hum of the office drifting in. The click of a stapler. The steady, monotonous buzz of the copier spitting out page after page. The muffled sound of voices. Through the frosted glass across the hall, another couple argued softly in Conference Room B. Everything was the same, yet everything had changed.

I kept my head down, letting the motion of alphabetizing legal documents wash over me. There was something almost meditative about it. Prenuptial agreements, custody agreements, and divorce decrees. Love stories, stripped down and labeled. Heartbreaks that unraveled one sheet at a time.

I slid a file into the cabinet. The metal felt cool beneath my fingertips, and then I reached for the next in the stack. Andrews, Phillip and Michelle. Mediation scheduled. Property division, still pending. I remembered them. He had a nervous laugh, and she wore perfume that lingered in the air after she left. It had been floral and a little too sweet for my taste.

Behind the glass, voices sharpened. Tension splintered, rising. Something about the dog, or maybe the lake house. It didn't matter. The arguments all bled together after a while. Promises made, promises broken. Did the walls ever get tired of holding so much heartbreak?

To my left, Sharon, our office manager, answered the phone with her signature singsong voice. "Good morning, Alden & Associates." At least ten years older than me, she still looked spry. Her lipstick was never smeared. Her bun was always perfect.

Across the room, Ted shuffled his papers and sipped burnt coffee. His eyes flicked to the clock every few minutes. Even though the day had barely started, his mind was already halfway out the door.

Janie, my assistant, breezed by with a stack of mail. Her perfume trailed behind her. The sharp citrus scent always made me think of summer, no matter what time of year it was.

I caught a glimpse of her smile as she handed off a package to Anthony, who ran the back office. Anthony always wore the same navy sweater, whatever the weather.

The copier groaned, coughing out another set of forms. I tucked a loose strand of hair behind my ear and tried not to think about the couple in Conference Room B. People who once couldn't go a day without hearing each other's voices now couldn't agree on who got the snowblower. I wondered if my parents were ever happy, before Alaska, before everything got cold.

Marriage? Overrated. I filed the next document and tried not to wonder how many love stories had ended in rooms just like this.

I tucked another file into the cabinet, realizing my name was hidden somewhere in those hanging folders. My signature on the dotted line. My divorce, stamped and filed and final.

I paused for a moment and picked up my coffee cup. The coffee was lukewarm, and a bitter film coated the roof of my mouth every time I sipped. I absently swirled the red straw in circles, watching the pale liquid slosh against the sides of the styrofoam cup. Then the swirling stopped. Forget-me-nots decorated the outside of the cup. I swallowed hard. Tiny blue blossoms marched around the rim like they were mocking me.

My eyes drifted to the frame on the corner of my desk. Christmas, years ago. Troy, the kids, me. Smiles frozen mid-snap. I remembered the scratch of Alex's wool sweater against my arm and the sharp pine smell of the tree in the background. And there he was. Troy. Planted right in the middle, impossible to crop out.

A knock pulled me back. I glanced up.

Amy leaned around the doorframe, her hair catching the light like spun copper. "Bad time?"

The tightness in my chest eased. "Not at all. Come in. Did we have lunch planned today?"

She crossed the room and dropped into the chair opposite me, the scent of her dry shampoo adding a fresh note to the stale office air.

"Well, now we do! How's your week going?" she asked.

"Oh, you know." I pressed the straw against the side of the cup. "Just wondering when men got out of the 'knight in shining armor' business."

Amy winced in mock sympathy. "Oof. That bad, huh?"

"It's nothing out of the usual." I shrugged. "I'm just starting to wonder if anyone actually gets a 'happily ever after' anymore."

Her gaze flicked to the photo frame, then back to me. "They must. Otherwise, one hundred percent of marriages would end in divorce."

I laughed softly, though my throat felt dry. My eyes betrayed me, sliding toward the frame again.

"Do you miss him?"

"Troy?" My voice came out sharper than I intended. "He

checked out of our marriage so long ago that I stopped missing him before he ever served the papers. But . . ." I tapped the frame's glass with my fingertip. "This is my favorite picture of the kids. And he's right in the middle. I can't rip him out without ripping them, too."

"So take a new picture."

"It's hard to get everyone together. Lauren's busy with the kids. Braxton's always traveling for work, and Alex is in his second year of college." Saying it out loud left a hollow ache in my chest. It was as if naming the distance made it expand.

Amy leaned forward. "You know, there are apps that could cut Troy out entirely. Poof. Gone. Like he was never there."

I raised an eyebrow.

She groaned. "I lost you at 'apps,' didn't I?"

"Yep."

"Give it here." She reached for the frame, her rings clinking softly against the glass. "I'll bring it back tomorrow when I pick you up for your surprise."

My head snapped up. "Surprise?"

Her grin widened. "I booked us a glamour shoot at a local photography studio."

"What? Why?"

"To have fun!"

The word "glamour" immediately yanked me back to high school, when Amy and I used to raid her mom's makeup drawer and transform each other into would-be models. We'd strike dramatic poses for the mirror, convinced *Seventeen* magazine's "Great Model Search" would discover us any minute.

"I don't have time for—"

"You totally do." She turned toward the hall. "Janie, didn't we just put it on her calendar?"

Out front, Janie gave a thumbs-up without looking away from her screen.

"Thanks, Janie!" Amy called, planting both hands on her hips.

Janie and I usually talked via the intercom on my desk, but obviously that wasn't Amy's style. Shouting down the hall seemed to work better for her.

I shook my head. "Amy, I really don't think—"

"Come on. You could use a break, tomorrow is Friday, and I could use a smoking-hot picture of you to put on the dating sites I'm signing you up for."

Back then, it was silly, fun, safe. But now? The thought of getting glammed up for some random photographer I didn't even know made my stomach sink. And posting a photo on a dating site? No way. Absolutely not. Thank you very much.

My mouth dropped open. "You wouldn't."

"I already did. Signed you up for the glamour shoot. Not the dating site. At least not yet."

I lifted both of my hands in protest. The bitter coffee splashed over the cup in my hand. "Amy, stop trying to put me back on the horse. It went lame years ago." I set the cup down hard.

"Then I guess I shouldn't tell you I gave a guy your number last night?"

The coffee suddenly tasted metallic on my tongue. My stomach dropped. "What? Who?" Then I remembered. *Jake.*

At that moment, the intercom on my desk buzzed and I flinched.

I pressed the button. "What is it, Janie?"

A faint crackle, then Janie's voice. "Call for you on line one."

Amy leaned forward, eyes gleaming. "Well, well—"

"He's calling now?" My voice cracked. Even though I had told Amy she could pass on my work number, the realistic part of me just assumed Jake wouldn't call.

The phone rang again, shrill and immediate, making me jump so hard I nearly knocked the coffee cup off my desk. Amy nodded, delight dancing in her eyes.

"For real, it's Jake?" I hissed. "I haven't spoken to this man in over thirty years!"

Amy clasped her hands in front of her. "Don't worry about that now, just answer it."

I slammed the intercom button again. "Tell him I'm busy."

"Wait a sec, Janie!" Amy yelled out the door. She wagged her finger at me. "Oh no, you don't. You answer that phone!"

I shook my head so hard it made me dizzy.

"Why not?"

"Because . . . because . . ." Words refused to line up. My mouth went dry. My pulse thrummed in my ears.

Amy narrowed her eyes. "Because you still have feelings for him?"

"Don't be crazy." The denial came out too quickly.

"Then answer the phone."

"I'm not going to—"

Before I could finish, Amy picked up the phone on my desk. "Hey, Jake," she sang, winking at me.

I glared at her, mouthing, *No.*

Amy mouthed back, *Yes.*

On the other end, I could hear Jake's voice filtering in, confused. "Amy? Did I dial the wrong number?"

"Nope," Amy chirped. "Kelly's right here. Have at her!"

She shoved the receiver toward me, triumphant.

I shook my head. Amy rolled her eyes.

Then she leaned down, whispering so only I could hear. "Didn't you say a big case could make you a partner? Jake's done really well for himself. This could be your break."

I exhaled, long and ragged. Every nerve in my body was a live wire.

Amy pressed the receiver into my hand like she was passing me a ticking bomb. She mouthed, *Talk to him.* Then, in a flash, she swept out of my office, Christmas photo in hand and the powdery aroma of dry shampoo trailing behind her.

I pressed the receiver to my ear. "Hello?" My voice barely sounded like mine.

A pause.

"Kelly?" His voice was warm and low. It was like hearing a song I hadn't played in years but still knew every note to. "Kelly, is that you?"

My heart missed a beat. There was no dramatic gasp, and no Hollywood clutch at my chest. Just a slight quiver. Barely there. But I felt it all the same.

"Uh . . . Kelly? Hello?"

And just like that, my mind fractured—half here in my office, half slipping back in time.

Kelly
Eagle River, Alaska
September 1986

THE BLEACHERS TREMBLED

under the stamp of boots and the hundreds of voices that roared for Ben Bailey.

I cheered along with the others as Ben slipped past a defender and sent the football arcing downfield as if his entire future hung in the laces. The crowd detonated when the receiver snagged it in the end zone. Metal rattled under me. A cowbell clanged somewhere behind my head. Yet even as I cheered for Ben, my thoughts were on someone else entirely.

I was huddled on the top row, and my thighs had grown numb against the frozen aluminum. Both of my hands were wrapped around a paper cup of hot chocolate, which had actually stopped being hot ten minutes ago. My breath came in little clouds, and I considered calling my dad to pick me up early. The outfit that had seemed cute when I left the house—layered pastel sweaters and a denim mini with tights and legwarmers— was not built for Alaskan football nights. Not even close.

"I told you," Amy rasped beside me, voice shredded from cheering. "This is Ben's night. MVP. Calling it."

"Good for Ben," I said, trying to make my teeth stop chattering. I didn't say the other thing, the only thing that really mattered: Jake still hadn't shown up.

I hadn't seen him since Tuesday in history class, when he'd pressed one headphone gently against my ear just long enough for "True" by Spandau Ballet to float between us, and then he grinned like he'd gotten away with something. We weren't a couple—nothing had happened, not really—but sometimes he looked at me like I wasn't just the new girl from the Lower 48 with too much hairspray and too few layers.

Then, as if I'd summoned him with my thoughts, Jake appeared at the base of the bleachers. My breath snagged mid-cloud.

Letterman jacket. Hoodie. Jeans. His hands were jammed into the kangaroo pocket. His hair was wind-messy, and there was a crescent of dirt across his cheek like he'd sprinted here straight from shoveling snow or helping his brothers fix a bike. He ignored the crowd and looked up, like he already knew where I'd be. When his eyes found me, they lit up in a way that made my chest ache.

"Sorry I'm late," he said after he climbed to the top to join us. His breath puffed out clouds in the cold, and a smile was tucked into the corner of his mouth. "Had to help my mom with something."

I opened my mouth, but whatever I meant to say dissolved into fog. I couldn't feel my legs. I could barely think.

"You're freezing," he said, already shrugging out of his jacket. He wrapped it around my shoulders without asking. It was heavy and warm, and then—God help me—he slid in beside me and tucked his arm around me like we'd been doing that forever.

My heart thudded so hard it drowned out the cheerleaders. The jacket smelled like boys and laundry soap, Ralph Lauren Polo, and the faintest hint of woodsmoke. Heat moved through the fabric and up my spine.

"Better?" he asked, looking down at me with those ridiculously gorgeous eyes. The kind that could've landed him on a Teen Beat poster without even trying.

"Yeah," I managed.

We watched a few plays in silence. Amy shouted Ben's name

like he could hear her above the din. I didn't move. I didn't even blink, afraid the moment might crack at any second.

"Jake!" A high, bright voice cut through the cold from down by the fence.

I turned. Bridgette—cheer captain, with eyeliner sharp enough to slice and lips always shiny. She was all bounce and glitter, a spotlight masquerading as a person.

Jake lifted a hand. Not a shy hello. A full-armed, enthusiastic wave. He even smiled.

My stomach twisted. He didn't say anything. He didn't have to. I felt the subtle shift, his attention untying itself from me and floating down the bleachers like a balloon that knew where it belonged.

When the game ended, Amy and I moved to the girls' bathroom. Amy insisted we celebrate after our team won. I, for one, wanted to disappear into my legwarmers. Instead, I ended up at the movies—wedged between Amy and the aisle. A cherry Icee sat in my hand, untouched until the top turned to syrup and the bottom to ice.

The lights dimmed and previews boomed across the screen. Ben and Amy crunched popcorn as if it were going out of style. Somewhere in the back row, Jake kissed Bridgette.

I saw it. Just a flicker when the screen flashed bright enough to put the whole theater in silhouette. His hand at her jaw. Her ponytail slipped off her shoulder as she tilted her head forward. It was a second. It was enough.

My throat cinched. The screen blurred. Amy leaned close, her whisper hot against my ear. "Ignore her. She throws herself at anything with a decent smile."

"I'm fine," I lied, taking a long pull of red sugar through the bent straw.

I wasn't fine because I wasn't Bridgette.

I was the girl he'd wrapped his coat around under the lights and in the middle of the roar. But I wasn't the girl he kissed.

Jake
Boise, Idaho

JAKE LEANED OVER THE COUNTER,

the phone pressed loosely in his hand, his other palm flat against the cool granite. The kitchen smelled faintly of brewed coffee and the lemon oil his housekeeper used on the wood floors.

He straightened at the sound of her voice. It was steady, clipped, unmistakably hers. But then there was silence.

"Uh . . . Kelly? Hello?"

"Yes?" she finally answered, cautiously.

He reached out and grabbed his coffee mug tightly, the heat biting into his palm. He let go and swallowed, his mouth suddenly dry. "Kelly Richardson? From Eagle River?"

For a beat, there was silence, only the faint hiss of the line filling the space. Jake's pulse thudded in his ears. He could picture her. Older now, sure, but still the girl who had once scribbled his name into the margins of her notebooks.

"Yes," she said finally. "Who is this?"

Jake exhaled, pressing his hand to the edge of the counter as if bracing himself. "It's Jake. Jake Forester."

They finally got through the awkwardness of talking again after all these years.

"Hey, Jake. It's . . . been a long time."

"Too long. How have you been?"

Kelly
Boise, Idaho

I tried to laugh, but it came out thin. "How have I been? You know, I'm . . . hanging in there." My eyes rolled at my own awkwardness, because, really—*hanging in there*?

He hesitated. "Sorry to call out of the blue. Ben and Amy gave me your number. Thanks for taking my call, Kelly."

The way he said my name—low, certain—shook something loose in me. I held the silence a beat too long, clutching it like a lifeline, steadying myself against the ground that suddenly felt less certain beneath my feet. "Hi."

"I . . . uh, yeah, thanks for answering. I wasn't sure you would."

I tried for breezy, though my hands trembled and my mouth tasted like nerves and stale coffee. "You caught me filing the remains of other people's love stories. In a file cabinet, you know. Perfect timing."

He laughed, soft and familiar. And just like that, I was seventeen again—hands behind my head on the hood of his car, with the cold night biting at my skin and the sky wide with the brightest of stars. My chest ached with the memory.

"Listen," he said carefully. "I'm not calling to . . . I mean, I don't want to make things weird."

Too late, I thought, but the words stayed stuck behind my teeth.

"I need a lawyer," he said finally. "Nicole's . . . well, things aren't working. For real this time. And honestly, I don't even know where to start."

I closed my eyes, pressing a thumb to the hollow of my throat, willing my breathing to calm.

The office around me faded, even the muffled argument behind the frosted glass. It was just his voice and mine, suspended between what was and . . . now.

"I'm sorry, Jake," I whispered, and meant it. "That's . . . I'm sorry."

That's not fair.

That's life.

That's crazy that someone would walk away from you.

I wasn't sure which phrase had tried to come out.

"She said she's tired of trying," he admitted. "We have seven kids. I don't want to lose them."

My chest pinched sharply. I pressed a hand to it, as if I could hold in the hurt. I pictured him, head bent, one hand gripping the phone, and the weight of everything he couldn't fix pressing down on his shoulders.

"I'm not looking for a favor," he rushed to add. "Just . . . I trust you. And I figured if anyone could help me see clearly, it's you."

The taste of burnt coffee lingered on my tongue. I drew in a slow breath. "Jake, maybe what you need isn't a lawyer. Maybe you need a counselor. Maybe it's not too late to work it out."

He went quiet. "You really think so?"

"I think you should try." My pulse thundered in my ears, but I kept my tone calm. "For your kids. For your marriage. If there's still a chance, you should take it."

He exhaled, shaky, and for a moment, it felt like he was right there beside me. "That sounds like you."

"Like what?"

"Like someone who still believes in good endings."

My eyes stung. I turned toward the window. The Boise sky was hanging dull and gray above the rooftops. The hearts and flowers from a few days ago were gone. Now, horns blared and people rushed through their lives. Yet all that dimmed beneath the thrum of his presence on the line.

Jake Forester wasn't just a name from my past anymore. He wasn't a what-if tucked in a box. He was real. His voice was close.

I steadied myself with the papers on my desk. *This* is real life, I reminded myself—case numbers beneath my fingertips. Yet Jake's name didn't have to be on one of these files. Not if there was a chance. "I believe in trying, Jake. Especially when it's hard."

He didn't answer right away. Finally, he cleared his throat. "I miss talking to you."

My grip on the phone tightened to a white-knuckled hold. The cool plastic pressed against my cheek. I was at work, I reminded myself. Doing my job. Helping someone in need. Nothing more.

"That's . . . kind of you to say," I managed, forcing my voice to be even and professional. "But I think it's best if we keep this about your case. If you'd like to discuss the next steps, I can guide you through the process. Or refer you to mediation. Or–"

"Or we can meet for coffee," he interrupted. "There's too much to discuss over the phone."

I blinked hard, my throat tight. "Um, I don't–"

"Come on, Kel. You're the only person I'd trust with this sort of thing."

I smacked myself lightly with the papers on my desk, wincing. "When?"

"Tomorrow?"

"I have some meetings, and then Amy's dragging me into one of her schemes–"

"Sounds like Amy," he said with a smile in his voice.

"Let me look into next week–" I offered, trying to stall.

"What about tomorrow night?"

I tipped my head back, staring at the ceiling tiles as if they could rescue me. *Say no. Say no.*

"Please, Kel. I'm desperate."

The word caught me off guard. *Jake desperate?*

Every brick I was attempting to use to build a wall between us crumbled. I bit my lower lip, attempting to keep a level head. "Okay. Tomorrow night. Say . . . seven?"

"Works for me. I'll text you the address. See you then."

"Bye."

The line went dead.

I sat there for a moment, clutching the receiver, nearly hyperventilating. My hands trembled as I pulled up my contacts on my cell phone and typed in his name and the number saved on Caller ID on my desk phone.

Jake Forester. The letters glowed on the screen. My breath caught as if I'd written them on my heart all over again.

Jake
Boise, Idaho

JAKE HURRIED FROM THE KITCHEN

and took the stairs to his bedroom two at a time. Even though he was the only one at home, he closed the door behind him after he entered. "Alexa, play Def Leppard."

The room filled with the opening chords of "Photograph," the guitar riff sharp and familiar. It tugged him straight back to the late eighties. The ache of remembering collided with the surprise of it. How long had it been since he'd listened to anything just for himself?

He scanned the room, frowning at the mess. A shirt was slung carelessly over the chair. Yesterday's jeans lay crumpled on the floor. The unmade side of his bed looked like it hadn't seen order in weeks. With a grunt, he bent down, scooped up clothes, and tossed them into the hamper. The guitar solo blared as he pulled the sheets tight, smoothing the wrinkles with a brisk hand.

In the bathroom, steam curled as he turned on the faucet. The water ran hot and fast. He leaned over the sink, splashing his face. The mirror caught him at an angle he didn't love—shadows under his eyes, stubble edging toward scruff.

He reached for his razor. The scrape of metal against skin mingled with Joe Elliott's voice belting through the speakers. The song vibrated the walls.

He pressed the razor to his jaw, the sharp glide cutting through the hum of Def Leppard. With his free hand, he unlocked his phone, tapped a number, and set it on the counter.

"Jake?" His coworker's voice crackled through the speaker, tinny against the tile. "What's up?"

"I'm coming into the office tomorrow," Jake said, swiping the razor down, foam gathering in neat lines.

Cam said, "You sure you're ready? You can take a little more time if needed. We're holding things down pretty well here—"

"I'm sure." He rinsed the blade under running water, the droplets splattering onto the counter. "I'll be in that part of town."

"Sounds good, man. The guys and I will catch you up to speed when you get here."

"See you then." He tapped the phone screen with the back of a damp knuckle, ending the call.

The music filled the silence again. *"I don't want your photograph . . ."*

Jake ran the razor one last time along his jaw, then rinsed, splashing water across his skin. He patted his face dry, inhaling the clean scent of shaving cream and citrus soap, trying to wash away more than just stubble.

Tomorrow loomed in his chest like a drumbeat. *Kelly.*

An hour later, the line of minivans and SUVs inched forward, brake lights glowing in the late afternoon haze. Jake drummed his fingers against the steering wheel, the faint hum of Def Leppard still lingering in his ears from the drive over.

The air inside the car smelled faintly of soap and aftershave, cleaner than it had been in weeks. A to-go coffee cup rattled in the console every time he shifted.

The school doors swung open, and a tide of kids spilled out. Backpacks bounced and voices rose high with end-of-day energy. Jake spotted his crew instantly—the familiar shuffle, the way they moved like a loosely tied knot. He rolled down the window and leaned out, a grin stretching across his face. "Hey guys! How was school?"

They froze mid-step, staring at him like he'd grown a second head.

"Woah, Dad!" Tyler shouted, breaking into laughter. "When did you shower?"

Jake barked out a laugh as he pushed the door open. The late sun was warm against his freshly shaved skin as he rounded the hood. "I never actually stopped showering, Ty."

"Could've fooled us," Sadie quipped, her tone dry but her eyes bright with amusement.

He gestured for Chris to take the driver's seat, tossing him the keys. Chris caught them easily, but didn't move. He stood there just blinking at Jake as if he were waiting for the punchline.

"You shaved," Chris finally said, skeptical.

Jake tugged at his jawline, still smooth. "I did."

Rae slid into the back, buckling her seat belt with a triumphant grin. "And you're not wearing pajamas."

Jake grinned, spreading his arms like a magician revealing a trick. "What can I say? The stranded-on-a-desert-island look was getting old."

The kids laughed with relief. It made the air in the car feel lighter as backpacks swung and zippers clinked. But Chris's brow furrowed as he slid behind the wheel. His silence was louder than the chatter of his siblings.

Jake caught it. Of course he did. "Something wrong?" he asked gently.

Chris just shrugged, adjusting the mirrors with exaggerated precision. Then, without answering, he pulled the car smoothly away from the curb.

Jake sank deeper into the passenger seat, the seat belt tugging across his chest. The scent of fresh soap still clung to him, but Chris's silence settled heavily. Jake rested his elbow against the window, watching the school recede in the mirror.

For the first time in a long while, he felt a glimmer of hope for the future. He just wasn't sure his son believed it yet.

Jake
Boise, Idaho

Jake sat on his knees in the corner of Lily's room, fumbling with an Allen wrench. A half-assembled bedframe sprawled out on the floor, stubborn as a mule. Each time he tightened a bolt, the thing tilted, mocking his effort.

Princess bedding waited in its shiny package against the wall—Lily's birthday request that was over a month late. Leo had been easy. He'd asked for a new bike. Out of everything she could've chosen, Lily wanted this. A big girl's room. And he was the one who had to put it together, as if he had any idea of what that meant. Thankfully, Rae had picked out a few things online and had them shipped. Too bad his oldest daughter had too much homework tonight to help everything come together.

Jake rubbed the back of his neck, staring at the frame like it might offer answers. His contribution so far had been limited to ordering a few items and some clumsy elbow grease. He knew it wasn't enough. Not compared to everything Nic used to do—the organizing, the soft touches. The way she made every room feel like a haven.

Still, he was here. Trying.

His phone was balanced between his shoulder and ear, voice steady for the health client on the other end. "The best part of our program is there are four elements," he explained, tightening another bolt. "First, the food. Next, the structure that moves you toward optimal health. There's the community, and then there's me—as your coach. Someone you can count on."

He'd said the line thousands of times. He'd carried those words onto stages, into boardrooms, and even into work-from-home calls in this mansion. But none of that mattered when the house was quiet and the bedframe mocked him. None of it mattered when the kids looked at him with eyes that often asked, *What now, Dad?*

The woman hesitated on the other end. "I'll get back to you after vacation, okay? I do need to improve my health, but it's Italy after all."

Jake let his voice soften. "Sure. I'll be here."

The call ended. The wrench slipped from his hand and smashed into his thumb. Pain shot through him, stupid and sharp. He hissed under his breath and sat back hard on his heels. The wrench rolled across the gleaming hardwood, clinking against the baseboard.

He closed his eyes, taking in what he could around him: the faint sounds of the kids getting ready for bed down the hall, the low hum of the refrigerator downstairs, the drip of a faucet somewhere, the ache of too much silence. This house had never felt so cavernous. The vaulted ceilings, the wide echoing hallways, the oversized rooms. The marble counters and gleaming floors reflected the afternoon sun, but instead of warmth, the light only seemed to highlight the emptiness. He missed doing life with someone—sharing the ups and downs of family and life.

And then Kelly's voice replayed in his memory—gentle, steady, achingly familiar after thirty-two years. At first, it had lit something inside him, a rush of joy he hadn't felt in so long.

But then, just as quickly, the weight settled in. That one moment of connection had reminded him of everything he didn't have anymore. Someone who listened. Someone who cared.

He realized, with a jolt, that he'd spent years trying to prove himself to Nicole. Trying to be enough. But in her eyes, he'd always fallen short. And maybe . . . maybe he'd been doing that with God too. Striving, performing, and hoping his effort would measure up. Only to come face to face with his own inadequacy.

Jake dropped his head into his hands, breath ragged. "I don't know what I'm doing, God," he whispered, the words spilling into the quiet room. "I can't fix this. I can't fix me. But I don't want to stay stuck. Please . . . show me how to hope again."

The prayer was shaky, imperfect, but as soon as it left his

lips, something flickered inside him. The slightest glimmer of hope, fragile but real.

His gaze landed on the unopened bedding, a splash of pink and purple against the cream walls. He dragged a hand across the cool plastic wrapping and told himself this mattered. Even if the rest of his life was unraveling, even if he didn't know how to walk this road alone, he could at least do this one thing for his youngest daughter.

The bolt refused to line up, though, no matter how many times Jake twisted the wrench. He sat back on his heels, thumb throbbing. Then he heard footsteps padding down the hallway.

"Dad?"

He turned to see Becca in the doorway, her hair a tangle, pajamas too short at the ankles. Behind her, Lily clutched a stuffed unicorn, eyes wide with curiosity.

Jake cleared his throat. "Hey, girls. Thought you were watching a movie."

"It's boring," Lily said, wrinkling her nose. Then she spotted the bedframe. "Are you building my bed?"

"Trying," Jake admitted, forcing a smile. "But this thing's fighting me."

Becca stepped inside, serious and determined in that way she always was. "You're doing it wrong."

Jake arched his brow. "Oh yeah? Are you a furniture expert now?"

She shrugged, kneeling beside him. "You have to hold the piece straight before you tighten it." She pressed her small hands against the slanted frame, bracing it steady. Jake tightened the bolt again. This time, it held.

"Well, I'll be . . ." He gave her shoulder a playful bump. "Guess I should've hired you as my foreman."

Becca beamed. Lily climbed into his lap without asking, dropping her unicorn so she could point at the unopened bedding. "Can we put it on now?"

Jake swallowed the sudden lump in his throat. He tore open the plastic package, the fabric spilling soft, pink, and purple across the floor. Together, the girls smoothed the sheets, tugged the comforter straight, and tucked the edges. The room began to look less like a project and more like a home he was helping to create.

When they were finished, Lily crawled onto the bed and patted the spot beside her. Jake lay down gingerly, feeling the frame hold beneath his weight. Becca climbed up too, curling against his other side. The scent of laundry soap and ketchup from dinner clung to their clothes.

Jake closed his eyes for a moment. He listened to their giggles, the rustle of sheets, and the muffled pressure of wind against the windows.

"You okay, Daddy?" Becca whispered.

Jake opened his eyes, staring at the ceiling. "I think so," he said softly. "As long as I've got you two . . . and your siblings, of course."

Lily's small hand found his, her fingers sticky but sure. Becca leaned her head against his shoulder. And for the first time in weeks, the mansion didn't feel so empty.

Leo and Tyler burst in then, tumbling onto the floor with a chaotic energy that always left Jake both exhausted and grateful. Becca left to take her evening bath.

Jake rose and tucked his youngest daughter in. Lily curled up in the bedding like it was a nest. Leo and Tyler immediately started sword-fighting with two empty wrapping tubes.

Jake leaned back on his heels, watching them. Their laughter filled the big room, chasing away the quiet. And in the middle of it all, that whispered prayer seemed to echo back, not in words but in giggles and shrieks and sticky little hands.

It was a reminder that maybe—just maybe—God had heard him. And that this flicker of hope was more than his imagination.

Kelly
Boise, Idaho

I COULDN'T SLEEP THE NIGHT

before. My mind had been on Jake and our brief conversation. I'd played and replayed every sentence over in my mind, wondering why he insisted on meeting tonight, especially when I'd made it clear I thought he should try for a second chance with his wife.

The fact that Jake pressed for us to meet meant that he was certain his marriage was over. He needed advice because no matter how much I had urged him to try, he knew it wasn't going to work. But was there more to it than that?

I didn't want to get my hopes up. My chance with Jake was long gone. We were two different people now. What we had was something in the past. I told myself to keep that in mind, and through the night, I pushed down every glimmer of hope that attempted to break through.

At one point, I rolled over and whispered into the darkness. "Lord, you know my heart better than I do. If Jake is just supposed to be my client, let me accept that. Help me be wise and not let old feelings tangle with what's real today. And if there's more . . . if you're writing a new story here . . . then I place it in your hands. I trust you with him. I trust you with me." The prayer wasn't polished, but it quieted the ache enough to let me breathe.

My lack of sleep didn't keep Amy from bursting through my front door in the morning like she was dropping the hottest surprise since Oprah handed out cars. She arrived at my bungalow with a garment bag in one hand and a curling iron in the other.

"Birthday photo shoot!" she announced, voice booming with all the drama of a game show host. "Fifty is fierce, my friend. Time to remind the world."

I'd tried to forget it was my birthday month. I'd also desperately tried to forget I was turning fifty.

I groaned from my place on the couch. "Amy, I deal with divorces. I file paperwork for broken people. Sometimes I give them advice or plead their case. I'm not exactly photo shoot material."

She flopped the bag onto the kitchen table like it was a treasure chest. "You're a beautiful woman. No excuses. We're doing this."

Within thirty minutes, I learned that Amy would be doing my hair, but a real makeup artist would be meeting us at the shoot.

By the time we pulled up to the photography studio, I was already regretting every life choice that had led me to this moment, including befriending Amy in high school. The building itself looked like an abandoned warehouse. Yet once we stepped inside, it was like crossing into another world.

Bright bulbs framed a row of vanity mirrors. Racks of sequined dresses—if you could call two feet of fabric a "dress"—glittered like disco balls. And then there was *her*. The makeup artist.

She glided toward us like she was auditioning for a perfume commercial. Her skin was so flawless I doubted sugar had ever crossed her lips. Her ponytail was sleek enough to slice through glass, and her body? Trim in a way that suggested kale was her love language.

I sent Amy a desperate look, silently begging for rescue. She ignored me, of course, already pawing through hangers of neon feathers and metallic leather like a kid at a yard sale.

"Tell me I'm not wearing those," I hissed.

Amy's eyes sparkled with the kind of mischief that had gotten us both grounded in high school. "Oh, you're definitely wearing these."

I gasped.

"Okay. Actually, I brought something that would fit you better."

I breathed a sigh of relief.

The makeup artist gestured for me to sit. The vanity lights blazed so hot I swore they were cooking my pores. The air smelled like hairspray and pressed powder, and I suddenly felt like I'd stumbled backstage at Miss America.

A brush skimmed across my eyelid, soft as butterfly wings, but what it left behind was anything but delicate. "I can't believe I let you talk me into this," I muttered as the eyeliner tugged. It kept going. And going.

To my temple. To my hairline. Possibly to the next zip code.

Amy clapped her hands. "Yes! Drama! Keep going!"

"Drama?" I squeaked. "I bet I look like Cleopatra's exhausted cousin."

The makeup artist didn't even blink. She just swirled another brush across my cheekbones like she was preparing me for my magazine debut.

And I? I just prayed that none of these photos would ever see the light of day.

When the makeup artist was done, Amy approached with a hanger draped in something silky. She held it up as if it were a crown jewel. A short wrap dress in deep sapphire blue, cinched at the waist with a thin belt. The fabric shimmered just enough to look expensive, the neckline just low enough to make me consider a second layer of Spanx.

"Um," I said slowly, eyeing the hemline that looked like it might declare war on my knees. "Are you sure this is going to look flattering on me?"

The makeup artist, who couldn't have been more than twenty, leaned back with a smug little smile. "Trust me, when we're done with you, every man on the planet is going to swipe right."

"Swipe right?" I repeated, clutching the hanger like it might self-destruct. "What is that, a dance move?" The chair beneath me squeaked when I shifted, nerves buzzing under my skin.

Amy snorted so hard she nearly dropped the feather boa she carried. The artist just shook her head like I'd asked if Walkmans were still a thing.

After I finished dressing, the makeup artist added the final touches. The brush whisked across my cheekbones, leaving behind a faint floral scent mixed with the chalky tang of setting powder. My lips tingled as lipstick went on. At that moment, I'd have given anything for a mango Lip Smacker.

"Okay," the artist finally announced, spinning me toward the mirror. "You're all done."

When I saw myself in the mirror, I blinked once. Then again.

My reflection stared back at me. My eyes were rimmed in smoky black. My lips were so red they could stop traffic. More than that, my lashes looked like they might take flight.

"Oh gosh," I breathed. "I look like Elvira."

Amy leaned forward. "No, you don't."

"Amy," I deadpanned, still frozen. "I can't move my face."

"The makeup has to be dramatic," Amy said with confidence. "Otherwise, in photos, it all just blends. Now come on!" She clapped her hands like a coach revving up the team. "Let's go show your ex what he's missing."

I groaned and pressed a fingertip against my cheek only to find it refused to budge. I wasn't sure if my pores would ever forgive me.

But Amy was already tugging me out of the chair, her excitement practically vibrating through her grip. My stomach flipped as we headed toward the photography area, every sense buzzing. When I settled onto a chair, with plenty of leg showing, hot lights warmed my skin. As a final touch, Amy wrapped the white boa around my shoulders.

Then, a new thought entered my mind. *Please, God, don't let Jake see me like this.*

Music pulsed faintly in the background and the air felt charged. The photographer tilted his head. He squinted at me through the lens like I was a rare bird he couldn't quite classify.

Duran Duran's "Rio" blasted through the studio speakers, Simon Le Bon crooning about dancing on the sand while I tried not to look like a taxidermied flamingo.

I lifted my chin. Crossed my arms. Tried a sultry smile. Even then, I was sure I looked like I was practicing for my mugshot.

"You're doing great!" Amy called from the sidelines. "Just try not to scrunch your eyes up so much when you smile."

I widened them. Big mistake. The photographer actually flinched.

Amy blinked. "Never mind. Scrunch away. Serial killer chic is not the vibe we're going for today."

I sighed, dropping my hands to my hips. "Is it your turn yet?"

"Not this time!" Amy shot back. "Now think Christie Brinkley—circa her Billy Joel era!"

"Pretty sure Christie never had eyeliner stabbing her tear ducts," I muttered, trying another pose that felt like "confused flamingo" meets "should I have stretched before this?"

That's when my phone rang.

I fumbled for my phone. My heart stopped. Jake's name glowed on the screen.

"It's Jake!" I squeaked, my voice an octave too high.

In her excitement, Amy hip-checked the poor photographer so hard his camera nearly toppled off the tripod. "Answer it!"

"I'm trying!" My thumb refused to cooperate, smearing the screen with foundation as I poked at every button except the one I wanted. Finally, the green icon lit up, and I pressed the phone to my ear.

"Jake?" I said breathlessly, praying he hadn't heard the thump of Amy and the photographer colliding behind me—or Simon Le Bon still singing about Rio like the man had stock in chaos.

"Jake," I said more calmly. "We're meeting tonight, right?" *Right?*

Jake
Boise, Idaho

JAKE DRUMMED HIS FINGERS

on the steering wheel as Kelly's voice filled the car through the speaker.

She seemed a little flustered when she answered.

"I know you said you can't meet until tonight," he said, keeping his tone casual, "but I'm in the area and thought I'd drop off the paperwork for you to look over. Are you in the office?"

"No," she answered, a note of hesitation in her voice. "I'm . . . at a photography studio, of all places."

He frowned. "Really? Why?"

"One word. Amy."

Jake chuckled under his breath. "Her crazy scheme."

"Exactly."

"Where's the studio?" he pressed.

"Uh . . ." Kelly didn't answer.

"Is it the one at Capitol and Main? I've taken my teens there for prom photos before."

"Well, it uh . . . yes," Kelly's voice squeaked out.

"I'm heading that way now. Drop a pin. I'll find you."

"Oh, no, Jake, I'm really not in a position to—"

Jake ended the call before Kelly could finish her protest. He knew that tone—half fluster, half defense—and he wasn't about to give her room to talk him out of it. He tossed the phone onto the passenger seat, the screen glowing once before going dark.

The lightest of rain misted across the windshield. Soft streaks caught in the sweep of squeaky wipers. His pulse thudded too loudly for such a quiet street.

By the time he pulled to the curb outside the photography studio, nerves had fully set in. He killed the engine. The tick of cooling metal filled the silence, sharp against the drizzle. Neon from a buzzing sign across the street painted the wet pavement in flickering pink, while the smell of damp asphalt and exhaust hung in the air.

He leaned toward the rearview mirror, smoothing down his hair with one hand. "Kelly Richardson," he murmured, low enough that only the steering wheel heard. "What are you like after all these years?"

The folder of paperwork crinkled in his grip as he climbed out. Drizzle speckled his face, calm and almost sweet. Straightening his shoulders, he tried to gather up the confidence he wasn't sure he had anymore. And then—she was there.

Kelly stepped out of the studio before he made it halfway. Her heels clicked against damp concrete. She stumbled, almost tripping, and his chest tightened with reflex memory. He wanted to reach for her, steady her like he used to, but she caught herself before he could.

For a moment, he didn't recognize her. She wore a large robe over a dress. Heavy makeup masked her features—dark liner, too-red lipstick, some makeup artist's handiwork written all over it. But beneath it? It was her. Wasn't it? The same Kelly who once laughed across diner booths, who hummed along when he fumbled through Bryan Adams on his guitar.

Jake tried to find that girl under the gloss and contour, the one who wore neon sweatshirts and smelled faintly of strawberry shampoo. He searched her face, desperate for a glimpse of the Kelly he'd carried in memory all these years. But the harder he looked, the more he realized the truth: no one is like they used to be. The girl he knew didn't exist anymore.

In her place stood a woman who carried herself with

confidence, wearing armor in the form of lipstick and perfectly styled hair. A divorce attorney, making her living in the aftermath of broken vows, picking through the rubble of other people's sorrows.

The thought hollowed him. He forced a tight smile, hiding the pang of disappointment. Whatever flicker of recognition had sparked in him a moment ago, he smothered it before it could spread. *Don't be a fool, Jake.*

He drew in a breath, erecting a wall around his heart, brick by brick. It was safer that way. Safer to keep her at a distance, even if every instinct in him ached to close the space between them.

Kelly
Boise, Idaho

Jake. He looked older. Lines around his eyes, a touch of gray at his temples. But the smile—his smile—was still the same, and those same dark, warm, mysterious eyes.

It's you . . . It's always been you.

"Kelly," he said, his voice rougher than he probably intended. "Hi. Wow, I almost didn't recognize you. You look—"

"Before you say anything," I cut in too quickly, forcing a lightness I didn't feel, "I don't normally look like this." I pulled the belt of the robe tighter around me, making sure no skin showed.

A short laugh escaped him, warm but cautious. "Okay."

I traced the edge of my sleeve with my fingertip, slow and deliberate, like smoothing fabric could steady me.

My gaze dropped to the folder instead of his eyes. "Do you have the paperwork?" The words clipped out evenly, professional. My other hand gripped the strap of the belt of the robe so tight my knuckles whitened. My smile was polite, practiced—something I'd perfected for courtrooms and clients.

When he handed the paperwork over, our fingers

brushed—paper usually doesn't conduct electricity, but maybe the rain worked its magic. The electricity was sharp enough to make me catch my breath.

"Thanks." I hugged the folder against my chest like armor. My voice came out cool, even, distant. "I'll review everything before our meeting tonight."

His smile tugged crooked, uncertain. "Ha. Okay. Well, it's good to see you, Kelly. I wish it were under different circumstances, but—"

"Me too." The words slipped out crisper than I meant, so I quickly pressed my lips into something that resembled a polite smile. "Okay, then. See you tonight."

"See you."

The silence that followed was odd—not the easy stillness we once knew. This silence was crowded. Heavy. Filled with things we didn't say, questions neither of us was brave enough to ask.

I wanted to ask about his kids, how his mom was doing, and if he still played the guitar. I wanted to know if he still thought of me when he saw forget-me-nots. Instead, I shifted my weight from one heel to the other, smoothing my sleeve again, every gesture carefully composed. Professional. Controlled. Untouchable.

All while painfully aware that the eyeliner Amy had talked me into probably made me look like I'd joined a Mötley Crüe tribute band.

Jake nodded once, politely, and turned toward his car. His figure disappeared down the slick sidewalk, rain glinting off his shoulders. My heart sank, and I felt like I'd stumbled into a movie scene no one had bothered to give me the script for.

I tilted my head, watching him go, and my chest tightened with something I didn't want to name.

Then I glanced skyward. "Really?" I muttered under my breath. "The first time I see Jake Forester, I look like this and he looks like that? At some point, you're gonna have to find someone else to pick on."

Whimpering—yes, actually whimpering—I shoved the door open and ducked back inside.

Amy was waiting at the window, practically fogging up the glass like an overeager golden retriever. As I trudged past, she spun around.

"So? How'd it go?"

"How did it go?" I tossed my arms skyward. "Let's see—he looks like he could moonlight as David Beckham's twin, and I look like I take shifts in the red-light district. How do you think it went?"

Amy's laugh burst out so loud the photographer gave us the side-eye.

"It's not that bad," she said, grinning.

I skewered her with my best courtroom glare, the one that shut down opposing counsel in depositions.

"Okay, okay," she surrendered, palms raised. "It's a little bad."

"A little?" I jabbed a finger at my eyeliner, which screamed caffeinated-toddler-with-a-Sharpie. "I can't meet him for coffee looking like this. Come on, help me get it off."

Amy hooked her arm through mine, smug and unrepentant. She steered me back toward the makeup station like she'd planned the whole ambush all along.

"Admit it," she sang, practically gloating. "You had fun."

I sighed, surrendering just a fraction. "At least the music was good."

Amy giggled, just as she had ages ago.

"At least the music was good," I muttered again, softer this time, as if saying it twice could turn the whole mess into nothing more than a funny story.

But my heart knew better.

Somewhere in the background, my favorite high school band was still playing. Simon Le Bon was crooning again about dancing on the sand.

I groaned. "Great. Even Duran Duran is mocking me now."

Amy just grinned wider, already reaching for the makeup wipes.

Kelly
Eagle River, Alaska
October 1986

WE WERE BACK AT THE LAKE

again, Jake and me, stretched out on the hood of his car. The paint beneath my palms still held the warmth of the day, although the night air had already turned cool. Above us, the stars stretched vast and endless, pricked bright against the black. The fire a few feet away crackled and sighed, throwing up sparks that looked like they were trying to join the constellations. The lake lapped softly at the shore, steady and rhythmic, a quiet pulse beneath everything.

We slid back into an easy silence. He rolled the guitar pick across his knuckles and let it fall. It made a tiny plastic click against the metal hood.

"What do you want to do after college?" I asked, surprising myself. The question felt bigger than the night.

"Change the world," he said, as if he were ordering fries.

I huffed a laugh and nudged his shoulder with mine. "No, seriously."

"I am serious."

I tipped my chin at the guitar he held. "Through music?"

"Maybe." He considered the neck, the frets, his hands. "Whatever it is, I just want to make a difference. Help people."

The embers rose and vanished. The lake lapped against the

shore. I looked up at Polaris—steady, stubborn. The earnestness in his voice gripped something deep inside me.

"Me too," I whispered.

Our eyes held for a moment longer than they should have, the space between us charged with unspoken things. Then his fingers curled around the neck of the guitar. The moment his hand hit the strings, a hush fell over everything.

He started to play. It was a soft, wordless melody that curled around us like mist off the lake. Notes rose and fell, brushing against my skin.

"That's pretty," I said, barely above a breath. "Did you write it?"

He glanced at me, eyes shining with something I didn't dare name. "It's just a little something I've been working on."

I watched him, utterly enchanted, as his fingers danced across the frets. The scent of pine deepened in the cooling air. Somewhere in the distance, an owl hooted low and steady.

Jake played on, and I leaned back against the hood again, letting the music wrap around me. Then, he stopped playing, letting the last note drift into the quiet.

Finally, he looked at me. And I swear, the stars held their breath.

Silence stretched between us, not awkward, just familiar. Still, my heart pounded, every inch of me aware of his presence.

"Have you ever thought that maybe we should . . ." Jake's voice trailed off, hesitant.

I turned toward him, watching as his fingers inched just a little closer to mine. "We should what?"

His gaze flicked to me, then away. He cleared his throat. "That we should . . . write to each other when I go away to college?"

A chill of disappointment settled over me. *Oh.*

The reality of everything hit me. Jake would be graduating and going away, while I would be stuck here for my senior year.

"Um, yeah," I said, pitching my voice higher than it wanted to go. "That's a good idea. Why are you talking about that now?

College is at least a year away. We both have the rest of this year of high school."

He nodded, thoughtful, the fire painting his profile in strokes of gold and shadow. If anything good came from us moving to Alaska, it was Jake.

"I just want to make sure we don't lose each other, you know." He shrugged. "And it helps to know that you'll always be there even when I'm far away."

I tipped my face back to the sky and found Polaris again. Around it, the constellations kept moving, attempting to find their unique place. My emotions were like those stars. Would my heart ever find its true home?

I told myself it was enough to know where north was, and maybe someday we'd get there together.

"Don't worry, Jake." My words released with my breath. "I'll always be there. You watch. You'll always be able to count on me."

Kelly
Boise, Idaho

I WAS LATE. OF COURSE, I WAS LATE.

I should have felt flustered, rushing across town, but instead I sat there at a red light, letting myself breathe. Letting myself remember.

Because before I could walk into that café, before I could meet Jake's eyes again, I needed to collect myself. I needed to admit the truth I'd carried for decades—that I'd let pride keep me quiet instead of confessing what I really felt. All the ways I'd let fear write my story instead of hope.

Back then, I didn't have the language for regret. I was seventeen, still reeling from the move north, still trying to figure out who I was supposed to be in a place where everyone else seemed to know already. I was ruled by hormones and heartbreak and a frontal lobe not nearly ready for what I asked of it.

I'd raised three teenagers since then. I'd watched them unravel under the weight of growing up—acting before thinking, pushing people away when they meant to draw them close, blurting things they didn't mean because feelings came faster than reason. I'd given them grace. Finally, I'd learned to give some to myself, too. Still, it didn't stop the wondering.

How would life have been different if I'd dared to tell Jake how I really felt? If I'd dropped my walls, just once, instead of hiding behind them? Maybe things would have worked out. Maybe not. That was the part I could never decide.

But we were here now. And for the first time in years, I could be thankful for that. If nothing else, I could be a friend. Someone steady. Someone to sit with him through the hard parts. For now, that would be enough.

The light changed, pulling me back to the present.

My car rolled forward, tires hissing against the wet asphalt, and I came to a stop directly across from the café. My eyes lifted to the window, and my heart jolted.

There he was. Jake.

He sat at a table by the window, shoulders squared, his hands folded over a mug.

I gripped the steering wheel tighter, pulse drumming faster than the rain streaking the windshield.

Normal, I reminded myself. *Tonight I look normal.* No smoky eyeliner. No clown-red lipstick. No serial-killer eyes like I'd half-feared the first time I'd caught my reflection in prom photos. Just me. My hair brushed smooth. My favorite blouse and jeans.

I was parked right in front of the café, but Jake didn't notice. His gaze was fixed on the café door. It didn't take me long to make my way there and go in.

Inside, the café looked warm, suspended in its own pocket of time. Golden lamplight softened the edges of brick walls and worn wooden tables. A saxophone whispered from the overhead speakers, low and slow, like the soundtrack to a memory you weren't sure you wanted back. I drew in a breath, letting it settle deep. Then I smoothed the place where my blouse was tucked into my jeans, and I strode toward Jake.

✦ ✦ ✦

Jake
Boise, Idaho

Jake's coffee had gone lukewarm, untouched, as he stared at the door of the café. Occasionally, he glanced at the swirl of dark liquid as if answers might surface there, but his gaze always went back to the door. It finally creaked open.

She appeared in the frame like a silhouette cut from light. Kelly Richardson.

For a second, Jake forgot the air in his lungs. This wasn't the makeup-smeared, flustered Kelly he'd seen earlier. This was her—clean-faced, understated, more herself than the version he'd seen earlier. And in that instant, he was taken aback in a completely different way.

Kelly finally looked up, her eyes caught his, and the world narrowed to a single held breath.

Jake was on his feet before he'd thought it through, manners drilled in by a lifetime of habit.

His breath caught as Kelly approached.

"Hey," she said, brushing hair from her face.

"Hey," he managed.

Kelly paused and studied him. She looked at him. Not past him. Not through him. *At* him. Jake shuffled a little, shifting his weight.

"You look good." The words were out before he remembered this was supposed to be about the help he needed, nothing more.

"Thanks," she replied. She sucked in a breath, and he noticed the quick pulse on her smooth neck. It fluttered like a paper lantern in the breeze.

For a moment, it was just the two of them. No broken vows. No ring lines on their fingers. Just two people who cared about each other, standing under a string of café lights. The lights flickered as if trying to remind them of something they'd lost.

She moved another step toward him, a half-smile flickering across her face. He extended a hand. "Thanks for meeting with me."

Her fingers slipped into his, warm, steady, briefer than he wanted.

"No problem," she said lightly, though he could hear the careful edge in her voice.

They sat. A waitress appeared, pen poised, and a practiced smile on her face.

"Black coffee, please," Kelly said.

The waitress nodded and drifted off, leaving Jake hyperaware of the small distance between them and the excited energy that danced in the air they both breathed.

Kelly gestured vaguely to her face. "Better?"

The corner of Jake's mouth tugged upward. "Just like I remember."

For a moment, he simply looked at her, taking in the little things—the way her hair curled slightly at the ends. The soft flush on her cheeks.

Jake cleared his throat, leaning back to soften his focus. "So how have you been all these years?"

"Mostly good. Some bad. It's been so long." Her words were measured, careful, as though they were dancing around old landmines.

He gave a short laugh. "Funny how we both ended up in Idaho, huh?"

"It wasn't my plan," she admitted.

"Mine either," he said. "But I love it." He paused, unsure how much to reveal. "To be honest, I'm a little nervous. Meeting with you."

"Why?"

"Because I never thought I'd find myself in this situation." He let the words out slowly, deliberately. "I'm not even sure what the next step is."

"That's why I'm here," she said gently. "To help you figure it out."

Gratitude tugged at him, heavy and unexpected. "Thank you."

The waitress returned with her coffee. Kelly thanked her, wrapping her hands around the mug as if absorbing its warmth. When the table cleared again, she met his eyes. "Why don't you start by telling me what went wrong between you two?"

Jake exhaled, long and low. "We just . . . grew apart. I think it started with the pillows."

Her brow furrowed. "Pillows?"

"At the beginning of our marriage, we always slept next to each other," he said, voice tightening as memory pulled at him. "But once the kids came along, Nic grew more distant. Said she needed her sleep. She said that being too close kept her awake. She started putting pillows between us. I didn't fight it. Now I wish I had. I wanted to be supportive."

Kelly's expression softened with something like recognition. "Really? That's funny. My ex-husband did the same thing."

Jake blinked. "He did?"

She shrugged, lifting her cup for a sip. Steam curled around her face. "I wouldn't say our problems started there, but that certainly didn't help."

Jake gave a dry laugh. "Yeah. Prom night doesn't usually set the stage for a happy ending."

Her eyes flicked to his, a wry glint there. "Especially when the guy you like is kissing Bridgette Martin while you're stuck with Troy Henderson."

Jake groaned, dragging a hand down his face. "God, don't remind me. What was I thinking?"

"You weren't." Her voice softened, though the sting was still there. "Neither was I."

Silence stretched, not uncomfortable, but heavy with all the years that had passed.

Jake wasn't sure how much to share with her. They'd come for a different reason, yet he'd gained enough wisdom over the years to know he shouldn't let this chance pass without saying what was on his heart.

Finally, he leaned back in his chair, exhaling hard. "You know, I've replayed that night more times than I'd admit to anyone else. Thought maybe if I'd handled it differently . . ."

"Maybe if I had too," she cut in gently. "But we were kids, Jake. Hormones, bad decisions, and an underdeveloped frontal lobe. Not exactly a recipe for wise choices."

That made him laugh—a real laugh, quick and unguarded. "You sound like a mom."

"I am a mom," she shot back. "Three times over."

His mug froze halfway to his lips. "Boys or girls?"

She nodded. "Two boys, one girl. She's the oldest. All out of the house now. And yes, when they were kids, I considered buying stock in Pop-Tarts."

Jake choked on his coffee. "I have seven."

Kelly smiled. "So I've heard." She wrinkled her nose when she smiled. "Of course, that must seem pretty normal since you have lots of siblings. I still marvel at how your mom managed to handle all those kids while looking so glamorous and running a business as well. How is she?"

Jake felt his smile slip away. His fingers tapped on the tabletop. "My mom's dying."

The words cracked something open inside him. Saying them aloud hurt in a way he hadn't expected.

Kelly's hand twitched like she wanted to reach for his, but she stayed still, her eyes holding his instead. "I'm so sorry, Jake."

He nodded, throat tight. "It's been coming for a while, but it still feels like a sucker punch every time I think about it."

"I know that feeling," she whispered. "Losing someone slowly is its own kind of grief. You're bracing for the goodbye every single day."

The café grounded him to this time and place, both the hiss of the espresso machine and the murmur of other voices. Yet what stood out most was the raw weight of her listening. Really listening.

Then Kelly straightened, her shoulders squaring as though something inside her had clicked back into place. "Jake," she said carefully, "are you asking me to be your attorney?"

He blinked, caught off guard. "Would you?"

Her lips pressed together, the barest smile tugging at the corner. "How can I say no?"

The warmth between them cooled instantly. She reached into her bag, pulling out a slim notepad and pen. "Okay then. First things first, how old are the kids? Are all of them minors?"

Jake leaned back. "The twins are six, Leo and Lily. Becca is eight. Tyler, ten. Sadie just turned twelve. Chris is fifteen, learning how to drive. Rae's seventeen."

Kelly nodded, scribbling. Her hand moved quickly, but her eyes didn't meet his. "Custody—what do you think would be best? Do you want full custody, shared, something else?"

He swallowed hard. "They need me. They need both of us, really. But Nicole isn't interested in the day-to-day anymore."

Her pen stilled for just a second. He caught the faint crease between her brows before she smoothed it away, professional mask sliding back into place.

"Okay," she said softly, and the click of her pen punctuated the distance now between them. "Assets. Do you and Nicole have a primary home together? Savings, retirement accounts, property in both names? I looked through some of your paperwork earlier, but I need to know absolutely everything."

Jake rubbed his temple. "Yes to all of the above, but then a lot more. It's messy."

His voice sounded flat, but inside he was unraveling. Because every time she looked down at her notes, he remembered how she used to look up at him instead, blue eyes wide and curious when he'd strum his guitar under the stars. Every time she smoothed her hair back behind her ear, he remembered her leaning across diner tables, whispering secrets like they were building something no one could take away.

Now she was asking about bank accounts and property lines. Now she was the one putting walls between them. And Jake couldn't blame her. He'd been the first to build his own.

"Most divorces are messy," Kelly said, her voice calm, steady. Too steady. "We'll take it one piece at a time."

Jake wanted to tell her to forget it. Forget the files, the signatures, all of it. They could talk like friends, like the kids who once looked at each other across a crowded gym and thought the whole world was waiting.

But he couldn't. He needed help. And deep down, he knew Kelly was the only one who could give it.

So he nodded, forcing the words out. "Yeah. I've got some more paperwork here."

Her eyes flickered with regret. Or it could be a relief. She slid the folder toward her side of the table, pen poised.

And just like that, the conversation that had almost cracked wide open folded neatly back into lines, signatures, and official words.

An hour later, Jake pushed through the café door and watched

Kelly cross the street to her car. He paused beside his truck, gripping the handle but not opening it. His reflection wavered in the glass. He looked older, heavier in ways that had nothing to do with weight.

The conversation replayed in his head, but it wasn't Kelly's questions about custody and assets that stuck with him. It was the way her hand twitched, like she almost reached for him. The crease in her brow when he mentioned Nicole. The flicker in her eyes when she took the folder, like she wanted to say something else, but swallowed it down.

And he'd gone along with it. He'd let the moment shrink into paperwork and signatures because that was safe. Because business was the only language they could speak without breaking something open that they weren't ready to face.

Jake dragged a hand over his face, breath fogging in the damp air. He hated it. Hated that thirty-two years of silence had led them to this—bank accounts, custody questions, clipped voices over coffee.

He leaned against the truck, head tipped back toward the gray sky. "God," he whispered, voice hoarse, "I don't know what you're doing here. But if there's more to this than business, you're going to have to show me. Because right now . . . it feels like I lost her all over again."

The rain ran cold down his collar, and for a moment, he let it. He finally pushed off the truck, climbed in, and started the engine.

But through it all, the tiniest ember burned. He'd heard her voice. He'd seen her eyes. He felt the brush of her hand again. And deep down, he couldn't shake the sense that maybe—just maybe—this wasn't over.

✦　✦　✦

Kelly
Eagle River, Alaska
January 1987

Jake's basement smelled like buttered popcorn and Aqua Net hairspray, the twin perfumes of every Friday night we'd ever spent down there. The couch cushions sagged beneath us, threadbare plaid fabric scratching the backs of my legs where my jeans had ridden up. A stack of VHS tapes leaned against the old Zenith TV, the screen glowing faintly blue as *The Return of the Living Dead* flickered to life.

We were piled together, four teenagers pressed into one couch: Amy and Ben on one end, Jake and me on the other. A bowl of popcorn was balanced precariously between us.

Synth-heavy music bled from the opening credits, tinny from the basement speakers. My heartbeat quickened, and I swore the shadows down here always looked darker when we watched scary movies.

The first jump-scare hit, and both Amy and I squealed, popcorn flying like confetti. Jake and Ben howled with laughter.

"This movie is so dumb!" I shouted, grabbing a handful of popcorn and tossing it straight into Jake's face. The salt and butter stuck to his cheek before sliding down his shirt.

He grinned at me, eyes catching the dim light, all mischief. "Then why are you scared?"

I stuck my tongue out at him, my heart racing faster than the movie warranted.

Ben and Jake exchanged a look and suddenly crouched low, arms stiff, groaning like the undead.

"Brains . . ." Ben intoned, lurching toward Amy.

"Benjamin Bailey, you stop that right now!" Amy shrieked even as she laughed.

Jake shuffled closer, hands outstretched. "Must . . . eat . . . brains . . ."

"Jake, don't you dare!" I squeaked, clutching a throw pillow to my chest like a shield. The fabric smelled faintly of Downy and basement dust.

But he kept coming, and the next thing I knew, Amy and I were both screaming, swinging pillows wildly. Feathers and popcorn flew everywhere, laughter echoing off the wood-paneled walls. The movie faded into the background, forgotten, as the pillow fight took over. It was an all-out war of shrieks, smack-thuds, and uncontrollable giggles.

Jake's mom showed up and offered us snacks. She was the

cool, beautiful mom that everyone wished they had. We quieted down after that.

An hour and a half later, the credits rolled in silence. Amy and Ben were passed out, sleeping at the far end of the couch. Amy's head was tucked against Ben's shoulder. The popcorn bowl lay on its side, kernels scattered across the shag carpet. Jake and I were left sharing one pillow. Our shoulders were pressed against each other in the quiet.

I turned my head at the same time he did, and suddenly we were inches apart. He reached up, slow and tentative. Then Jake brushed a strand of hair behind my ear. His fingertips lingered for half a second against my cheek, feather-light.

I held his gaze, and my pulse skittered. Shy. Pure. The beginning of something. Then, for one suspended moment, with the hum of the VCR and the faint rustle of Amy shifting in her sleep, the whole world felt like it existed only here.

Jake
Boise, Idaho

EXHAUSTION CLUNG TO JAKE AS

he trudged into his bedroom. The room was dim, the only light spilling from the hallway behind him. His gaze drifted to the guitar propped in the corner. A ghost of a memory lingered in his mind. He thought of nights when Kelly had sat on the hood of his car. She'd listened and smiled like he was her whole world. His shoulders sagged. The ache of it cut deep.

Frowning, Jake flipped on the light at the bedside table and then sat on the edge of his bed. The mattress dipped beneath him. He glanced at the pillows neatly lined up through the middle. It had been a wall of fabric standing between what had once been "them."

Jake inhaled sharply and then pulled open the drawer of his bedside table. He dropped his wedding band inside. The soft clink of metal echoed louder than it should have. The ring's circle gleamed in the low light. He glanced away and then shut the drawer. For a moment, his hand lingered on the handle.

There were things he hadn't told his kids. Things he couldn't bear to say out loud. Like how Nicole had already found someone else. How the woman who once promised forever had been planning her exit while he was still fighting to hold the pieces together. The kids thought the separation was mutual. They didn't know about the betrayal, and Jake wasn't sure he wanted them to. Protecting the image of their mother seemed easier than shattering it.

He sat there long enough to strip away the last ounce of hesitation. Then, with one sweep of his arm, Jake shoved the line of pillows off the bed. They tumbled to the floor with a muffled thud.

Switching off the lamp, Jake stretched out diagonally across the wide mattress for the first time in years. The sheets smelled of laundry soap and a hint of loneliness. His body sank deep into the space, and he closed his eyes. This moment felt like freedom, even if it came with a sting.

But freedom wasn't the same as peace.

His thoughts turned back to Kelly at the café. Her smile had warmed something in him he thought had gone cold. Her gaze had softened when he admitted his mom was dying. And even though her style of clothing had changed, Kelly had worn those silver hoop earrings—the ones she probably thought he wouldn't remember. But he did.

She'd agreed to help him, and he wondered again how they'd ever drifted apart. Things were different back then. It hadn't been as easy to communicate. The unanswered calls. The changed addresses.

Yet even before that, the day Jake had boarded the plane for college, he'd felt sick to his stomach. Because deep down, he knew something had ended without either of them saying goodbye.

"You don't just forget your first love," he murmured to the ceiling. "Not when she was everything."

A weight pressed against his chest, heavy and insistent. Was Kelly a temptation? A distraction he had no business inviting back into his life? Or . . . was she a second chance he didn't deserve but couldn't ignore?

Jake shut his eyes and exhaled hard. "God, I don't know what I'm doing here," he whispered into the dark. "I don't want to make another mistake. If she's a temptation, take it away. If she's meant to be part of my life again, show me how. Just . . . don't let me mess this up."

His words faded into the quiet, a prayer released into the

silence. He didn't feel lighter exactly, but surrender carried its own kind of relief.

Turning onto his side, Jake pulled the comforter close. Then, somewhere between memory and prayer, he let exhaustion carry his thoughts away, and he remembered something he hadn't in a while.

He rose and walked to his closet. In the back, behind his hiking boots, Jake found the box with the old cassette. Kelly's mixtape. The one she made in high school. She'd written her name in pink bubble letters. He hadn't been able to throw it away.

He slipped it into the boombox that Nicole had taunted him for keeping and then hit play. The old machine crackled before the first few notes of "I Will Always Love You" bled into his room. Whitney Houston. Taylor Dayne. Bryan Adams. Roxette. It all came rushing back.

The dances. The field behind the school. Her voice when she read him parts of her journal. Her jelly shoes tapping on the sidewalk. The scent of her hairspray, strawberry lip gloss, and flower-scented lotion. All of it.

"Maybe it's a second chance." The thought rose with the music. "I'm not giving up this time," he whispered. "Not on her. Not on us."

Jake stood and wandered to the window. He flattened his nose against the cool glass. Then he slid the window open. Somewhere below, a siren wailed. So much had changed. So much was the same. Now, all these years later, a couple of interactions—one humorous, one serious—stirred up everything he'd tried to bury all those years ago.

Kelly
Boise, Idaho

The first thing I did when I walked through the door was kick off my shoes. They clattered across the wood floor, landing somewhere near the bookshelf. My toes ached, grateful to be free. I collapsed onto my couch with a sigh. I wasn't sure what to think. It had been too easy to talk to Jake, as if thirty-two years hadn't passed. Yet, that was the problem. Those years had passed, and I'd walked through mountains and valleys over the years. Dark, dark valleys.

I wasn't the naive teenager I once was. I couldn't just pretend we could pick up where we'd left off. Men had broken my heart, Jake included. With my job, I helped hurting women every day.

I could see from the look in Jake's eyes that he was attracted to me, but deep down I wondered if the real attraction was to her . . . the young Kelly. The girl I used to be. Moreover, I'd seen many of my clients jump into rebound relationships immediately. Most of the time, they didn't work out.

The only thing worse than being an old flame was being a rebound, then being left for a second time. I wasn't sure if I could face my heart being broken by Jake Forester again.

I snuggled one of the couch pillows tight to my chest, thankful I was now Jake's lawyer. Ethically, we couldn't date. We could, though, stay friends. Keeping Jake in the friend zone—at arm's length—seemed the best solution to this problem.

My phone buzzed across the coffee table. Amy. Of course. I swiped it up.

"Hey, Ames."

On her end, I could hear the familiar sounds of her kitchen—wine being poured, the faint scrape of a chair. Then the lilting swell of romantic music, something jazzy, filled the background.

"So?" Amy's voice was curious and a little too eager. "How did it go?"

I leaned back into the couch cushions, pressing a palm to my forehead. "Well, I'm going to be his divorce lawyer. How weird is that?"

I heard a muffled laugh, then the shuffle of movement. Ben must have been in the room because the music grew louder, richer.

"How was it talking to him again?" Amy's voice had softened, and it carried a mischievous edge.

I hesitated, staring at the ceiling and watching the shadows shift with each car that passed on the street below. "Good," I admitted, my voice low. "I mean . . . he's Jake. I just . . . can't get too close."

In the background, Ben must have been trying to pull her into a dance. I heard the faint shuffle of shoes, her laugh, the swat of her hand against his arm.

"Why not?" she asked.

"Because I don't trust my own judgment," I said. The words came sharper than I expected. "That's why I'm a divorce attorney and not a marriage counselor."

Amy's laugh tinkled through the line, but it wasn't at me. "Ames?" I asked, suspicion prickling.

Her laughter grew louder. Then I heard Ben's voice—teasing, warm—before Amy's muffled protest.

"Hey, wait—didn't you say something about a class reunion coming up?" I asked, trying to sound casual.

"Oh, that," she replied, breath airy. "I passed it off to the people still living in Alaska. We might go . . . not sure yet."

I blinked at the ceiling, a slow realization settling in. Had her sudden enthusiasm for planning been about nostalgia—or about nudging me toward Jake? The thought pricked, bittersweet. Maybe it wasn't the reunion she'd been hoping to rekindle. Maybe it was something . . . someone.

"Sorry," she finally managed between giggles. "Ben's decided we're Fred Astaire and Ginger Rogers tonight."

A moment later, Ben's voice came through the receiver. "Hey, Kel. I'm going to steal her away now, okay?"

I smiled despite myself, curling deeper into the couch. "No kids tonight?"

"They're at a sleepover," Amy replied, breathless, clearly being twirled across the kitchen.

"Have fun," I said softly, meaning it.

The call ended, and I dropped my phone onto the cushion beside me. Silence filled the bungalow for only a breath before the faint echo of music threaded through my thoughts. Duran Duran's "Rio."

The song had been playing earlier at the photo shoot, all glitter and bravado. Now, though, the memory replayed differently. Slower. Softer.

I tilted my head back against the couch, staring at the ceiling but seeing something else entirely. The plaster above me blurred into a dance floor, the pulse of colored lights shifting across polished gym floors, jewel-toned gowns, and tuxes two sizes too big. The weight of hope pressed like a heartbeat in my chest, and I allowed myself to get swept away with it.

For a moment, my living room disappeared, replaced by the electric hum of my high school years. And at the center of it all, there he was—Jake Forester, smiling like I was the only girl in the room.

The ceiling came back into focus, plain and unremarkable, but the ache lingered, caught somewhere between the girl I was then and the woman I had become.

Jake
Boise, Idaho

THE MORNING SUN STRETCHED

across the balcony, flooding the planks with gold. Jake sat in the light, guitar balanced on his knee. His fingers moved over the strings, coaxing a melody that rose and fell with quiet urgency. The sound carried into the cool air, mingling with birdsong, filling the empty spaces of the house behind him.

When the song broke, he set the guitar aside and reached for a worn leather journal. Flipping it open, he began scribbling lyrics with an energy he hadn't felt in years, words tumbling faster than his pen could keep up. Then, noticing the time, he decided to surprise the kids with breakfast.

Soon, Jake's movements were quick, intentional. He became energized by the rhythm as he flipped pancakes. In a second pan, he cooked the bacon. The bacon sizzled, and the coffee steamed fresh in the pot. He couldn't remember the last time he'd made himself coffee.

One by one, the youngest kids shuffled down the stairs in pajamas, rubbing sleep from their eyes. Leo and Lily paused in confusion at the sound of the kitchen alive again. Next came Tyler's feet thundering down the stairs.

"Dad?" Tyler's voice broke the spell first, wary but curious.

Jake turned with a grin. "Hey guys! I've got bacon and pancakes. Help yourselves."

Lily squealed. "Yes!"

"Awesome!" Leo echoed. Both twins darted forward, grabbing plates bigger than their heads. They rushed to the table, where a pitcher of warm syrup was waiting. When the older kids were little, Jake used to make pancakes and bacon every Sunday before church. It encouraged the kids to get up and get ready. It made him sad now to think the younger ones didn't know that tradition.

The other kids followed, tentative but grateful, all except Chris. Chris lingered near the doorway, arms crossed, suspicion etched across his face.

"You haven't made breakfast for us like this since—" Chris stopped himself, his voice catching. "—in a while."

Jake held his gaze, flipping another pancake onto the stack. "It's been a while since I did a lot of things."

The spatula hovered for a moment before Chris spoke again, low and cutting: "Does this mean you're over Mom?"

The room froze. Forks stilled midair, pancakes forgotten. All the kids stared at him, heartbreak hanging heavy in the silence.

Jake drew in a breath, steady but weighted. He looked at each of them. His entire world was gathered in this kitchen. With a sigh, he searched for words that wouldn't break them further.

"It means," he said slowly, "I've wallowed long enough. It isn't fair to you guys, and it isn't fair to me."

The kids turned instinctively to Chris, waiting for his verdict. He studied his father, then gave a slight nod.

"Next time," Chris said, grabbing a plate, "make sausage too."

Relief rippled through the room. Jake laughed and tossed a kitchen towel across the counter at him. Chris grinned, dodging it, and the rest of the kids relaxed. They dove into their breakfast with the easy chatter of normalcy.

"By the way," Chris added between bites, "nice to see you brushed your hair. You keep this up, and you don't have to crouch down in the car when you drop us off in the morning."

Jake arched his brow. "Wasn't gonna anyway."

The kids chuckled, and Jake turned back to the stove. The smile tugging across his face was more real than it had been in years. The scent of bacon and maple filled the air, and for the first time in too long, the kitchen felt alive with hope for his future—for *their* future.

Jake only hoped the mistakes of his past weren't too big an obstacle to hurdle in his future.

Jake
Eagle River, Alaska
August 1987

The bass pounded hard enough to shake the hood of his car. The boombox was turned all the way up, and he wondered if it might blow a fuse. Jake felt it in his sneakers, in his chest, like the speakers had plugged straight into him. The air smelled like fried dough and cotton candy, sweet and heavy, mixed with the sharp tang of engine grease from the rides grinding in the background. It was the usual state fair mess—too loud, too bright—but with Kelly standing there, it felt different, like all of it had tilted toward her.

Taylor Dayne's voice spilled out over the dirt lot: *"Tell it to my heart, tell me I'm the only one . . ."*

Jake rubbed his damp palms against his jeans, then stuck out his hand before he could think better of it. "Dance?"

Kelly arched an eyebrow, her smile playing at the corner of her mouth. "Here? In the parking lot?"

"Why not?" he said, aiming for confidence, though it came out more crooked.

When she slid her hand into his, warmth rushed up his arm, settling somewhere low in his chest. He pulled her in, careful, like one wrong move might make her change her mind. All around, the fair kept on. Kids yelling, the clatter of rides, the smell of corn dogs drifting past. But it all faded when she looked at him.

The sky overhead was stubbornly bright, the kind of endless daylight an Alaska summer never seemed to run out of. It made the whole night feel stretched thin, like it could last forever. Jake set his hand on her waist, tentatively. She looped her arms around his shoulders, easy, like she'd done it a hundred times before.

"You're terrible at this," she said, soft but teasing.

"Guess I just need more practice," he answered, forcing a grin. His pulse was hammering too fast.

He wanted to say more. To tell her she was too perfect, too much of a dream to last. That every guy he knew liked her, and he still didn't get why she was here with him, that he'd be leaving for college soon, and he didn't know how to tell her how he felt.

But the words stuck. Fear kept him quiet.

So he held her, moving awkwardly to the music, trying to pin the moment to memory without realizing it would come back to him again and again. That night. That moment. The unspoken words. The regret.

Kelly
Boise, Idaho

I FLIPPED ANOTHER PAGE OF

the file and nearly choked on my coffee. My mug thudded onto a yellow legal pad, accidentally sloshing a brown crescent into the margin. I swiped the back of my wrist through the spill.

I looked around, sure I was on *Candid Camera*. This had to be a joke, right? Nope, no one was giving me the least bit of attention. No one jumped out of the coat closet to declare, "Surprise!"

I swallowed hard, unsure of how I felt about this new information. My eyes snapped to the column of figures as if the numbers might rearrange themselves if I stared hard enough.

"Janie?" My voice came out sharper than I meant. A pen rolled off the stack of pleadings and pinged against the floor.

Footsteps clicked down the hall. Janie appeared in my doorway, already pushing her glasses up her nose with one finger. A cordless phone was tucked under her arm. "Yeah?"

I tapped the page with my pen—once, twice—the click too loud in the quiet office. "Does this say Jake Forester is worth twenty million dollars?"

She didn't even blink. "Yep. He made some through health coaching, some through—"

"Franchised smoothie shops . . . investing in tech companies and other startups," I interrupted. I was already riffling through the packet. Paper whispered against paper. "And yes, being a top health coach for over twenty years made more than I ever thought possible. Clearly, I've gotten into the wrong business." I skimmed past valuations, margin notes, and photos of storefronts. My mouth went dry. "And since there's no prenup, I assume his wife is going for half. Who's her attorney?"

"Mr. Reed."

A humorless breath slid out of me. Of course. I pinched the bridge of my nose with ink-smudged fingers. With a calming breath I sat up straighter, smoothing my blazer as if that alone could pull me back into the center of myself. "Of course it's Reed. Get him on the line for me?"

"On it." She was already dialing as she backed out of my office, receiver pressed to her ear. "I'll patch him through."

Everything grew quiet in my office once again. The HVAC system hissed softly, and somewhere down the corridor, the copier groaned and spat out pages. I leaned back, chair creaking, and let the file slip from my grip so it fanned across the desk. I touched the edge of a smoothie shop photo with my thumbnail, and then pulled my hand back like I'd been burned.

Twenty million. The number looked ridiculous sitting in black ink on white paper. I tried to anchor it to Jake in my memory, but failed. The boy who scribbled lyrics on notebook paper. The young man who drove with the windows down so the wind could carry our singing into the Alaska sky. The one who once told me that a person could live on love and ramen if they wanted something badly enough. Obviously, he'd gotten past the ramen.

Now holdings, LLCs, structured notes, a brokerage statement with commas in places that I'd never seen before.

My desk phone buzzed once—an internal line lighting up. I stared at it while my pulse flicked against the underside of my jaw. I took a sip of coffee that had gone lukewarm and then set the mug down, ignoring another buzz.

I rubbed at the knot in my temple, wondering what I'd gotten myself into. The stakes were high in more ways than one.

When I started to twist a strand of my hair between my

fingers, I caught myself and smoothed my hair instead. *Act professional. Act neutral. You can do this, Kelly.*

With a sigh, I stacked the pages and squared the corners against the desk until they lined up just so. My thumb hovered over a handwritten note—no prenup confirmed, respondent seeks equitable distribution.

"Line one," Janie called from the doorway, leaning in, palm over the handset. "Mr. Reed in thirty seconds."

"Thanks." My voice found the flat, even place where it lives during depositions. I flipped to the financials again, scanning for leverage. For any weak seam I could tug. My pen tapped a staccato against the margin—a nervous habit that my opponent would spot in an instant. I set the pen down and then laid it carefully across the top of the file instead. I wasn't the Kelly from high school. This Kelly knew how to win for the sake of her clients. This had to be no different.

I slid open the top drawer, pulled out a fresh sticky note, and wrote two words in neat block letters: *Stay factual.* I stuck it to the edge of my monitor for backup support.

The phone rang—one clean, businesslike trill. I drew a breath, steadied it, and hit SPEAKER. "Mr. Reed," I said, smoothly, "thanks for taking my call."

"Always a pleasure," came his practiced baritone.

While he talked—preliminary disclosures, timelines, civility—I watched the coffee ring drying on my desk. My thumb found the edge of the file, tracing the raised grain of the paper. Part of me listened with the courtroom half of my brain. The other part filled in a picture I hadn't invited: a bouquet the color of sky left on a wet bench.

Kelly
Alaska State Fair
August 1987

THE AIR SMELLED LIKE KETTLE

corn and cotton candy, sugar thick enough to cling to my hair, with a faint undercurrent of diesel from the Tilt-A-Whirl grinding in the distance. Neon lights from the Ferris wheel pulsed in pinks and blues across the corn maze fence, painting Jake's face in a shifting glow as we walked. Gravel crunched under my Keds, and somewhere behind us, a group of girls squealed when one of the boys dropped his funnel cake.

I slowed near the fence, crouching low when I spotted the tiny pops of blue tucked in the weeds. Forget-me-nots. Their petals were soft, fragile, almost glowing under the buzzing lights strung overhead. I gathered a handful carefully, inhaling their faintly sweet, earthy scent.

"You're really into forget-me-nots," Jake teased, his voice low, amused.

I glanced up, brushing dirt from the stems. "Mostly because of the story. It's romantic."

He tilted his head, giving me that grin that was equal parts teasing and disarming. I gasped. "You seriously don't know the story behind our state flower?"

"Nope." He shoved his hands into his jeans pockets. "Enlighten me."

So I did. "Legend has it, a knight was walking along the riverbank with his true love and picked her one of these flowers. But his armor was too heavy—"

"Occupational hazard," Jake muttered, grinning.

I rolled my eyes and finished. "The knight fell into the river. But before he sank, he threw the flower to her and said, 'Forget me not.'" I held the blossoms closer to my chest. "The name stuck."

Jake let out a laugh, shaking his head. "That's the most depressing thing I've ever heard. You call that romantic?"

I shrugged, but my heart was pounding harder than it should have been. "I call it beautiful. His last wish was for her never to forget him."

Our eyes locked, and the fair blurred. The voices, the rides, the smell of frying corn dogs—all of it dimmed until it was just Jake and me, heat curling low in my stomach. He opened his mouth like he wanted to say something, then hesitated. Instead, he shrugged off his letterman jacket and settled it across my shoulders. The fabric was warm and it smelled like leather, faint detergent, and something that was just . . . Jake.

Before I could say anything, a flash went off.

"You guys are too cute!" Amy sang, shaking the Polaroid in her hand.

I grabbed it and laughed nervously as the picture slowly developed in my palm, the image bleeding into focus while Jake turned to talk with Ben. My cheeks burned.

Amy leaned close, whispering, "So . . . has he asked you out yet?"

I shook my head, clutching the Polaroid like it could tell me the future. "Not yet. What if he doesn't like me?"

"He does," Amy said firmly. "Boys are just stupid sometimes."

Across the way, Ben asked Jake something, and Jake's glance flicked back to me so fast I felt it like a touch. My chest tightened.

Then Bridgette swept in.

Her hair was teased to the sky, her leather skirt barely covering her thighs, her perfume sharp even in the fried-dough air. She eyed Jake up and down with a smile that made me want to shrink.

"Lookin' good, Jake," she purred, twirling a strand of hair and smiling like there was a secret only she knew.

Heat climbed my neck. Jake cleared his throat. "Uh . . . thanks."

"You still coming to my cousin's bonfire next weekend?" she asked, leaning in just enough to make my stomach twist.

"Probably." His voice was casual, but his eyes flicked toward me.

"Mmm. Make sure you say hi." She let her fingers trail lightly down his arm before sauntering off, her laughter floating behind her like Aqua Net and trouble.

I swallowed hard. "You guys used to go out, right?"

"Yeah," Jake murmured, rubbing the back of his neck. "But that was forever ago."

"It doesn't feel like forever," I whispered, trying to keep my voice steady.

He turned toward me, close enough that I could feel his warmth even through his jacket—his jacket still draped over my shoulders. "Hey." His voice softened. "There's nowhere else I'd rather be right now than right here. With you."

I wanted to believe him. I really did. But as Bridgette's laughter carried across the fairground, I couldn't stop watching her walk away.

✦ ✦ ✦

Jake
Boise, Idaho

Jake stood in his home office, a warm coffee mug between his palms. The rich, nutty scent curled up with the faint tang of printer ink and lemony wood polish from the housekeeper's latest pass.

Outside the expansive glass windows, the mountains rose jagged against a sky the color of tarnished silver. A breeze teased through the open vent, carrying the faintest trace of pine.

His phone lit up on the desk. Caller ID: Kelly.

He swiped to answer. "Hey, Kel." It wasn't until he'd answered that he realized it seemed so easy just to act as if decades hadn't passed, as if he hadn't felt the sting of her disconnecting her number so long ago. He didn't need to think about that. It was the past. He needed her now, and Kelly had answered.

Her voice rushed in, brisk but warm. "Hey, I talked to your wife's lawyer. Would you be free to come into the office this afternoon to talk strategy?"

Jake shifted the mug to his other hand, brushing crumbs from the edge of his desk. The screen of his computer glowed with a screensaver of colorful smoothies. He tapped the keyboard, and his calendar filled the monitor, squares packed so tightly with meetings it felt like a wall. Once he'd told Cam he was back in the game, his partner had filled his schedule.

"I've got client meetings all day," he said.

There was a beat of silence, then her voice softened, teasing. "Is this the health coaching side of your business?"

"Yeah," he said, the word stretching into a smile. He leaned against the desk, steam rising into his face as he sipped. The taste was intense, dark, and slightly bitter. "It's the best. I love helping people realize their goals and find a new passion for life."

For a moment, he thought about telling Kelly that he'd work something out. Cam could cover some meetings if necessary. But deep down, Jake hoped that since his day was full, they could maybe meet up this evening.

A rustle came through the line—papers shifting. "So you're changing the world after all," she said. "Just like you always wanted to do."

The sound of her words warmed him more than the coffee. He grinned, straightening, glancing again at the mountains outside. "Trying to, at least. One person at a time."

"Well," she said, voice dipping back into professional mode, "we can talk on Monday—"

"What are you doing tonight?" The question slipped out before he could change his mind.

A pause. He pictured her blinking, looking up at some courthouse ceiling, brow furrowed.

"Well, I have a hot date with a towering pile of paperwork."

Jake chuckled, setting the mug down. The ceramic clinked against the wood. "If it can wait, you could come to the Spring Break Carnival."

Confusion flickered in her tone. "Why would I—"

"I've got a booth there every year," he said. "Telling people about our health coaching business. Selling smoothies. Even have a dunking booth. It's kind of like the state fair, just a little smaller. Should be fun."

"Oh, well . . ." Her voice faltered, uncertain. He could almost see her caught between duty and something she didn't want to name. Sparks? Interest?

"We could go over everything afterward," he offered, softer now.

On the other end, there was the muffled echo of a door closing, along with fading voices. He imagined her pushing forward, papers in hand, always hurrying somewhere.

"Sure," she said at last. "I can make that work."

Relief loosened something in his chest. "Great. I'll text you the details."

"Perfect. See you then."

The line went dead, leaving Jake in the stillness of his office.

He turned back to the desk, but the calendar's crowded boxes blurred. He focused enough to realize he was a few minutes late to a meeting.

Jake grinned as the video conference pulled up, the screen brightening with the familiar faces of his team.

"Hey!" Coach Brian's voice boomed through the speakers, followed by laughter from a few of the others. "Look who's back from the dead!"

The jab was good-natured, and Jake couldn't help the chuckle that slipped out. He adjusted the earbuds in his ears, the soft plastic tugging at his skin. "Sorry that I've been MIA. What did I miss?"

The screen filled with voices, each chiming in over the other. Someone rattled a chip bag too close to their mic, the crunch like static in Jake's ear.

"You finally let the mountain man look go, huh?" another coach teased.

Jake rubbed a freshly shaved jaw, smooth beneath his fingertips. He leaned back in his chair, the leather creaking as he sank into it. His eyes flickered across the tiny boxes of faces tiled on his screen. Behind each one was a slice of life: a cluttered kitchen counter, a bookshelf stacked too high, a muted toddler running through the background. It felt noisy, chaotic, alive.

As the laughter settled, Jake's gaze drifted toward the window again. Snow still clung to the mountains' far ridges. He breathed deep, letting the sight settle his pulse. For the first time in weeks, he didn't feel like an outsider logging in late. He felt present—connected.

"All right," he said, rolling his shoulders, fingers poised above the keyboard. "Catch me up."

The voices rang out, eager, ready to pull him back into the rhythm he'd been missing.

Jake
Boise, Idaho

The carnival sprawled out before Jake like a canvas of sound and color. He breathed in the smells of sweet fried dough, tangy onions, sizzling sausages, and buttery popcorn. It really did remind him of the state fair. The only thing missing was the odor of hay and barn animals on the breeze.

A carousel's music drifted in, half-drowned by the shriek of kids daring the roller coaster. Neon bulbs blinked against the fading gold of sunset, giving the carnival an electric heartbeat.

Jake sat perched at the dunking booth, sleeves rolled, his shop's banner fluttering overhead. The twins flanked him. Lily sipped on a smoothie. Leo squinted at the prize shelf like he had a battle plan. The blender whirred behind him, rattling the plastic table stacked with sample cups, glossy brochures, and his own cards for the smoothie business.

Sadie, Tyler, and Becca tore through the crowd toward Jake. Their faces were painted in swirls of glitter and animal whiskers. The trio clutched a handful of ride tickets like treasure. Even with all the noise, their laughter cut through the chaos, pure and sharp.

"Can we go on some rides?" Becca's voice pitched high, excitement vibrating in every word.

"Sure." Jake waved them toward the midway. "Just stay together."

"Thanks, Dad!" Sadie pulled some tickets from the ball in her hand and shoved the rest at him. "Hold on to these for us, will you?"

The ticket pile hit the counter—three sticky, tangled balls of paper. Jake stared at the mess, then pushed them toward the twins. "New assignment. Untangle these."

"Aye aye, captain!" Leo saluted, already tugging at the first knot. Lily rolled her eyes but leaned in to help, their shoulders bumping.

Jake smirked. "And find a place to keep them so they don't get mixed up with other people's."

A beat later, tickets flew through the air like streamers, the twins laughing as they pelted each other.

"Yep," Jake muttered under his breath. "That's exactly what I meant. Nailed it."

It wasn't long before Sadie, Tyler, and Becca had returned. From out of nowhere, Chris and Rae showed up too. It was as if their "Dad's up to something" radar had gone off, and they were trying to figure it out.

Maybe he'd been too cheerful as they'd set up the booth. He'd have to watch that. Would it be weird to pretend to be depressed and moody just to keep his kids at bay? He didn't have time to consider if it would work because, in the blink of an eye, he spotted Chris determinedly lifting the mallet at the strongman game in the next booth over, only to bring it down and ring up the lowest possible score.

Rae clapped dramatically. "Wow. Incredible. So strong," she deadpanned, bowing.

Jake let out a belly laugh, startling the people near him.

But Jake's laughter cut short as he spotted someone in the crowd. The golden evening light stretched across Kelly as she approached. Her hair hung straight, falling to her shoulders. She wore a long, flowing skirt and a white blouse. She seemed too put together to belong here—and yet, somehow, she fit so perfectly. For a moment, Jake almost believed the whole carnival had been designed as her backdrop. Her clothes whispered of Milan or Manhattan, not state fairs and dust. Yet the sight of her hit him like a memory come to life.

For a second, his mind flickered backward. Teen Kelly walking through the Alaska State Fair, sunlight slanting across her hair. A giant stuffed bear had been tucked under her arm. Jake's arm brushed hers every other step. The glow then. The glow now. It was the same.

The past dissolved as Kelly drew close. Her expression was unreadable, but her presence was undeniable. His chest tightened. Jake's breath caught before he smoothed it into something casual.

"You made it!" Jake called, louder than he'd meant. The words tumbled out with more relief than coolness.

Her eyes swept across the booth, the twins, the chaos. "I did."

"Thanks for coming." He stood straighter, brushing his hands against his jeans as though he could wipe his nerves clean. "Let me introduce you to my family." He turned, raising his voice. "Hey, guys—come meet Kelly Richardson. She's an old friend of mine from Alaska."

The blender hummed low behind him, the scent of strawberries and vanilla rising warm and sweet. Fireworks cracked faintly in the distance, but all Jake felt was the thrum of his pulse as Kelly stepped closer. Her sweet perfume threaded through the cotton candy haze, a reminder that some memories never dulled, no matter how many years had passed.

Kelly
Boise, Idaho

JAKE'S SEVEN KIDS CAME AT ME

all at once, a blur of color and movement, like the carnival itself had gathered speed and crashed into me. Well, not all of them were kids. Two were teens, and they joined the younger ones gathering around me in a circle so tight I could feel their body heat radiating against the cooling evening air.

"Hi, kids." I forced brightness into my voice. "Nice to meet you."

The words felt too simple for the weight of seven pairs of eyes fixed on me. Their gazes flicked up and down, cataloguing every inch. My blouse that probably looked out of place here, the faint gloss on my lips, the little effort I'd made to look like someone who belonged.

"Hello," they said nearly in unison. Their voices were flat and cautious, like a choir that hadn't yet learned the melody.

The smell of fried dough and sizzling meat swirled around us, but I could still catch a whiff of bubblegum, and one girl's face paint, and sunscreen clinging to another's skin. The awkward silence stretched as thick as the spring air.

Rae's eyes lingered on me the longest, sharp and assessing. She glanced at my clothes, my makeup, then crossed her arms tight over her chest. It was as if my presence had exposed something she didn't want anyone else to notice.

Before I could think of something to bridge the space between us, the older kids were tugged away by their friends. That left the twins—Lily and Leo—bouncing on their toes, their faces painted with crooked stars.

They tugged on Jake's sleeve, their voices eager, sugar-tinged. "Can we go to the funhouse?"

Jake's eyes flicked to me. Mischief danced within them. "Well, that depends on whether this lovely lady right here wouldn't mind taking over your jobs."

Their heads swiveled toward me, pleading eyes wide, palms pressed together like tiny supplicants.

I laughed, my voice betraying the flutter low in my stomach. "How can anyone say no to that?"

"Yay!" they shouted in tandem before racing off, their sneakers pounding against the trampled grass.

I turned back to Jake. "So, uh . . . what exactly do I have to do?"

He moved aside, the faint scent of aftershave mixing with popcorn oil and cotton candy in the air. Then Jake gestured me toward the booth. His shoulder brushed mine as he leaned close. "Take tickets from people who want to dunk me and put them in this bucket here. Then give them three balls each."

"That's it?"

Jake placed a hand over his heart, feigning offense. "What do you mean, that's it? This is a very complicated job, Ms. Richardson. One that cannot be taken too lightly."

I laughed, the sound bubbling up in a way I hadn't expected, surprising me almost as much as him.

"I promise," I said, grinning, "to do my due diligence."

For a beat too long, he just stared at me. The noise of the carnival seemed to fade around us. His expression softened as if my laughter had pulled him somewhere else entirely. Then he cleared his throat, stepped back, and climbed onto the dunking tank with a practiced ease.

"Step right up!" His voice rang out, playful, commanding. "Anyone who wants to see a middle-aged man fall into a giant tub of water—get in line!"

And to my surprise, a line formed quickly. A string of kids and teenagers clutched tickets and grinned with anticipation. The bucket in front of me was filled with scraps of paper, my hands automatically passing out balls. The sounds around me sharpened—the smack of rubber hitting wood, the squeal of laughter as the target wobbled, the splash of water waiting to be unleashed.

Jake pointed at one boy in line, tall and wiry, his cap tilted backward. "Pitchers excluded, Brad!"

"I don't see that written down anywhere, Mr. F.!" Brad shot back, grinning.

Jake rolled his eyes, muttering something under his breath. I laughed again, the sound blending with the carnival chaos— wild, uncontained, alive.

And for the first time in a long time, I felt that way too.

✦ ✦ ✦

Jake
Boise, Idaho

The first notes of "Put Your Arms Around Me" drifted from the speakers of a nearby ride, carried on the warm, sticky air. The song wrapped itself around the fairgrounds, weaving through the laughter, shrieks, and the mechanical groan of the Ferris wheel. Then it landed squarely in Jake's chest.

Kelly was behind the booth now, sleeves pushed back, and moving with surprising ease. Her fingers grasped tickets from eager hands. Then she dropped them into the bucket and passed out balls like she'd been born for this small-town chaos. Her perfume—something floral and clean—rose each time the breeze shifted, mingling with the burnt sugar of cotton candy, warming his senses.

The thud of balls missing the target echoed against the wooden backboard. It was followed by groans and laughter from the throwers.

Jake shouted encouragement, his voice hoarse from cheering,

but his laughter bubbled up between every word. Water sloshed below him. Its damp scent crept into his nostrils. The chill teased his skin in anticipation.

From the corner of his eye, he caught Sadie, Tyler, and Becca spinning wildly on the Tilt-A-Whirl. Their hair flew, and their laughter carried above the music. They looked weightless and unburdened, lifted beyond the problems of this world, and those in their home.

Lily and Leo reappeared at the booth. Their mouths were dyed blue and pink, and sticky cotton candy clung to their fingers. They thrust a tuft toward Kelly, and she shook her head with a polite smile. The twins giggled and devoured it themselves, sugar melting on their tongues.

Jake's gaze shifted again. This time to Chris. Standing off to the side, he was half-listening to some pretty teen girl, but his eyes kept straying back to Jake. There was curiosity there, a flicker of something softer than the guarded silence Jake had grown used to. He clung to that look like a lifeline.

Then Brad stepped forward, all limbs and teenage swagger. He was a few years older than Chris, but they'd been on the same swim team one summer. Brad was known as one of the best athletes in town.

Jake scrambled theatrically on the platform, arms flailing. "Easy on me, Brad!" he called. It didn't help. The ball cracked against the target with a clean, satisfying smack.

The trap gave way, and Jake plunged into the tank. Cold water swallowed him whole. The shock of the icy water bit at his skin, rushed into his ears, and stole his breath. He surfaced, sputtering, and the world roared back to life—the chorus of the song, the crowd's cheers, the smell of hay dampened by spilled water.

And above it all—Kelly's laugh, bright and unguarded. He twisted toward it, droplets running into his eyes, and found her doubled slightly at the waist. Her hand was pressed against her chest as she laughed with everyone else.

For a moment, she looked seventeen again, radiant in the golden glow of the fair, as if time had folded in on itself.

Jake clapped his hands together, applauding Brad, water

streaming down his arms. The boy grinned, triumphant. And from the corner, Chris smiled too, tentative but real. Jake felt something shift. Like something had unknotted in Chris. Maybe—just maybe—the sadness that had been wearing Chris down was starting to lift.

Then his eyes found Kelly's again.

A hush seemed to fall inside him even as the carnival kept spinning. Music thumped, voices shouted, the lights blinked in every color. Yet all Jake felt was the pull of her gaze.

His chest constricted, and his breath stalled, as if the space between them held everything they hadn't said in years. It lasted only a heartbeat. But it was enough to remind him why he'd never really stopped waiting.

Kelly
Boise, Idaho

TO ME, THE FAIR HAD ALWAYS

been a final exhale of the last breath of summer. This spring carnival brought back all of those memories. The sky had deepened to navy, and strings of light bulbs flickered as vendors unplugged extension cords, shutting down for the night. The smell of fried batter and smoke from sparklers lingered, tangled with the cool bite of night air.

I stood beside Jake at the booth. Our shoulders brushed every so often as we counted tickets into neat piles. My fingers were tacky from the paper stubs. I smiled as I breathed in the faint sweetness of cotton candy, which mingled with the citrus scent of his aftershave.

I turned to him. "I think it's safe to say your booth was the hit of the night."

"Thanks for helping out." His tone was warm and casual, but his eyes lingered.

I wanted to look away, but was afraid to at the same time. Afraid this was just a dream. Afraid I'd wake up tomorrow and none of this would be real. "No problem."

The space between us grew thick—too charged for something as simple as counting tickets. My pulse stumbled, and I cleared my throat. Finally, I forced myself to glance away to watch

Jake's kids weaving fire through the dark with sparklers. "So, I've got some paperwork in the car . . ."

Before I could escape to work, Jake gestured toward the funhouse at the edge of the fairgrounds. Its mirrors glinted in the dim light, distorted reflections flashing like a dare.

"Want to run through before they start tearing it down?"

I blinked at him. "A funhouse?"

"Yeah, why not?"

I laughed softly, shaking my head. "Come on, Jake. Get serious."

"I am serious." He grinned, already starting toward it. "Let's go!"

I stayed rooted, my arms folded against the night chill. He glanced back at me, his silhouette caught against the glow of carnival lights.

"You're seriously gonna make me do this alone?"

I said nothing. Instead, I jutted out my chin, and my feet remained immovable.

He raised a brow. "Man. You've changed."

The words stung sharper than I expected. "What's that supposed to mean?"

"The Kelly I knew would've already run in ahead of me and told me to try and keep up."

My chest tightened. He turned then, slow, deliberate, his back retreating into the thinning crowd.

"All right. Suit yourself."

The air buzzed with laughter and the faint crack of sparklers, but all I could hear was the echo of his words.

I looked around—the emptying booths, the trail of families heading for the exits, the dust curling at my feet—and then back at Jake, his shoulders squared against the dark.

No more regrets. No holding back.

"I can't believe I'm doing this," I muttered, but a smile tugged at my lips before I could stop it. Something light, something reckless, sparked in me.

I gathered my skirt and broke into a run. Without hesitation, I darted past him toward the funhouse entrance. "See you on the other side!" I called, breathless, my laughter trailing behind me.

I glanced back long enough to see Jake's grin flash in the shadows. "Oh, no you don't!"

His footsteps thundered after mine as I disappeared inside. Immediately, the glow of the carnival dissolved into mirrors and colored lights.

Jake
Boise, Idaho

The first room swallowed Jake whole. It was almost entirely dark, humming faintly with hidden speakers. Splashes of neon paint streaked the walls and ceiling, glowing like constellations under black lights. A mirror loomed ahead, warping his reflection into a funhouse parody of himself.

"Kelly?" His voice echoed strangely, bouncing back at him.

"Yeah?" Her reply came faint but sure, from deeper inside.

He moved forward, pushing through a tangle of vinyl-covered poles that swung against his arms and shoulders. They squeaked under his grip, smelling faintly of plastic and lemon disinfectant. He nearly tripped, his sneakers catching on the rubber mat.

His breath puffed out in the cool air. "You gettin' the feeling this place was made for much smaller people?"

Her laugh floated back, warm and teasing. "You're just figuring that out now?"

"Come back." He reached out a hand, sliding it along a pole for balance. "We'll find our way together."

"Oh no you don't, Jake Forester." He could practically hear the grin in her voice.

"What?"

"You think I don't know you'll race ahead of me the second I come back there?"

"I would never!"

"Hay bale maze," she shot back.

He winced, grinning despite himself. "Okay, one time—"

"Paintball."

"Forgot about that one."

"The three-legged race at Founder's Day Picnic—you do know you're supposed to stay tied to your partner, right?"

"That was the old Jake Forester," he countered, laughing under his breath as he shoved through the last of the poles. "The new Jake Forester isn't nearly as competitive."

Her voice softened, almost as if she were just talking to herself. "Doubt it."

A flash of her hair caught his eye as she darted ahead, slipping into the next room. The challenge tugged at him, pulling him forward like a magnet. He barreled through the obstacles with less grace than force, poles smacking against his sides, and chased her into a labyrinth of mirrors.

Light fractured in every direction. It bounced his reflection back at him in a hundred distorted angles. He spotted Kelly ahead—her silhouette, her laugh, the shimmer of her dress in the neon glow.

"Nice try, Richardson—" He reached for her, only to crash into cold glass. The impact rattled his teeth.

Her laughter spilled out, bright and unrestrained. "I'm not there, Forester."

They wove through the hall, catching fleeting glimpses of each other. His hand brushed glass. His reflection crossed hers, their voices weaving through the dizzying maze. Each time he thought he was close, Kelly slipped away, just out of reach.

Finally, he stopped, breath tight in his chest. Across from him, Kelly stood frozen too. They were feet apart, eyes searching. Was it really her—or just another reflection?

Slowly, he lifted his hand. She mirrored him. His palm pressed to the glass—except it wasn't glass.

Her fingers met his. Warm, alive.

The music shifted, garbling. Natasha Bedingfield's *"Live your life with arms wide open"* from "Unwritten" bled into the opening chords of John Waite's "Missing You." And with it came a rush—Friday night dances, stars wheeling above them, the press of her sweater against his denim jacket, and the softness of her hand in his.

The mirror maze fell away. There was only her hand in his, and the weight of everything they'd lost. And maybe everything they might still find.

Kelly
Boise, Idaho

The music wrapped around me, pulsing through the mirrored halls of the funhouse—"Unwritten" blurring, then bending into something older, something heavier.

And suddenly, I was seventeen again.

Jake's hand in mine. His jacket scratchy against my bare arm as we danced under the streamers and fairy lights of the gym. The world was small then. Just the two of us swaying, the smell of his cologne mixing with floor wax and too-sweet punch.

I remembered the way I'd leaned into him, how safe it felt. Until I noticed her—Bridgette—standing off to the side, her eyes locked on us, hungry, calculating. That had to be at the second Alaska school dance. The one when I realized I really did like Jake.

The memory cracked, and I blinked back into the present. Jake's eyes caught mine across the maze of mirrors, brown and warm and searching. The same eyes. Older, sadder maybe, but still his.

Another flash. A few dances later. Amy tugged me back into the bathroom after my mascara smudged. Both of us giggled as we fixed ourselves in the mirror.

When I'd stepped back into the gym that night, Troy was there.

"You know, Kelly, if high school handed out penalty flags for being too cute, you'd be benched already," he'd said, attempting to loop a hand over my shoulders.

I'd laughed. It was an easy, bubbling sound I hadn't expected.

I'd managed to slip away, and that's when I saw Jake watching. He had frozen mid-step across the gym floor, and I'd felt the moment shift. A fork in the timeline neither of us chose, but both of us felt.

I pushed that memory out of my mind. That was then. This was now.

Jake moved closer, and I felt my pulse trip. His shoulder brushed mine as he shifted near, and the air between us buzzed like static.

Electricity over his closeness fought with fear. *Oh God . . .* the beginning of a prayer filled my mind, but stopped short. The truth is that it wasn't too often that I turned to God for answers anymore. It almost seemed easier to figure things out on my own. That way, when things went south, I only had myself to blame.

I'd spent too many nights praying that God would bring Jake back into my life, only to be disappointed. My faith was fragile enough, and I didn't need doubts of God's love for me to fill my mind. God had been so silent for so long. Yet at that moment, unexpected words filled my mind. *Answered prayers are not quick fixes.*

My roommate Trish had told me that phrase decades ago. Was it the truth? Could this moment be the answer to all those prayers I'd prayed? Had God been weaving a new story all along?

Jake and I were different people than we'd been back then. The storms of life had battered each of us. Yet they had also shaped us into the people we are today. And yet, maybe this was just who we needed to become for *now.* Perhaps the answer to my prayers had been no back then because God had been preparing each of us for a distant yes. A yes we could make to each other with confidence.

We'd both become people who prioritized our families and clients. Perhaps now we could draw closer, with a deeper understanding that, while the past had been full of pain, it had also given us many gifts. Maybe now it was the moment when we could truly appreciate all those things and each other. As friends, of course.

The memories came harder now, like snapshots too bright to ignore: The prom, Jake with Bridgette, her hand sliding up his arm as he tried to pretend he didn't notice me watching. Or leaving with Troy, my chest hollow, the music too loud, the gym spinning. Jake turning away, shaking his head.

We were past the point of playing games. Time had brought maturity. Regrets had paved the way to this second chance. My breath caught at the realization that we'd somehow found our way back to each other. God, our North Star, had led us here, to now.

The mirrors threw back a thousand versions of us, but none of those refracted images mattered. I looked up and saw the real Jake standing before me. It was him, right in front of me.

His chest was rising and falling like he'd just run a mile. I felt the heat radiating off his body. I breathed in the scent of aftershave clinging to his skin. I took in the last droplets of water still in his hair from the dunk tank.

We stood inches apart, breathless, like the universe had pressed pause. His gaze dropped to my mouth, then lifted back to my eyes. I swallowed hard. I swore time folded in on itself. Past and present, crashing together, making it impossible to tell where one ended and the other began.

I thought he might kiss me. I thought I might let him.

But before I could move, before I could decide, another memory filled my mind. I could clearly see the gym door slamming behind me. I'd been too quick to act then, and I'd regretted it. Was that memory a warning? Could it be a reminder that sometimes choices are made too quickly and leave scars that last for decades? If this were the right time for us, then it would still be the right time tomorrow.

Still, my hand tingled where his had been. And my heart beat loud enough to drown out everything else. *Lord, show me. Help me. I don't want to hurt Jake. I don't want to be hurt. Lord, please . . .*

Jake
Boise, Idaho

"Kelly?" The word slipped out of Jake's lips, part trepidation, part hope.

He watched as her lashes fluttered. Although his heart pounded, he told himself not to rush. Not to scare her away. Moreover, he was still married. Nicole had left their marriage ages ago, but he would still uphold his vows.

Kelly's eyes widened slightly. For a moment, she looked like the girl he'd lost once already. So beautiful. So kind. More than he'd ever dreamed. Again, feelings of unworthiness knotted themselves in his throat, and Jake attempted to swallow them down.

It was almost as if his worried thoughts had built an invisible wall between them. With a fold of her eyebrows, a guarded expression replaced the hopeful one.

Two heartbeats later, Kelly took a small step back. She forced a smile. "Find our way out together?" Her voice sounded shaky, and every doubt Jake had about his worthiness tightened his shoulders, causing him to stand straighter.

Jake nodded, throat thick. When he reached for her hand, she didn't pull away. Her fingers were warm, delicate. He grasped them with the slightest pressure, and they remained steady in his hand. A breathless charge hummed between them as he led her through the final twists of the funhouse.

They stepped outside into the cooling night. The last streaks of sunlight had bled from the sky, leaving indigo threaded with the first shy stars. Kelly shivered, the kind of subtle movement he might have missed if he weren't watching her so closely.

Without a word, he shrugged off his jacket and draped it over her shoulders. The fabric slipped against her skin. He saw the memory flicker in her eyes. Years ago, he'd done the same. They both remembered.

"Thanks," she murmured.

"No problem." His voice came out rougher than intended.

In the field nearby, the younger kids darted through the grass. Sparklers painted streaks of light in the dark. Chris lingered with his friends, fist-bumping them goodbye. Jake felt the tug of time.

"It's getting late," he said at last. "I've gotta get my kids to bed."

"Oh, well—" She pressed her lips together. "I suppose we didn't get to that paperwork, did we?"

"You want to follow us home?" The words came before he could second-guess them. "We can talk after I get them settled."

She hesitated, then nodded. "Yeah. Okay."

They started toward the parking lot. Jake called out, his voice carrying across the darkening field. The kids came running, their laughter bright against the hum of cicadas and the distant crack of fireworks. All except Chris—he lagged, falling in step at the back, shoulders tense.

"Everyone," Jake said, "Kelly is going to follow us home."

Chris's brows pulled together. "Why?"

Jake stumbled for words, his tongue thick, his chest tightening. Before he could speak, Kelly's voice slipped in, calm and professional.

"I'm your father's old friend, but I'm also your father's attorney. We need to discuss a few things."

Sadie's sparkler hissed low, almost gone. She glanced up, voice small. "About Mom?"

Jake and Kelly both nodded.

The kids exchanged looks, their laughter dimming. Tyler's voice broke the silence, thin but earnest. "Can you make sure we can still see both our mom and our dad? My friend Billy—his mom has him all the time. He never sees his dad."

Becca chimed in, her tone solemn. "I have a friend where it's the other way. She's with her dad all the time, but never sees her mom."

Jake paused. He crouched slightly, meeting their eyes, feeling the weight of their fear. "That's why I hired Kelly. I want to make sure you guys are as unaffected by this as possible. And Kelly's going to help me with that. Right, Kel?"

Her eyes met his, steady. "Absolutely."

The younger kids' faces eased, shoulders relaxing. But Chris and Rae still looked unconvinced. Shadows clung to their expressions.

Jake straightened, clapping his hands together with false brightness. "Now then—who wants to pick up smoothies on the way home?"

The younger ones cheered and bolted for Jake's SUV. Burnt sparklers were stomped out and then thrown into a nearby bin. Jake tossed the keys to Chris, who caught them reluctantly. His eyes flickered between his dad and Kelly.

Jake pretended not to notice the doubt there. But he felt it. He always did.

Kelly
Boise, Idaho

THE SIGN ON THE DOOR READ

"CLOSED," but the lights inside glowed as if they were waiting for me. I sat in my car longer than I should have, telling myself I had no business being here. With any other client, I never would've let the day bend this way, bleed past boundaries. But Jake wasn't just any client.

He was Jake.

The boy who once made me smoothies before Algebra finals. The man whose name I'd whispered in the dark of dorm rooms, hoping distance couldn't erase him. Well, until I missed him so much that I thought my heart would break, and so I decided it would be easier just to pretend he was dead.

And now, Jake would be the client who would soon be sitting next to me in a courtroom battle. One I guessed would be too messy to wrap neatly in affidavits and clauses.

It should have been simple: a lawyer helping a father fight for his kids. That's all. But the light spilling across the dark street told another story. It stretched out in a golden band, pulling at me, beckoning me like it had the right.

A few minutes later, I pushed the door open and stepped inside. The scent of fresh fruit and vanilla washed over me, undercut with a sharp note of citrus cleaner. The place was cozy, lived-in, alive in a way most health food shops never are.

And then there was Jake—moving behind the counter as if he'd done it a thousand times, his presence filling the room so completely it felt like I was stepping not just into a shop but into something far more dangerous. His kids were already spread out across the tables. Their voices rose and fell like background music.

The chalkboard above his head listed smoothies with names that made me grin. *Wake Me Up Before You Mango-Go* promised a sunny burst of pineapple and mango. *Pour Some Berry on Me* looked like a wild mix of every berry imaginable.

There was *The Fresh Mint of Bel-Air*, cool with chocolate and mint, and *Knight Smoothie Rider*, bold with chocolate and espresso. For the health nuts, *Kale Me Softly* winked from the bottom corner, paired with apples and lemon.

Jake caught me reading, and the corners of his mouth tilted up like he knew the names were part of the charm. Before I could order, he set a tall cup in front of me. The smoothie was pale pink and frosty. Condensation beaded down the plastic.

"Here you go."

I took a sip, and cold sweetness slid across my tongue. The burst of strawberry was bright, the yogurt creamy. My eyes widened before I could stop myself. "Wow! That's delicious."

His grin was boyish, almost shy, though I could see the pride glinting in his eyes. "There's no reason healthy food shouldn't taste good. And that one has extra protein powder. I need you to be in tip-top shape." He winked.

I pretended his wink hadn't just sent a chill down my spine. To deflect my emotions, I glanced up at the chalkboard again. "Are all of these your concoctions?" I took another sip.

Jake leaned one elbow on the counter, following my line of sight. "Most of them, yeah. And this one—" He tapped the chalk beside *Sweet Child O' Lime*. "That one goes way back. I first made it for you the night before your Algebra final. Remember? You were cramming at my kitchen table, convinced you were going to fail." His voice softened, and his smile tugged with memory. "You said you needed a miracle, so I pulled out strawberries, lime, and whatever else we had in the fridge. You swore that smoothie gave you enough brain power to scrape out the C you needed."

The memory warmed me instantly. I laughed, covering my mouth with one hand. "I barely scraped by. If it hadn't been for that final, I would've failed the whole semester."

"And you passed." His eyes remained steady on mine, as if he could still feel the relief of that night. "I told you the smoothie had magic in it."

I hadn't realized his kids had gone quiet until I noticed them, huddled at a nearby table—now together as a group—watching us with curious eyes. One of the two little ones leaned toward the other, whispering, and a soft giggle followed.

Heat rose to my cheeks, part from the attention, part from the memory of who we'd once been—two teenagers, side by side over open textbooks, sharing a frosty drink through mismatched straws. For a heartbeat, the years between then and now felt thinner, like the past had only been waiting for us to pick it back up.

The spell broke when Rae, his oldest, sighed loudly. "Dad, I still have an essay to finish before tomorrow."

The twins, Lily and Leo, rubbed their eyes, their small bodies folded against each other in identical exhaustion. Their yawns came in unison, and it tugged at my heart.

The other kids—respectful, curious—seemed mostly pleased, even relieved, to see their dad smiling like this.

But Chris. His gaze lingered on me, steady and unreadable. My stomach flipped when I realized he was only a few years younger than Jake had been when I first fell for him. Chris had the same dark hair, falling just so across his forehead, though his eyes were lighter and more widely set. Still, when he smiled—Jake's smile—it nearly undid me.

Jake looked at me, set his jaw, and said, "All right—time to head out." He pulled a folded slip of paper from his pocket and slid it across the counter. "Here's the address."

Before I could respond, Sadie's hand shot up. "Can I ride along?" She glanced at me with hopeful eyes. She looked so like Jake—especially in the few old photos I'd seen at his childhood home. Her dark eyes, the curve of her brow—a carbon copy of him in miniature.

I hesitated, but she pushed. "I'll show you the way." She beamed at me, confident, eager.

Sadie chatted all the way as we drove, pausing from her descriptions of her day at the carnival and her favorite smoothie to tell me where to go. As we turned into the subdivision, my heart rate sped up. The houses stood tall, with manicured lawns and expansive driveways that were wide enough for two cars. I thought about how Boise had neighborhoods known for their stately homes—tree-lined streets, old revival styles, classical façades. This one—called the North End—especially, with its historic charm and handsome streets, was known for beautiful, graceful houses.

The neighborhood shimmered in the dark, each house lit up like a stage. Ornate lanterns glowed on stone pillars, casting long shadows across perfectly edged lawns. Driveways stretched wide, some with polished SUVs parked like trophies. It was all a little too perfect, a little too glossy, like the kind of postcard version of life no one really lives in.

Jake's house stood tallest on the block, its façade washed in a halo of light from carefully hidden spotlights. Brass fixtures flanked the arched doorway, their glow spilling onto the stone path in golden circles. The windows gleamed, most of their curtains drawn back to reveal crystal chandeliers and ornate draperies within.

It was the most beautiful house I'd ever stepped up to. And yet, as I followed Jake inside, a strange hollowness pressed against me. The marble floors gleamed, too polished to feel warm. Velvet drapes hung heavy against the tallest windows, shutting out the night. Every corner gleamed with effort—expensive, curated effort. This wasn't Jake. It was too ornate, too fussy. A house that seemed to demand admiration rather than invite you to sit down and stay a while.

As if reading my mind, Sadie glanced up at me. "Mama picked everything out. Daddy just wanted to make her happy." Her voice softened, her dark eyes—Jake's exact eyes—catching the light. "But Rae says he wasted millions trying to do that. And nothing can really make you happy on the outside if you want something else on the inside."

I stared at her, startled by the wisdom tucked into her young words. Sadie only smiled faintly, tugging my hand. "Come on. I want to show you my room."

She led me up a sweeping staircase. The carpet was thick beneath my shoes, and the railing was polished to a shine. At the top, the hallway branched like spokes of a wheel, lined with framed portraits—family vacations at the beach, Jake with a toddler on his shoulders, the whole brood dressed in Christmas pajamas before a twinkling tree. My chest tightened at the sight, a window into the years I had missed. I followed the pre-teen through one of the open doors.

Sadie's room was bright and unmistakably hers, even against the backdrop of the house's heavy grandeur. She had lavender walls with fairy lights strung in loose loops above her headboard. A bookshelf overflowed with well-worn novels, their spines cracked and bent. On the dresser sat a collection of trinkets—a glitter globe, a ceramic horse, a seashell painted with her name in crooked letters.

But it was the bulletin board that caught me. Photos tacked in layers, overlapping like a collage. Sadie, with her siblings in the backyard, Jake crouched between them, his grin wide and unguarded. One photo in particular pulled me back. It was a slightly younger Jake, his arm looped around a gap-toothed Sadie. His dark eyes lit with the same spark I remembered from his youth. My throat thickened.

"This is my favorite," Sadie said, pointing to a snapshot of Jake holding the twins. He held one in each arm, both babies squalling red-faced while he laughed like it was the best moment in the world.

I smiled, even as something inside me ached. "That's a good one," I managed, my voice thinner than I wanted.

Then a sound drifted down the hall. It was the low rumble of Jake's voice. Instinct pulled my attention toward the sound.

"Love you, Daddy," Leo called from one bedroom.

"Love you, Daddy," Lily echoed from another. Her voice was lighter, as though her words might drift straight into the stars.

"Love you, too, pumpkins. Sweet dreams," Jake replied.

The tenderness in his tone hollowed me out.

There were fewer photos of Jake's wife on the board, but the ones displayed told it all. Nicole was gorgeous, *just like Bridgette.* The thought sent my old insecurities rushing back.

My chest ached, not just for myself but for them. They hadn't asked for any of this. Divorce. Courtrooms. As hard as it was for parents, the children so often carried the heaviest load, navigating worlds they had no power to shape.

I shifted, and that's when I noticed her. Rae, leaning in the doorway of her own room across the hall. She was looking into Sadie's room, watching us.

Her arms were crossed tight, her posture sharp with defense. But her wary eyes never left me. She didn't speak, but she didn't need to. The message was clear enough. *You're not one of us.*

Heat rose in my cheeks, guilt prickling along my skin. I offered the faintest smile, but Rae's face didn't change. She turned and disappeared into her room, leaving the door ajar just enough to remind me she was still listening.

I thanked Sadie for showing me her room and returned to the hall. The house seemed suddenly quieter, the velvet drapes heavier, the marble colder.

Jake's voice drifted again from one of the kids' bedrooms, and I realized that no matter how ornate the house, no matter how carefully chosen the furniture, this was where the genuine love lived—in whispered goodnights, in the trust of little voices, in the guarded eyes of teenagers still trying to figure out where they belonged.

And I wasn't sure yet if there was a place for me in it, even as a friend.

When we returned downstairs, I sat at the kitchen table, and Jake made me tea.

I almost felt numb as I watched steam rising in lazy curls from the mug between my palms. I fiddled with the tea bag string, winding and unwinding it around my finger, trying to steady myself. The house smelled faintly of chamomile, soap, and something warm and masculine I couldn't quite name.

Jake leaned against the counter, sipping from a mug of coffee that smelled rich and dark, grounding. His shoulders looked heavy in the kitchen light, shadows stretching long against the cabinets. I was unsure how I felt about any of this, and so I turned my thoughts back to business.

"Seeing as there was no prenuptial agreement," I began, my voice careful but firm, "she is entitled to fifty percent of all assets. We can fight it."

His eyes lifted to mine, steady and unflinching. "No. I don't care about the money or the stuff. All that matters to me is that we share custody—and for my kids and me to find our new normal, one full of joy and peace."

His words caught me off guard. Most people lead with money, driven by anger or fear of loss. But not him. What I saw was pain, yes, but also a kind of integrity I rarely witnessed across a table littered with legal briefs. It stirred something in me—something I didn't want to name.

I reached across the table, my hand brushing the rim of my mug. "I promise to do everything I can to protect your kids and you, okay? Trust me?"

His gaze locked on mine, unwavering, the weight of it sending heat into my chest.

"Yeah," he said softly. "I trust you."

I swallowed, forcing myself to look away before the moment grew too large to contain. "Okay, then." I straightened the papers I'd brought with me, the rustle breaking the quiet. "Let's get to work."

But even as I spread the documents across the table, I could still feel his eyes on me—heavy, searching, and full of something close to hope.

Kelly
Boise, Idaho

DAYS BLURRED TOGETHER IN A

rhythm that felt almost domestic. His house became the place of late-night tea, stacks of notes spread across the table, and conversations that slipped between custody strategy and memories neither of us expected to surface. I didn't mind the hours. In fact, I found myself looking forward to them—his kids' laughter drifting down the stairs, the quiet steadiness of his presence beside me, the way his voice softened whenever he spoke about what he wanted for their future.

Still, when Jake was worried about the kids overhearing our detailed conversations about his assets and bank accounts, we found ourselves carting the paperwork elsewhere.

The bell above the coffee shop door chimed, and Jake held it open for me like it was the most natural thing in the world. My arms were full of folders, heavy with custody agreements and financial affidavits, but under his steady gaze, the weight of them felt somehow lighter.

I wondered when that had started—how he could still make me feel steady with just a look. Years had passed, whole lives had been lived, and yet one small gesture had the power to unsettle me.

Inside, the shop wrapped around us with coziness. The air carried the rich scent of espresso, cut with cinnamon and the faint bitterness of burnt milk froth. A milk steamer hissed in the background, voices murmured at nearby tables, and the low hum of indie music filled the spaces in between.

We claimed a corner booth, its vinyl cracked and soft from years of use. Between us, the table disappeared under a barrage of papers—custody filings, property valuations, yellow highlighter marks glowing under the coffee shop's amber lights. Jake leaned forward, elbows braced, his eyes narrowing at every clause.

Hours blurred into coffee refills and ink smudges. At one point, his head dropped into his hand, shoulders bowing under the invisible weight pressing him down. For a man built of such strength, the vulnerability of that gesture hollowed something in me.

Before I could think better of it, I reached across the table and rested my hand on his. His skin was warm, rougher than I remembered, the heat of it steadying me. "We'll figure this out," I whispered.

His eyes lifted to mine, and for a moment, the contracts scattered between us seemed to vanish. There was just him—tired, stubborn, but still fighting for the people who mattered most.

The moment stretched too long until Jake jolted upright. "Sadie's game. I'm late." His words spurted out, and his knee knocked into mine as he scrambled to gather the files.

I blinked, startled. "Then go."

But he looked up again, something sparking in his expression. "Come with me."

"Jake—" My hand gestured to the folders. This was my world: briefs, hearings, rules. A high school gym didn't fit.

He cut me off with a grin that carried the same reckless warmth it had back in high school. "Kelly. You've done enough heavy lifting for one night. Just come. You won't regret it."

And before I could protest again, he was already holding the door, evening air rushing in.

The gym was alive with cheers and buzzers. The air smelled of floor polish and salty popcorn. Sneakers squeaked, the basketball thudded in sharp rhythm, and voices rose in waves—cheers, whistles, and the blare of a fight song played a touch off-key.

I slid onto the bleacher beside Jake. My shoulder brushed his. His eyes flicked to mine—quick, grateful—before darting back to the court. Jake's voice cut through it all. He shouted Sadie's name until his throat sounded raw, cupping his hand to his mouth like a man who could will victory into being. His kids fanned out around him in loyal chaos: Becca spilling popcorn down her hoodie, Tyler hollering as though born with a megaphone, Rae tucked into the shadows with her arms crossed, Chris slouched with his phone glowing faintly, and the twins rubbing their eyes in synchronized exhaustion.

When Sadie looked our way, I lifted my voice, calling her name. Her head whipped around, her eyes lit, and the ball left her hands in a perfect arc. The swish of the net was swallowed in the roar that followed.

By the time the buzzer blared, sealing the win, the bleachers shook with stomping feet. Jake's younger kids spilled onto the court in a rush of joy. Their voices collided in laughter. He wrapped his arms around them, pulling his brood close, and somehow I was swept in too—Becca squealing in my ear, the twins clinging to my waist, Tyler grinning like we shared a secret.

For a moment, under fluorescent lights and echoing cheers, it felt alarmingly like family.

But then Chris lifted his gaze from his phone, sharp and assessing, and Rae's arms crossed tighter across her chest. Their wariness sliced through the warmth, reminding me of what I was: not theirs. Not really. I was a lawyer. A helper on paper.

My chest ached. Divorce was hard on everyone, but hardest of all on the ones who hadn't chosen it.

The scent of popcorn and sweat pressed too close. The celebration grew loud, with tangled limbs and laughter. For a heartbeat, I wanted to belong. And wanting that was dangerous.

Jake's laugh boomed above the noise. His arms looped around Becca, his hand steadying Leo, his head bent to press a kiss to Sadie's sweaty, damp hair. Even in the chaos, his eyes found mine.

"You fit here," he said quietly, almost in wonder.

The words hit too deep. My shoulder still tingled from his brush, my hands sticky from the twins' sugar-coated fingers. I had felt it too—that terrifying, glowing sense of belonging.

Yet the business suit I still wore grounded me. Custody motions. Affidavits. My role was clear.

I shook my head, forcing the words out steadily. "I'm here as your attorney, Jake. That's all."

His brow furrowed, and disappointment flickered. But he didn't push. Instead, he gave a slight nod. The gym still roared, but a space opened between us. Because as sweet as it felt to be part of that circle, I knew the truth. This wasn't my world. And the ache of wanting it only made me more afraid.

Jake
Boise, Idaho

JAKE LEANED IN THE DOORWAY

of Kelly's office, a paper sack warm in his hands. They'd seen each other nearly every day for weeks, and he was grateful. He'd also found an excuse to see her again today, and he'd picked up lunch. Just to be nice, of course.

The scent of roasted chicken and fresh bread drifted out of the bag he carried. Heads turned. He couldn't help but observe that whispers rippled between her coworkers, and he hoped this wouldn't get her in trouble.

"Jake." Kelly's cheeks flushed as she spotted him.

He set the bag on her desk and cleared his throat. "Thought you might need a break."

The awkwardness in her eyes softened when she laughed. It was a quiet, grateful sound. "You thought right."

They ate at the edge of her desk, plastic cutlery clinking against takeout boxes. Their conversation meandered from work to weather to nothing at all. It was ordinary, but not.

When Kelly pushed her chair back, gathering her briefcase, Jake stood too.

"Court?" he asked.

She nodded. "Yep. On Monday. It's a big case. You do remember that I have other clients besides you, right?"

He noticed nerves tightening her shoulders. "You'll do excellent," he said.

Kelly eyed him, and her brow lifted. Almost as if she didn't believe him.

"You always were the one who could get a whole room to listen. Do you remember the speech you gave back in high school? My senior year, right before graduation?"

Her eyes widened. "You remember that?"

"How could I forget?" His smile tilted, boyish. "You stood up there and told everyone that fairness doesn't mean treating people the same—it means giving each person what they need to stand a chance."

The words still rang true. And he remembered not just the speech, but the way her voice had filled the gym, how her conviction had silenced even the rowdiest kids. He remembered thinking then that Kelly Richardson had more courage than anyone he'd ever met.

Later, back at his office, Jake slumped into his chair. A voicemail notification blinked on his cell. He pressed play.

Nicole's voice spilled through, clipped and businesslike. "Jake, Mom needs me this weekend. Can you keep the kids? I'll pick them up on Monday."

He exhaled slowly. On paper, this helped his case—proof he was already carrying the heavier load of parenting.

But even more important than proving he was right, Jake didn't want his kids to be anywhere they weren't wanted for the weekend. He sent a quick text and told Nicole he'd keep them.

And this is what it had all come down to between them: voicemail messages and texts.

A knock on his doorframe pulled Jake back. He glanced up to see a familiar face. Ben leaned into Jake's office, hands stuffed in his pockets. Like a shadow, Amy was just behind him.

"Well, hey. Never knew you two just to drop by."

"Checking in," Ben said, his grin quick. "Amy has a house showing just around the corner in a bit, and since I'm waiting for supplies for my next painting job, uh, how're things with Kelly?"

Jake looked at Ben and cocked an eyebrow. He knew Ben

better than that. Ben's success was due to his planning. He never had to wait for supplies. Jake guessed that Amy had put him up to this.

"Don't look at me like that. We all see it." Ben chuckled, then shifted. Ben gave Jake a knowing look. "You know you have the subtlety of a fireworks display when she walks into a room, right?"

Jake stiffened. "She's my lawyer. There are rules. Boundaries. Entire continuing-ed courses warning against this exact . . . vibe."

Amy crossed her arms, unimpressed. "Uh-huh," she said. "And in high school, you were being respectful when you stared at her like she was the last slice of pizza, but never actually said anything."

Ben nodded solemnly. "RIP to opportunities lost due to chronic emotional caution."

Jake sighed. "I can't mess this up. It's too important."

Amy leaned closer, voice softening just a hair. "I'm not telling you to sweep her off her feet and ride into the sunset on a legal technicality. Just . . . don't leave her guessing. Last time, silence did the talking for you."

Ben nodded, shrugged, and pointed to Amy. "What she said. So play it safe, sure. But don't put her in emotional escrow forever."

Jake groaned. He attempted to wave them away. "Go, do your jobs. Be responsible adults. You have a mortgage to pay." They didn't move. Instead, they just stared him down, waiting for a better response.

Jake sighed. "Why are you two like this?"

"Because we love you," Amy said sweetly. "And because I refuse to watch you miss your shot *twice*. You can follow the rules and still show up."

Ben grinned. "Yeah. Tell her you like her. Then sign whatever disclaimers her lawyer-client handbook requires."

Jake tried not to smile. "You two are insufferable."

Ben and Amy eyed each other. "And correct," they said in unison.

Jake
Boise, Idaho

Saturday morning arrived with the sound of laughter and slamming doors. The twins thundered down the stairs in mismatched socks, Rae trailed after them with a book in hand, and Tyler was already begging for pancakes. Jake poured batter onto the griddle, and the kitchen filled with the sweet, buttery smell.

Nicole's absence still hung in the air, but the kids didn't mention it. They leaned into him instead—questions, jokes, even arguments, all funneled toward him like he was the center they orbited. He loved it. He dreaded it. Because he knew somewhere in the mix, Kelly would step into this rhythm, too, and the thought made his pulse trip.

For a moment, as he stood there with a spatula in hand, he let himself imagine it: Kelly at the table, her laugh carrying above the noise, the family circle expanding without effort.

But, just as quickly, he pushed the thought away. Too much time with her could hurt them both. He had to be careful. Too much time could go against you in court. Nicole was shrewd, and though she only knew Kelly's first name, he prayed she wouldn't piece together the rest. Kelly had gone back to her maiden name after her divorce, but Nicole's lawyer was expensive, and expensive meant thorough.

The smell of pancakes hit the air just as Leo shouted, "Dad, don't burn them!" and Jake barked out a laugh, shaking himself back to the moment.

Kelly
Boise, Idaho

Saturday blurred into stacks of paper and highlighted case law. I sat cross-legged on my living room floor, my client

Marissa's files spread around me like pieces of a puzzle. Every affidavit, every school report, every medical note had to fit together into a picture the jury could not ignore. I told myself I didn't mind the long hours, that the work was its own kind of anchor—but my mind kept wandering. To Jake. The way his steady gaze made the weight of a hundred documents feel lighter. The way my heart betrayed me whenever my phone lit with his name.

By Sunday morning, I was no better. I slid into a pew, Bible on my lap, willing my thoughts to stay with the choir, the sermon, the pages of Scripture. But they kept drifting to custody agreements and court strategy, to Jake's smile when he'd said I could get a whole room to listen.

Then Pastor Stonecliffe leaned over the pulpit, his voice steady and sure, quoting from the book of Amos: "Let justice roll on like a river, righteousness like a never-failing stream."

His words lit something in me. A memory surged: standing in that gymnasium decades ago, papers shaking in my hands, declaring that justice wasn't blind—it was supposed to be balanced. That a level playing field sometimes needed leveling.

That thought stayed with me all the way to the courthouse on Monday.

The courtroom always smelled the same—like paper that had been handled too many times, like old wood polished just enough to hide its years. As I settled at counsel's table, I felt that familiar mix of adrenaline and dread coil tight in my stomach.

My client, Marissa, sat beside me, her hands knotted together, knuckles white. She was a mother fighting to keep her children, and every inch of her body radiated fear.

I touched her arm lightly, steadying her. "We're going to get through this." My voice was calm, though inside my pulse pounded like the tick of the clock on the wall.

Across the aisle, opposing counsel leaned in toward his client—her ex-husband, Daniel. He was tall, broad-shouldered, his cuff links glinting under the fluorescent lights. He had wealth, a polished image, and a team of lawyers who had already stacked neat binders of evidence against Marissa. To anyone who didn't know better, he looked like stability itself.

But I knew better.

The bailiff's voice cut through the buzz. "All rise."

Wooden chairs scraped the floor as the judge entered. I stood, smoothing my skirt, heart rattling against my ribs. I was aware of everything: the low murmur of the gallery, the faint creak of the ceiling fan above, the way the fluorescent lights glared down, washing color from the room.

"Be seated." The gavel cracked, sharp and absolute.

The husband's attorney was first, parading Daniel onto the witness stand like a trophy. He painted him as reliable, steady—a man of means who could offer his children every opportunity.

"Unlike their mother," he pressed, "who has missed multiple workdays, who has bounced checks, who cannot maintain a consistent schedule." His voice carried a smug authority, punctuated by the scent of his bitter cologne as he passed our table.

Marissa sat rigid beside me, eyes wet but fixed forward.

When it was my turn, I rose slowly, gripping the edge of the table for half a beat longer than necessary. The weight of everyone's eyes fell on me—judge, spectators, even the gallery shifting in their seats. My throat was dry, but I forced myself to swallow, to breathe.

And then I remembered Jake's words, the way he had looked at me that afternoon with the take-out bag in hand and said I was the one who could get a whole room to listen. I thought of that high-school gym, my trembling hands, and the words I'd spoken all those years ago: fairness doesn't mean treating everyone the same—it means giving people what they need to stand a chance.

I stepped closer to the bench.

"Ladies and gentlemen, the law in Idaho requires us to consider the best interest of the child. Not the wealthiest parent. Not the parent with the flashiest car or the sharpest suit. But the parent who has shown, again and again, that her children's needs come first."

Daniel shifted in his seat, jaw tight.

"My client, Marissa, did not walk away from her responsibilities.

She walked toward them. When her youngest was hospitalized with pneumonia, she missed shifts. Not because she was reckless, but because she refused to leave her child's bedside. Those missed hours have been twisted into a perception of irresponsibility. But what do they truly show? Devotion."

I let the word hang, sharp as the scent of varnish in the air.

I gestured toward the financial binder Daniel's attorney had proudly displayed. "You've seen the spreadsheets. The bounced checks. But what you haven't heard is why. Daniel earns six figures, yet during their marriage, he closed joint accounts, cut Marissa off from funds, and left her scrambling to buy groceries. Ask yourself, who created the instability?"

Daniel's attorney jumped to his feet. "Objection—argumentative!"

The judge's gavel cracked. "Overruled. I will consider counsel's statement."

I steadied my breath, lowering my voice. "There's precedent here. Griggs v. Duke Power Co., 1971. The Supreme Court recognized that neutral policies—rules that look fair on paper—can still be discriminatory when they ignore real-life circumstances. Today, Daniel's side argues for rigid sameness: hours on a timesheet, checks that clear or don't. But sameness is not fairness. Justice recognizes reality. And the reality is that Marissa has been the one to show up. For every doctor's appointment. Every school conference. Every time a sick child was up at night."

Marissa's sob was muffled, but I felt it reverberate through the table.

The jury was listening. I could see it in the way their pens stilled over notepads. In the way their eyes flicked from me to Daniel and back again. He looked polished, yes, but also restless now, his foot tapping against the rung of the witness stand.

I leaned closer, drawing the jury in. "She is not the sum of missed hours or imperfect finances. She is a woman who has borne the weight of illness, motherhood, and betrayal. And today she asks only for what the law already provides: equity. Dignity. Custody that keeps her children where they feel safe and loved."

When I finished, the silence was thick, almost heavy. My hands trembled as I gripped the table again, but I didn't sit right away. I wanted them to see me, to see Marissa, and to feel the gravity of what hung in that space.

The gavel came down—sharp, echoing through the paneled room like a strike of finality.

"Court is adjourned."

Kelly
Boise, Idaho

Soon, we were called back into the courtroom for Judge Whitaker's ruling. Her words rang steady: Marissa was awarded primary physical custody. Daniel's polished façade cracked, his mouth hardening as his attorney whispered furiously beside him.

Beside me, Marissa collapsed, sobbing into her hands. Relief poured through her body like water breaking through a dam. I wrapped my arm around her shoulders, pulling her close, my own chest tightening with something fierce and protective.

Across the aisle, Daniel looked less like stability and more like what he was—a man desperate to control what he had already lost.

I gathered Marissa's papers as the gallery emptied, the scrape of chairs and shuffle of shoes filling the room. My heart still thundered, but beneath the exhaustion was a quiet satisfaction. For once, the law had met flesh and blood.

For a long moment, I couldn't move. The room smelled of wood polish and nerves, of too many bodies crammed into a space where lives were scrutinized and decided upon. The faint buzz of the ceiling light pressed down on me, mingling with the shuffle of papers as opposing counsel gathered his things quickly, along with the impatient cough of a juror eager to leave.

Then Marissa collapsed against me again, sobbing into my shoulder. Her tears soaked through the fabric of my jacket, hot and unrelenting. My arms went around her instinctively, steadying her when her knees gave way. She had fought so hard, had been called names and painted as careless, when all she had ever done was show up for her children.

I breathed her relief as though it were my own. And maybe it was.

The courtroom emptied slowly, its occupants' shoes clicking against the tiled floor, as the scent of stale coffee drifted in from the hall. I finally sank into my chair, every muscle aching as if I'd run a marathon barefoot. My throat burned, and my hands wouldn't stop trembling.

That's when my phone buzzed.

How did it go?

Just four words on a glowing screen. But I knew the voice behind them—low, steady. It was the voice that had anchored me since it slipped back into my life.

I won my case

I typed, fingers shaky but sure.
Almost instantly came Jake's reply:

Let's celebrate.

A smile spread across my face before I could stop it, wide and unbidden. The tension in my shoulders eased, and for the first time all day, I let my body relax into the hard wooden chair.

The room was nearly empty now. Only the scent of paper lingered, mixed with the faint tang of disinfectant. I closed my eyes for a moment, letting the weight of the day settle. The sound of Marissa's sobs, the sight of the jury leaning forward, the feel of victory still thrumming in my blood.

My lips curved again, softer this time. Victory had always been about rulings and outcomes. But tonight, victory felt like more. Like a door, slowly creaking open.

And somewhere in the quiet of my mind, I heard Jake's voice again: *You'll do excellent. You always were the one who could get a whole room to listen.*

Jake
Boise, Idaho

BOISE GLOWED THAT NIGHT,

streetlights flickering against damp pavement. The restaurant buzzed with chatter, the faint hum of jazz winding around the clink of glasses. Jake watched Kelly reach for her purse, her instinct pulling her back toward work, back toward the safety of papers and numbers. He reached out, covering her hand with his.

"Not tonight," he said softly.

Her eyes lifted, surprise sparking in them.

He raised his glass, the wine catching the candlelight. "To new beginnings."

Slowly, she smiled. Their glasses touched with a soft chime, and in that slight sound, Jake felt something stir awake that he hadn't dared to hope for again.

After dinner, the night air in downtown Boise carried the faint bite of autumn. It was cool against Jake's skin as he walked with Kelly by his side. Streetlights painted golden halos on the pavement. The hum of restaurants and bars spilled into the street. It was familiar: the low thrum of laughter, the clinking glasses, the occasional swell of music.

Then, ahead, the faint sounds of a guitar weaving through the evening air. Jake slowed, drawn by the rhythm, and without hesitation reached into his wallet. He tossed a twenty into the open case, where coins winked like tiny stars. The guitarist lifted his eyes in brief thanks, but never let the music falter.

It was then, out of the corner of his eye, that Jake noticed Kelly watching him. She had tilted her head, that familiar little gesture he remembered from so long ago. And when he turned—truly turned to take her in, time seemed to fold back on itself.

Her hair caught the glow from the streetlight, a halo softening the edges of the years. Lines framed her face now, but they only deepened the story she carried. And when she smiled—oh, when she smiled—the same delicate wrinkle creased her nose, as if thirty-two years hadn't dared touch it.

But it wasn't just her smile. It was her eyes. He saw them more clearly than ever before. Not the sparkling innocence of the girl he'd once loved, but the layered depths of a woman who had lived, who had endured both joy and loss. There was wisdom there. And pain. And something else—something that made his chest ache with recognition.

Back then, he hadn't realized what God had placed in front of him. He hadn't known it was a gift. But standing beside her now, he saw it plain as the neon light spilling across the pavement.

Kelly. His first love. Still a masterpiece in the making.

The guitarist's melody trailed after them as they walked, delicate notes rising and falling like the echoes of some half-forgotten dream. Jake shoved his hands in his pockets, feeling awkward, though he couldn't have said why. Maybe it was the quiet between them. Maybe it was the weight of thirty-two years pressing down all at once.

When he dared glance at her again, Kelly was smiling, that same familiar wrinkle tugging at her nose. The sight undid him. He had forgotten how much he'd loved that little quirk, how it had felt like a secret only he got to see.

"You always did that," he said softly.

She tilted her head. "Did what?"

"That thing. With your nose when you smile. You haven't changed . . . Well, I guess you couldn't. It's part of you."

Her laugh was quiet, almost shy. "Thirty-two years, Jake. I've changed a lot."

He studied her face, the fine lines etched by time, the gravity in her gaze that hadn't been there before. And yet, beneath the years, he saw the same girl he'd once held on a summer night, the girl he'd let slip through his fingers without realizing she'd been a gift from God Himself.

"Not the things that matter," he said. His voice cracked a little, but he didn't care. "I look at you now, and I wish I had pushed my worries aside. I never thought I was good enough. Not for you, especially. I was so caught up in my mind that I didn't trust the love I saw in your eyes. If only I could have believed. If I had truly seen what we had, I . . ." He stopped, searching for the words, but they tangled on his tongue.

Kelly's eyes softened, and for a long moment she only looked at him, as if measuring the truth in his face. Then she whispered, "Maybe you weren't supposed to see it then."

The words hung between them, heavy, yet full of grace.

Jake swallowed, his throat tight. "Maybe. But I see it now."

For the first time that evening, she didn't look away.

The guitarist's music faded behind them as they turned down a quieter street, the hum of neon replaced by the hush of night air. Jake matched his stride to hers, every step stirring old memories he hadn't known he'd kept.

He stole a glance at her. Long, light brown hair spilled over her shoulders, threaded now with silver. He thought of the girl she'd been—hair flying in the wind when she rode her bike down Main Street, laughing without care. Thirty-two years had softened that wildness, etched faint lines at the corners of her eyes.

"You know," Jake said finally, "I still remember the way you used to look at me. Like I was more than I was. Like I could actually be somebody."

Kelly's gaze flicked to him, sharp and surprised, before softening. "Jake . . . just, no. You were already somebody. I didn't make that up."

"Maybe. But I think about it sometimes. How much I needed that back then. I didn't even know it." He gave a low laugh. "Guess I was too stubborn to see God was handing me a gift, wrapped up in freckles and shy smiles."

She stopped walking and turned to face him fully. The streetlight caught her features, and he saw not only the woman she was now but the shadow of the girl she had been. "Life doesn't always give us what we want," she said gently. "So many silly mistakes. So many misses between us. We've both been knocked down by life, haven't we?"

The truth of it stung. He thought of the years lost—choices that had carried him far from her, mistakes that carved regret into his bones. And yet here she stood, close enough that he could trace the wisdom in her gaze, and the sorrow too.

"Still," he murmured, "I can't help but wonder what it would've been like. You and me."

Her smile was faint, tinged with something that looked like ache. "I wonder that too. More than I'd like to admit. Then again, we wouldn't be the people we are now, would we?" She swallowed as if emotion had caught in her throat and she was trying to swallow it down. "I just wanted you to see me, Jake. Sadly, I played games. I enjoyed the attention of the other guys. I'll admit that. Yet all the while, I wished it were you."

For a moment, neither spoke. The world around them hushed, as though waiting. Then Jake reached out, hesitant, and brushed a loose strand of hair from her face. His hand lingered, not quite touching.

"I see you now, Kelly," he whispered. "Not just who you were. Who you are. And I'm not blind anymore."

Her breath caught, and the wrinkle appeared at her nose once again. And he saw it again . . . that love in her eyes. It was both a memory and something new. His heart quickened.

The guitarist's melody still faintly clung to the night air. He squeezed her hand, and they continued walking. Jake felt lighter for having dropped that twenty in the case, but heavier for the memories stirring in his chest.

Beside him, Kelly tilted her head, her eyes tracing his profile. "Do you still play?" she asked.

He glanced at her, surprised. She remembered. "Here and there when I can. I still write some too. I wrote a song for Nicole when things were falling apart, but . . ." He hesitated, pressing his lips together, the pain sudden and sharp. "To be honest, I think she stopped listening quite a while ago."

Kelly didn't answer right away. Instead, she flipped her hair back over her shoulder, her steps slowing as if she were letting his words sink deep.

Jake cleared his throat, softening the admission with a wry smile. "But I'm happy to report I've started playing again."

Her gaze lingered, steady and kind, the lamplight catching a shine in her eyes. "That's great, Jake. If I've learned anything about how people cope after divorce, the ones who thrive are the ones who don't let it steal the joy from the things they've always loved." She paused, her voice gentling. "I'd love to hear you play again sometime."

Her words landed in him like a weight and a gift all at once. He smiled, slow and genuine, letting them rest there. "I just may take you up on that."

For a heartbeat, she looked as if she might ask when—but Jake gestured ahead toward his SUV, breaking the moment. "Here's mine. Where are you parked?"

"I walked," she said lightly. "I live a few blocks from here." She started forward, tossing a glance over her shoulder. "Thanks for dinner. I have another call with Nicole's lawyer tomorrow. I'll call you after."

"Richardson." His voice stopped her.

She turned back, brow raised. "What?"

"I am not letting you walk home alone at night. Get in."

Her mouth quirked in half-protest. "Really, it's no trouble—"

He stopped her with a look.

Kelly shook her head, exhaling, but the corners of her lips curved in surrender. "Fine."

She crossed to the passenger side, and Jake hurried ahead to open the door. For a moment, as she slid in, their eyes met, something unspoken pulsing between them—a memory, a hope. Was it all right to hope? He closed the door gently and circled around to his side.

When the engine hummed to life and they pulled away, Jake's chest tightened. Responsibilities, children, the wounds of the past— there was too much at stake to let himself imagine. And yet the thought pressed against him anyway: what it might be like to be seen again, cared for again, loved again.

✦ ✦ ✦

Jake
Boise, Idaho

Jake pulled the truck to the curb in front of Kelly's bungalow. The low-slung house sat back from the street, its wide porch stretching beneath a slanted roof. Weathered cedar shingles gave it a lived-in warmth, softened by climbing roses that curled lazily along the railings. Built in the 1920s, it carried the charm of a place that had sheltered generations, its broad windows glowing faintly as though holding on to the day's last light.

The neighborhood smelled of fried onions drifting from the diner down the street, layered with the powdery sweetness of laundry detergent coming from a vent below. A car rolled past, bass thumping, before the night settled again into the quiet buzz of crickets.

Kelly unclipped her seat belt. The metallic snap echoed in the still cab. She pushed open the door quickly, as if she couldn't get out fast enough, letting the cool air rush in and steal away the fragile warmth that had hung between them during the drive.

"Good night," she said, her voice firm, brisk—closing the moment before it could linger.

Jake frowned. He wasn't ready to let her slip away like that. He turned the key, killing the engine, and shoved open his door.

She stopped mid-step, brows lifting when she heard his boots crunch against the pavement. "What are you doing?"

"Walking you to your door," he said, moving toward her. "I want to make sure you don't slice yourself open on those rusty saw blades masquerading as a staircase."

Her lips twitched. Not quite a smile. It was closer to annoyance, though he caught the flicker of amusement she tried to hide. "You know, I've been walking up and down these stairs all by myself for nearly a year now."

"Don't care."

His tone was steady, not teasing. It was the kind of voice that reached straight through her defenses, unsettling her more than she wanted to admit. She rolled her eyes and turned toward the stairs.

The metal railing groaned under her touch as she ascended. Jake followed, his hand brushing the cold iron. The steps vibrated faintly beneath his boots, every squeak and creak making him test his balance.

Her perfume drifted back as she moved, light and citrusy, achingly familiar. He hadn't smelled it in years, yet it had the power to stop his breath.

"When was this place built?" he asked, his voice low in the quiet.

"A hundred years ago." Pride colored her tone. She let her fingertips trail along the brick wall, as if she were defending an old friend.

"And they haven't updated it since?"

She glanced back at him, eyes narrowed. "Why does everyone think that just because something is old, it's trash? This place has charm, character—watch that hole there."

Jake stepped wide to avoid the jagged dip in the porch. Bits of crumbling stone scattered beneath his heel, gritty against the sole of his boot.

"Oh yeah," he said with a slight grin. "This place has charm coming out the wazoo."

Her glance over her shoulder was quick, sharp, but softened at the edges. The porch light above them flickered, catching the curve of her cheek. Their eyes held for a breath longer than he expected.

At the landing, Kelly fit her key into the lock. Her fingers trembled just enough for him to notice.

When she opened the door, the front hallway smelled of fresh-cut flowers and old floor wax. Somewhere beyond her bungalow a distant neighbor's radio crackled with a low jazz tune.

"Well," Kelly said softly, pushing the door open. "This is me."

Jake nodded, but didn't move. The weight of the years, of everything they hadn't said, stretched taut between them. He shoved his hands into his jacket pockets, anchoring himself before he could reach for something he wasn't sure he had the right to touch.

"Get inside, Kelly," he murmured.

She lingered, lips parting like she might say more—might undo years of distance with a single word. Instead, she smiled at him so faintly that it almost broke his heart.

"Good night, Jake."

The door clicked softly behind her.

Jake stood there longer than he should have, staring at the worn paint, listening for the muffled sound of her footsteps inside. When the silence finally swallowed him whole, he turned and descended the stairs. Each step felt heavier than the one before, as if he were leaving behind something he wasn't sure he could ever get back.

At home, the house breathed its nighttime breath—furnace low, the clock in the hall marking out small, stubborn seconds. He set the coffee for morning, turned off the kitchen light, and paused in the doorway of his office where the guitar leaned in the corner, patient as always.

He went in and sat with it across his knee, letting his fingers find what words could not. Melody first, because melodies don't lie; they only confess. Then words, not a list to keep him straight, but a song to carry what he couldn't say to anyone but God.

He wrote, haltingly at first, then with the surety that comes when the heart stops hiding:

BOISE NIGHT

*STREETLIGHTS ON WET PAVEMENT, CANDLES IN YOUR EYES, A
    WAITER SETS DOWN GLASSES, TWO CAREFUL ALIBIS.*
*WE TOAST TO SOMETHING WEIGHTLESS, LET THE MUSIC HIDE
    THE SEAM—*
*NEW BEGINNINGS, NOT THE KIND THAT STEAL, THE KIND THAT LET
    ME BREATHE.*
*I WALKED BESIDE YOUR LAUGHTER WHERE THE NEON HUMS AND
    FADES,*
*A BUSKER STITCHED THE EVENING WITH SIX HONEST, WEARY
    STRINGS.*

I TIPPED HIM FOR THE MERCY OF A MELODY THAT KNOWS, SOME
    DOORS YOU KEEP FROM OPENING, SOME ROADS YOU NEVER GO.

SO I'LL KEEP BOTH HANDS ON THE WHEEL, DRIVE THE LONG WAY BY
    THE RIVER.
LET THE WANTING LEARN TO KNEEL, LET THE BETTER MAN DELIVER.
IF A PRAYER CAN HOLD A LINE, LET IT HOLD ME THROUGH THIS
    WEATHER—
I CAN LOVE YOU IN THE LIGHT WITHOUT CROSSING IT TO GET THERE.

YOUR HAIR IN STREET-LAMP HALOS, SILVER THREADING SUMMER
    BROWN,
THE WRINKLE AT YOUR SMILE THAT THIRTY YEARS REFUSED TO
    DROWN.
YOU SAID MAYBE TIME WAS HONEST WHEN IT KEPT US FROM
    THAT FIRE—
I SAID MAYBE I WAS BLIND; NOW I SEE, AND STILL I'M TIRED.
I WALKED YOU UP THE IRON STEPS THAT SANG BENEATH OUR FEET,
YOUR DOORWAY BREATHED OF LEMON OIL AND SOMEONE ELSE'S HEAT.
YOU TOLD ME, "GOOD NIGHT, JAKE," SOFT—LIKE A PORCH LIGHT LEFT
    FOR STORMS;
I TOLD YOU, "GET INSIDE, KELLY," AND KEPT MY HANDS WARM.

SO I'LL KEEP BOTH HANDS ON THE WHEEL, DRIVE THE LONG WAY BY
    THE RIVER.
LET THE WANTING LEARN TO KNEEL, LET THE BETTER MAN DELIVER.
IF A PRAYER CAN HOLD A LINE, LET IT HOLD ME THROUGH THIS
    WEATHER—
I CAN LOVE YOU IN THE LIGHT WITHOUT CROSSING IT TO GET THERE.

THERE'S A VOW THAT STILL HAS BREATH,
    AND A HEART THAT WON'T KEEP QUIET;
I WILL LAY ONE DOWN TO LIVE,

TILL THE TRUTH OUTLASTS DESIRE.
IF GRACE IS JUST A NOTE
    A TIRED GUITARIST FINDS,
LET ME PLAY IT SOFT AND CLEAN,
    KEEP THE MELODY IN TIME.

SO I'LL KEEP BOTH HANDS ON THE WHEEL,
    TAKE THE LONG WAY, DRIVE IT STEADY.
WHEN THE RIVER DARKENS STEEL,
    LET THE MORNING SAY I'M READY—
NOT FOR TAKING WHAT AIN'T MINE,
    BUT FOR STANDING IN THE WEATHER.
I CAN LOVE YOU IN THE LIGHT,
    AND KEEP ALL OUR FUTURES BETTER.

STREETLIGHTS ON WET PAVEMENT,
    A DOOR I DIDN'T CLOSE—
I'LL LEAVE IT TO THE DAYLIGHT.
    AND THE GOD WHO ALWAYS KNOWS.

He set the guitar down and read the words once, then again. They didn't solve anything. Songs rarely do. But they put a hand on the wild part of him and asked it to sit a while and listen. Outside, the night thinned toward morning. Upstairs, his kids slept. Jake folded the page, slid it beneath the guitar's neck, and let the silence say the rest.

Kelly
Anchorage, Alaska
September 1987

EARLY FALL IN ALASKA DIDN'T

arrive all at once. It slipped in quietly, brushing color along the hillsides like someone dragging a paintbrush dipped in gold and cranberry. Fireweed tops had turned to cotton, the final sign summer was over. The first dusting of snow—termination dust—rested on the Chugach Mountains like a promise and a warning.

Birch leaves clinked like coins in a pocket as the wind passed through. The air smelled like woodsmoke, damp earth, wet wool, and the last of the wild blueberries crushed beneath boots. Daylight still stretched long, but the angle of the sun had changed. It was lower, softer. You felt the season turning in your bones before you ever saw it.

It was cool, not yet winter-cold, but cold enough to make one's breath visible in the mornings. Puddles were already thinking about freezing. My boots crunched over gravel as I followed Jake across the airport lot, stepping around frost-glazed leaves and the first thin lace of ice at the edge of a mud puddle.

Inside the terminal, I hugged my arms around myself. My denim jacket was more fashion than function, and the chill seeped into my bones. Overhead, fluorescent lights buzzed, a faint headache waiting to happen. The old flip-board clattered out new departure times, mechanical and final, like a clock I couldn't turn back.

Jake's duffel bag landed with a dull thud on the smudged linoleum.

He was leaving. Seattle first. Then maybe somewhere bigger. Somewhere warmer. Somewhere that wasn't me.

"I guess this is it." Jake raked a hand through his thick hair, and it fell across his forehead in that boyish way that made my chest ache. He looked toward the window. "Runway is gonna be rough. Everything's still thawing."

I nodded, though the strap of my purse was biting into my shoulder. If I shifted it, I was afraid something in me might crack, too, like pieces of my heart rattling loose where he could see them.

Amy stood a few feet away, her hands tucked into her sleeves, watching. Silent, steady. She always knew when words would only make the ache worse.

Then came his mom's voice, sharp and impatient, slicing through the terminal. Boarding would start any minute. I'd learned not to take her tone personally. It wasn't just me—it was the world. Still, I wondered, what would she do without him?

Jake turned back to me, and the air around us stilled. Even the airport seemed to hold its breath. *This is it. He's going to kiss me. Finally. Please.*

But he didn't.

Instead, his hand brushed a loose strand of hair behind my ear. His fingers skimmed my cheek just as the boarding chime pinged. Somewhere, a toddler laughed—and then cried. *Perfect timing, universe.*

"I'll write," he said.

I nodded again. But what I wanted to say pressed against my teeth: *Don't forget me. I love you. Stay. Please stay.* The words wouldn't come. They stuck like molasses in my throat.

His eyes flicked to my mouth—just for a second. A breath caught between us.

And before I could think—before logic, fear, and that old instinct to play it safe could clamp down—I leaned in and kissed him.

It wasn't dramatic. No sweeping music, no grand cinematic dip. Just a soft press of lips, as instinctive as breathing. As impossible to stop as the tide pulling toward the moon.

For a second, he didn't move. I could feel the surprise in the way his breath stalled against my cheek, the tiniest startle in the curve of his mouth. My fingertips brushed the fabric of his sleeve, barely there.

A whisper of a touch. Not a declaration—just a question. *Are you still mine in some quiet corner of your heart? Because I am still yours in all the noisy corners of mine.*

And then I pulled back an inch. His eyes opened slowly, like he was waking from a dream he wasn't ready to leave. His forehead rested against mine for one suspended heartbeat. The world hushed around us, nothing but warmth and what-ifs between us.

I didn't breathe. I wasn't sure I remembered how.

"Now boarding Group A for Seattle . . ."

Reality snapped tight between us.

Jake blinked, breath unsteady. "Kel . . ."

I shook my head, suddenly mortified, heat flooding my cheeks. "I—I just—sorry. I don't know why—"

He swallowed, eyes searching mine as if he wanted to say everything but couldn't say anything at all.

"Don't apologize," he said quietly.

Jake hefted his duffel bag and took one small step backward. Then he turned.

At the gate, he looked over his shoulder, lifting two fingers in a half-wave.

My hand came up automatically, mirroring his. My lips still tingled. My heart was a wildfire. And I stood there wishing time worked like the movies—where the hero turns back, runs to you, chooses you. Instead, the universe just kept on boarding Group A.

He walked calmly down the jetway, but my heart raced on. It was still pounding twenty minutes later when the plane rolled back from the gate.

I stood at the window, watching until the blinking white taillight shrank to a pinprick against the glare. Until even the pinprick disappeared.

Amy moved closer, arms folded tight.

"I think this is it," I whispered, forcing the words out. "I might not see him again for a long time."

Her eyes softened, but she didn't speak. She didn't have to.

"But he is the one," I said. Not was. *Is.*

The sun slipped behind a cloud, and I pulled my jacket tighter. Fall had arrived, but the hope of summer still clung on. And so would I.

And maybe, just maybe, I'd wait forever.

Kelly
Boise, Idaho

The sunlight streaming through my office window had no business being so bright. It glared off the glass of the neighboring high-rise, spilling onto my desk in sharp angles and making the stack of briefs and motions look harsher than they already were. I should have been reading them.

Instead, I stared past the glass and watched the city pulse. Cars inched through traffic, a woman juggled coffee and a phone call, and a delivery bike moved between lanes like its rider had no fear of death.

My mind wasn't here. It was back on a cracked bungalow staircase last night. Especially on the way Jake's voice had sounded when he said, *Don't care.* As if my safety, my life, mattered to him.

The sound of my office door creaking open snapped me back to attention. My boss strode in as if he did so every day. He didn't. Rarely had he come to my office.

"Mr. Alden." I sprang to my feet. My voice was too sharp. My smile was too forced. "Do you need something?"

He waved a hand, his suit jacket stretching across his shoulders. "No, no. I just thought I'd come see how the Forester case is going."

My throat went dry. "Um. Fine."

He studied me and his brow knitted. "Just fine?"

I blinked, pulled in a breath, tried again. "Sorry. It's going . . . well."

He smiled, satisfied enough with the correction. "Good. Langford and I have high hopes for this one."

I managed a smile, though it felt pasted on. "Me too."

He turned toward the door, already shifting to the next thing. "Don't forget! That corner office is waiting for you."

"Yes, sir."

The door clicked shut, and silence swelled in its wake. I let myself collapse into my chair, shoulders sagging. His words—*corner office, high hopes, good case*—echoed like they were supposed to be trophies. Once, they would have been. Now they just felt hollow, like a celebration I no longer wanted to attend.

I pressed my palms over my eyes. The neat stack of case files on my desk blurred behind me as the pressure mounted. They were a reminder of the climb I'd worked for, sacrificed for. But all I could think about was a flickering porch light, an older woman's words in Sedona, and a man who still walked me to my door even when I pretended I didn't need him to.

The latch clicked again. Janie didn't knock. She never did. She swept into my office like a burst of caffeine, with arms stacked with paperwork. Her grin lit up the room.

"I heard that!" she said, eyes wide. "Congrats, girl! Corner office—finally!"

My stomach sank. Of course, she'd been right outside, listening. She always caught everything.

I tried for a smile, but it slid off before it reached my eyes.

Her grin faltered. "Why don't you look happy?"

I exhaled, rubbing the bridge of my nose. "Because Jake and I dated in high school. He was my first love. And now . . ."

"Now what?" Her eyes sparked. "Wait—are you dating him? Because that—"

"Would be an ethical violation, I know." The words tumbled out too fast. "We're not dating. It's just . . . complicated. Memories. Old feelings I thought I had buried."

Janie dropped the files onto my desk, leaning in with that hands-on-her-hips posture that made her look more like my life coach than my paralegal. "Then turn them off until you finish this! You heard Mr. Alden. You've been grinding for this promotion for years. Don't screw it up now."

"Just . . . turn them off?" I repeated, half laughing, half incredulous.

She nodded firmly, bangs bobbing like punctuation marks.

I gave her a tight smile, the kind you put on for the camera when you just want to get the photo over with. "I can do that."

But even as I said it, I knew I couldn't.

"Good." She smirked. "And you get to practice right now because he came to sign papers. Mr. Forester is here."

My stomach dropped. "He's—what?"

She tilted her head toward the hallway. Sure enough, there he was. Jake. He leaned against the wall like it was built just for him. His hands were tucked in his pockets, and he wore an easy smile.

My throat went dry.

Janie, of course, was delighted. She laid the contracts on my desk. "Good luck," she mouthed before disappearing. Then, with an extra sway to her steps, Janie breezed past him.

I straightened my blazer, drew a breath, and wondered if it was even possible to turn off my feelings for Jake.

"Hey." Jake stepped inside. His smile was disarming, as always. "How are you?"

"Fantastic," I blurted too brightly. "Thanks for asking. Let's sign those papers, shall we?"

His brow lifted as if amused. He knew I was overcompensating. I couldn't hide anything from Jake.

I ignored his coy smile, leading him to the conference table where the paperwork was waiting in a neat stack. I set a pen down in front of him, my hands steady though my pulse was anything but.

He lifted the first sheet—the Petition for Dissolution of Marriage—and frowned. "Tell me something, Kelly."

I met his eyes cautiously. "What?"

"Why am I signing any of this when we both know Nicole's going to fight me on every last page?" His voice was low, weighted with disbelief. "She hasn't shown up for most of the kids' school events in a year, but suddenly she wants to drag me through court?"

I pressed my palms flat against the table, fighting to keep my tone even. "Because we have to build a record, Jake. Every petition, every proposed settlement—it shows the court that you tried. It matters."

His eyes narrowed, skeptical. "Even if she tears it all apart?"

"Yes," I said firmly. "Especially then. Judges want to see that one side has acted reasonably, in good faith. These documents are proof of that. Proof you're not the one playing games."

He let out a humorless laugh, the kind that snagged in my chest. "Funny. Nicole's the one who walked out. And I'm the one scribbling my name on forms like I'm the villain."

I swallowed, leaning forward just enough to lower my voice. "You're not the villain. You're the father trying to keep stability for your kids. That's what this shows."

His eyes searched mine, something raw flickering there. "You always were good with words."

"Jake," I said softly, almost warningly.

He smirked, but it didn't reach his eyes. "What's next?"

I slid the Marital Settlement Agreement toward him. "This covers the house, vehicles, bank accounts, and furniture. It's standard—"

"Standard," he repeated, cutting me off. His pen hovered. "Do you know what isn't standard? Coming home to find your wife gone, leaving nothing but a note and an empty closet. And now I get to divide up my life on paper."

"I know." My throat tightened. "But if you don't propose a division, she'll do it for you. And believe me, it won't look anything like this."

His jaw worked as he signed, each stroke of the pen sharp, almost violent.

I pushed the Custody Agreement forward next. "This outlines parenting schedules, holidays, vacations."

His gaze dropped to the section on Christmas. "She's going to fight this hardest," he muttered. "Suddenly she'll want every holiday, every break, even though she barely calls now."

"She can want it," I said quietly. "But the court will look at her history. Who's been there? Who's shown up? That matters more than claims on paper."

His eyes lifted, lingering on me. "And you'll be the one telling them that. You'll fight for me?"

I felt the air catch in my lungs. "It's my job," I said, a little too quickly.

"Your job," he echoed with a half-smile. "That's all this is?"

I forced my expression to be neutral. "Yes."

But his eyes told me he didn't believe me.

Finally, I slid over the Financial Affidavit. "Income, expenses, debts. It feels tedious, but it's crucial. Courts weigh everything from mortgage payments to credit cards."

He tapped the margin with the pen. "Nicole never cared about expenses. Or the businesses. Now suddenly they'll matter." He shook his head, sighed, then looked up at me again. "Why do I feel like I'm the only one fighting for something that should've been mine all along?"

"Because you are," I said softly. "But that doesn't mean you'll lose."

His smile was faint, wistful. "You always did know how to keep me in the fight."

And as his fingers brushed mine, just for a second when he pushed the papers back, I felt the truth of what he wasn't saying—that this wasn't only about winning in court.

My pulse stumbled, but I crossed my legs and leaned back like I hadn't heard him. *Turn it off. Turn it off.*

Jake bent over the paperwork, his hand steady as he signed. I let my gaze wander, watching the way his sleeves stretched over his forearms, the faint scar near his knuckle, the shape of his smile when he concentrated.

By the time he pushed the final page toward me, my heart was racing like I'd climbed a small mountain.

"Done," he said, sliding the pen back across the table.

I forced a smile, reaching for the stack. "Great. Thanks."

My voice sounded professional enough. But my hands—traitorous things—trembled as I gathered the papers.

We sat there, staring at each other, caught in that limbo where neither of us knew how to say goodbye. His eyes searched mine like they remembered too much, and I hated how much I wanted to let them.

My phone dinged. The sound sliced through the tension. I groaned, reaching for it. A text message from Amy popped up with a link.

"Oh no."

Jake leaned forward. "What is it?"

I winced. "I just got my photoshoot pictures."

"Really?" His mouth tugged into a grin. "Let me see."

I hugged the phone to my chest like a middle-schooler clutching a diary. "No way! It's so embarrassing."

He lunged across the desk, and before I knew it, we were in a full-on wrestling match for my phone. His laugh rang out—low, warm, entirely too charming. He won, of course.

"Jake!" I swatted his arm as he swiped. "Stop!"

And even though I felt my face reddening, I knew I couldn't continue to fight him. If I did, every office and cubicle would be emptied as my coworkers rushed in to see what the commotion was all about.

I released the phone, and he brightened the screen to get a better look. I wanted to disappear into the floor as he flipped through the photos. The whole time, he wore a wide, goofy smile on his face.

"Wow." His eyes widened and his eyebrows lifted. "You look . . . really uncomfortable."

Heat flooded my cheeks. "I was."

"So this isn't what you like to do for fun?"

I groaned. "Please. I wouldn't waste money on this. I don't have extra money to waste on this. This was all Amy."

Something shifted in his expression, a flicker of concern. "Forgive me if I'm overstepping, but I thought attorneys made good money."

I hesitated, then forced myself to say it out loud. "Not everyone is as kind as you are when it comes to sharing assets with their ex-spouses."

The words came out flat, heavy. My throat tightened.

"My husband went for the jugular," I added, quieter now. "I personally decided to concede so that he'd get off my back . . . and I could find some peace. So I had to start over from scratch."

The air between us stilled. I swallowed, fighting the emotion pricking at the corners of my eyes. Jake didn't move, didn't speak. Then I smiled. My armor.

"I'm doing much better now," I said brightly. "But I still don't feel like I've earned back enough to spend money on something so frivolous, you know?"

Jake didn't answer right away. He just watched me. His brow furrowed, as if he could see right through the cracks I was trying to patch.

"Come on." I leaned closer, forcing cheer. "Let's see what other winners I have in there."

We swiped through the rest of the photos together, laughing at the ridiculous ones—the half-blinked smile, the awkward hair flip, the one where I looked like I'd swallowed a lemon.

"So why did Amy think this was a good idea?" Jake asked.

"Something about making my ex jealous."

He stopped suddenly at a photo. His breath caught.

"Well," he said softly, "mission accomplished."

He turned the screen toward me. I blinked at it, surprised.

"Huh. That one's not bad."

"Not bad?" His eyes locked on mine. "You're just as gorgeous as ever."

The air shifted. My heart stumbled. His words hung there, too heavy to brush away.

I stood abruptly, fumbling for composure. "I should—"

"Yeah," he said quickly as he got up. "Me too. Talk later?"

I nodded, not trusting my voice.

He left, the door clicking behind him, and the moment collapsed into silence.

I rubbed a hand down my face, groaning into my palm.

This was going to be more complicated than I thought.

Jake
Boise, Idaho

THE LATE-AFTERNOON SUN

slanted through the park, gilding the tops of the trees and glinting off the pond, where kids tossed bread to the ducks. Jake jogged along the winding path with Ben at his side. Their sneakers pounded in rhythm with the steady thrum of cicadas.

"So," Ben puffed, tilting his head toward Jake, "things are going well with Kelly?"

Jake kept his eyes straight ahead, focusing on the trail. He'd just seen Kelly, as a lawyer. He didn't want to talk about all the other moments with her, where they talked about things other than his paperwork. Those moments Jake held close to his heart.

"Everything's settled with the divorce as far as splitting finances goes, but custody's still up in the air. We've got a court hearing coming up soon."

"Uh-huh," Ben said, not letting it go. "And . . . ?"

Jake frowned. "And what?"

Ben shot him a grin. "And you've been hanging out with Kelly daily. Are the same old sparks there?"

Jake exhaled hard, more from the question than the run. "For me? Like a raging fire. But right now, those feelings are off-limits. Which means we're just . . . friends."

Ben barked out a laugh. "Okay, then. So what's your next move as friends?"

Jake hesitated. "I'm thinking about taking her to do something special. You know, thank her for all her hard work. From what Amy's told me, she's always doing everything for everyone else—her clients, her kids—but it's been years since anyone's done anything for her."

Ben smirked. "Something special, huh? You're right. Doesn't sound romantic at all." Ben's teasing words hung in the air, lighthearted and needling in the way only an old friend could get away with.

Jake shot him a look, then shook his head. "I just want to show her that someone sees her. That she deserves nice things too. That she doesn't always have to hold everything up on her own."

"Someone like you?" His grin spread wide, unrepentant, daring Jake to react.

Jake only rolled his eyes and lengthened his stride, the muscles in his calves tightening as he leaned into the run. The gravel crunched sharply beneath his shoes, his body finding that old rhythm that had once been second nature.

"Oh no," Ben groaned behind him, his laughter broken with uneven breaths. "Don't do that. I hate it when you do that!"

But Jake didn't slow.

Instead, he surged forward, as if he could outpace not only Ben but the thoughts pressing heavy inside his chest. The air sliced past his ears, cool and clean. It burned into his lungs with each inhale.

The ache in his legs built quickly, fire spreading through every muscle, but he welcomed it. The hurt made him feel sharper, more alive.

The trail ahead narrowed, lined with tall grass whispering in the breeze. In a moment, their friendly jog turned into an escape. Release. Punishment and reward rolled into one. As the memory of Kelly's smile tugged at the corners of his thoughts, it became something else, too—hope.

Behind him, Ben's voice cracked through the air, part complaint, part admiration. "Fine! I'll meet you at the car!"

Jake didn't slow down. The path opened before him, dappled with golden light. Running was easier than answering questions with thoughts he didn't want to admit out loud—that Kelly wasn't just in his past anymore. She was lodged in his present, whether he was ready for that or not.

He glanced back over his shoulder. Behind him, Ben hobbled off the trail in the opposite direction, complaining about stubborn fools who thought cardio counted as therapy.

Jake pushed on, chest tight—not from the run, but from the truth pressing harder with every step.

Twenty minutes later and back around to the parking lot, Jake slowed as the gravel crunched beneath his shoes. His lungs were still raw from the run, and Ben was napping in his front seat.

As Jake drove Ben home, they joked around as usual, yet neither mentioned Kelly. By the time Jake pulled into his own driveway, the sweat had cooled on his skin and the golden haze of evening had settled over the house.

The smell hit him first—garlic, roasted vegetables, something warm and inviting.

Inside, Rae was bustling around the kitchen, setting plates with an energy that tugged a smile from him. Chris was sprawled on the couch, scrolling through a movie list with the younger kids huddled close.

"Hey, Dad," Rae called, glancing over her shoulder with a grin. "We made dinner tonight. And we planned a movie night with the little kids."

Jake blinked. His jaw dropped. "You . . . did?"

She nodded, sliding a casserole onto the table. "I overheard you on that work call, saying you needed time off for the lawyers to sign papers. We figured you could use a break, you know, after something hard like that. We thought you could use a little time for yourself."

Jake tried to be optimistic. He never wanted his kids to feel as if he didn't want them around. "A break?" He shrugged as if it were no big deal. "I'll get one next Saturday. Surely a dad of seven doesn't need more than that." He winked, thinking of his recent interaction with Nicole. "I hope you're not too bummed to have to stick around with your old man this weekend. Your mom told me she needs to help Grandma."

"Grandma?" Rae shook her head. "Her mom? That grandma?"

Her smile turned wry. "No. Grandma called herself. She said she misses us and feels caught in the middle of everything. She's coming to get us on Saturday morning, for the weekend. But Mom won't be there. She's . . . somewhere else. Not with Grandma."

For a second, Jake couldn't speak. His throat tightened, eyes burning with the kind of tears he didn't usually allow. He shouldn't let the lies sting anymore. But somehow they still did.

Rae's face softened as she reached for his arm. "I'm sorry you have to go through so much," she said gently. "But at least you have us, right?"

Jake pulled her into a hug, tucking her head under his chin. "I wouldn't trade any of the pain, Rae. Not a second of it. Because you're worth it. All of you are worth it."

Before he could say more, a crash erupted from the living room. Pillows flew across the couch. Shrieks of laughter echoed down the hall.

"Dad!" Chris shouted. "We need backup!"

Jake rubbed his brow, torn between exhaustion and the pull of their laughter. His mind wandered back, unbidden, to Kelly. Even in the shadow of Nicole's leaving, Kelly was a bright spot—steady, unexpected. Ben's words on the trail rang in his ears: *Something special, huh?*

Jake exhaled slowly, almost smiling. Maybe Ben wasn't wrong. "Something special" might not be enough. Perhaps it was time to think of something *extra* nice—and maybe even romantic—as a token of appreciation. But first . . . pillow fight.

✦ ✦ ✦

Jake
Boise, Idaho

An hour later, after the pillow fight, dinner, and a hug from the kids, who'd circled up for a movie, Jake stretched out across his bed. He lay with one arm tucked behind his head, the other holding his phone inches from his face. The screen glowed in the dark, throwing light across the lines around his tired eyes.

He swiped open the ticket confirmation again. Two digital passes. Def Leppard. Center seats. He couldn't stop the grin tugging at his mouth.

It had been years since he'd planned something like this—something fun, something spontaneous. Not for his kids. Not for work.

His thumb hovered over Kelly's name in his contacts. For a long moment, he stared. He almost convinced himself to close the phone and forget it. Then, with a sharp breath, he typed:

Are you busy this Saturday?

He set the phone on the nightstand, exhaling. For the first time in too long, he felt anticipation that wasn't tangled in custody hearings or client meetings. It was simple. Hopeful.

His eyes drifted across the room to the guitar propped in the corner. He sat up, padded across the carpet, and pulled it into his lap.

The wood was cool under his palm. The strings buzzed slightly out of tune. He tightened a peg, strummed, adjusted. Then he began to play.

The melody came slow, almost tentatively, like it had been waiting for him all these years. Notes of longing and memory. His voice followed, low and rough, filling the room:

> *Letters home, keep writing,*
> *Your words feel like light on my skin.*
> *Even a thousand miles away,*
> *You make me feel like I'm home again.*

He closed his eyes, letting the chords carry him back to dorm rooms and late-night letters. To the ache of missing her before life got complicated. His thumb brushed the strings softer now, coaxing the music into silence.

The last chord vibrated through the wood, lingering before fading. He leaned his forehead against the curve of the guitar and let out a long breath.

"Home again," he whispered.

And he couldn't help but wonder if, after everything, that's what it felt like for Kelly too.

Kelly
University of Alaska, Anchorage
September 1988

THE DORM ROOM BUZZED LIKE A

pinball machine. Music thudded, Love's Baby Soft clung to the air like fog, and clothes—shoulder-padded blazers, chunky belts, and miniskirts—were everywhere. Somewhere under it all, I was on my knees, trying to find my other earring. The pink one. Neon pink. My favorite.

"Trish!" I shouted over the blaring "Sweet Child O' Mine."

Trish, my pre-law roommate and queen of color-coordinated scrunchies and pantyhose, popped her head out of the closet. "Don't look at me. I haven't touched your radioactive Barbie jewelry."

Heather, perched on the top bunk with her legs swinging, snorted. She was painting another coat of electric-blue eyeliner onto her lids using a handheld mirror. "It's probably buried under Jill's dating calendar."

"I heard that," Jill yelled from behind the partition we'd rigged from a beach towel and duct tape. "And FYI, I've got the phone from 6:15 to 6:30. Don't even think about touching it."

The yellow rotary phone hung on the wall like a prize we never stopped fighting over. A Sharpie-penned schedule loomed above it. I still had the scar over my eyebrow from when a bottle of pink nail polish flew across the room during one of our wars.

"Relax," I said, tugging my sweatshirt off and smoothing my miniskirt. "I'm not waiting on a call."

Today felt like a day of celebration, and I wanted to look my best. The letter had been waiting for me in my little campus mailbox. A secret folded into paper, a promise. I hadn't told the girls. They wouldn't understand. Or worse, they'd tease me mercilessly.

"You got a letter from Jake Forester?" I could already hear Jill's laugh. "That Eagle River guy who played guitar and never kissed you at prom?"

It didn't matter what they'd say, because I remembered the way he'd held my coat open for me like it was something sacred. The way his eyes had lingered during worship nights at youth group, like he couldn't quite believe I was real. And this past summer? We'd stayed up until three a.m. many nights, sitting on the hood of his car, talking about the future—about writing and music and maybe, someday, meeting back in the middle. Now here it was. The future. His letter.

I found my favorite pink bracelet and slid it onto my wrist. Then I sat on the windowsill, my heart hammering against my ribs. I tore the envelope open with trembling fingers.

> KEL,
>
>   I FOUND THIS SONG IN THE BACK OF AN OLD NOTEBOOK AND THOUGHT OF YOU. I SWEAR, EVERY LYRIC STILL FEELS LIKE YOU. I'M WORKING NIGHTS AT THE MECHANIC'S. PLAYING WEEKEND GIGS WITH THE BAND. IT'S NOTHING FANCY, BUT IT'S HONEST.
>
>   ANYWAY . . . I HOPE YOU'RE GOOD. REALLY GOOD. I MISS TALKING TO YOU. AND IF YOU EVER WRITE BACK, I'D LIKE THAT.
>
>   ALWAYS, JAKE

There was a cassette tucked inside. His voice, waiting for me on tape.

I read the letter three times. Then smiled.

I folded it carefully, pressing the crease with my palm as though I could smooth the ache in my chest. The paper was warm from my hands. I slid it back into the envelope that was scrawled with my name in Jake's handwriting.

And then I wrote him back. It was a simple letter, thanking him for the tape and asking about his Christmas plans. It was just enough to let him know I wanted to meet up.

Finally, after sealing the envelope, I uncapped my Hot Coral lipstick—the shade I wore whenever I needed courage—and pressed a kiss to the back of the envelope before mailing it. Silly. Dramatic. Then I decided to put it in the outgoing mail before I changed my mind.

The hallway reeked of burnt coffee from the lounge. My sneakers squeaked on the linoleum. As I carried the letter down, Whitney Houston sang softly in my ears through my Walkman. Somewhere down the corridor, a radio buzzed tinny and thin.

Outside, the evening air was cool and scented faintly with wet grass from the sprinklers. The mailbox by the stairwell was dented and peeling, paint chipped by too many hands. I paused there, the envelope heavy in my grip.

It felt like more than words. It felt like me. My laughter scribbled into margins. My longings pressed into ink. My heart, folded and sealed, asking to be carried across miles.

I hesitated, my pulse loud in my ears. For a second, I almost turned back, ready to hide it in my desk drawer, safe but silent.

Then I thought of him. His laugh. His songs—even the silly ones—were filled with a kind of reckless hope that made me believe in forever. I slid the envelope into the slot. The metal flap clanged shut. I stood there, staring at the box as if it might somehow return the letter to me. But it didn't.

A breeze tugged at my sleeves, carrying the faint bite of juniper. My hands felt suddenly empty. I pressed my fingers against my heart on the walk back, trying to quiet the ache. The letter was gone now—out in the world, carried by strangers, maybe finding him, maybe not. But for the first time in a long while, I felt a sense of relief because the feelings weren't locked inside me anymore.

Back upstairs, the girls were still arguing over eyeliner and phone schedules. Jill wrinkled her nose. "Kelly, are you wearing my perfume?"

"Nope," I lied, even as the sweetness of her Giorgio Beverly Hills clung to my sweater.

Some girls had boys who brought carnations and spun them under string lights at formals. I had a letter. And somehow, in that moment, it felt like enough.

Kelly
Boise, Idaho

I should have been asleep. But instead, I sat cross-legged on my bedroom floor, surrounded by half-opened boxes like a soldier in the aftermath of a battle. You'd think by now I'd be done—settled, organized, life in neat stacks on clean shelves. However, I was still digging up skeletons from cardboard graves.

My phone buzzed against the carpet, startling me. The screen lit up with a name that made my stomach drop and flutter all at once.

Jake.

> Are you busy this Saturday?

I chewed my lip, my fingers hesitating over the keyboard like a girl who should have known better. Then I typed back:

> No. Why?

Seconds later, the reply:

> I've got something planned. Pick you up at noon?

My pulse leapt. Ridiculous, right? Like I was seventeen again, staring at the same name scrawled across the corner of my notebook, doodled into the margins of algebra problems I never solved. I set the phone aside and smiled at nothing, at everything.

Then I reached back into the box.

My hand brushed something flat and heavy at the bottom. I pulled it free and gasped.

My yearbook.

The one I thought I'd thrown away months ago, in a fit of moving-on bravado.

I let out a shaky laugh. "I threw you away . . . didn't I?"

But apparently not.

The book cracked open like an old wound, and as it did, a folded piece of notebook paper slipped free, fluttering into my lap. I froze, my breath catching before I even opened it.

That handwriting. I knew it instantly.

Jake's.

My fingers trembled as I unfolded it, smoothing the creases that time had softened. And then, as my eyes scanned the lines, it wasn't me reading at all. It was his voice, clear and steady, filling the room as if he were sitting beside me.

DEAR KELLY,

I WAS SURPRISED TO RECEIVE A LETTER FROM YOU. COLLEGE IS A BEAST. I CAN BARELY KEEP UP.

The edges of the paper blurred as tears filled my eyes.

I WISH YOU WERE HERE WITH ME. PLEASE KEEP WRITING. YOU MAKE ME FEEL LIKE I'M HOME AGAIN.

I pressed the letter to my chest, eyes squeezed shut, my breath shaky. All these years, I'd convinced myself that what we had was a high school fling. Too young to matter. Too sweet to last. But the ache in these lines—the rawness—proved otherwise. He'd felt it too.

I opened my eyes, the glow of my phone still faint on the nightstand. His newest message waited. This man, who once broke me, was offering something again. Something different. Something I hadn't dared let myself imagine.

And for the first time in a long time, I let myself wonder: *What if love hadn't given up on me after all?*

But with that hope came the dread. Because wasn't I already stretched too thin? Jake's custody case looming, the corner office dangling like bait before me. Did I even want it—the long hours, the endless pressure? Sure, my kids would cheer me on. They'd tease me about "Mom in her fancy office" and say they were proud. But it wasn't as if they needed me to rise to the top.

So who was I trying to impress? Mr. Alden? Mr. Langford? Myself?

I could almost hear Jake's laugh in the hallway of our high school, see Ben and Amy grinning as they teased me about my speeches—the way I'd command a room when I cared deeply about something. That was me. That was real. And yet here I was, wondering if I was chasing accolades instead of purpose.

And then the truth pressed in. Did the corner office matter if it meant I lost my peace? Did I need more applause when I was finally coming to the realization that God was still here with me, even when I didn't turn to Him as often as I should?

I laid the letter down carefully, as if it might crumble. My gaze shifted back to the phone, to the promise of Saturday. What in the world did Jake have up his sleeve? Whatever it was, it already mattered more than the promotion. Because for the first time in years, my heart felt awake.

I picked up the phone and typed a response.

> Saturday sounds perfect. Noon it is.

✦ ✦ ✦

Kelly
Georgetown Law School, Washington, DC
September 1992

My apartment smelled faintly of pencil shavings and cold pizza. Law textbooks were stacked high on my desk. Their pages bristled with yellow Post-it notes like porcupine quills.

I balanced the phone between my shoulder and ear, pen tapping like a nervous metronome against an open casebook.

"Jake's going to be in DC this week?" I asked, trying for casualness and landing somewhere near breathless.

Amy's voice crackled through the receiver. "He's going there for a conference. He started that organic smoothie shop in Denver, remember?"

I frowned at my law notes, but I didn't really see them. "No."

"I didn't tell you? Well, it's doing great, and he's looking to franchise. Anyway, he wants to see you."

I froze, the words catching in my chest. "He does?"

"Of course he does! He's flying in on Friday. He'll only be in town for a day, but he's hoping you guys can grab dinner before he leaves. I gave him your number. I hope that's okay?"

My pulse skipped. My pen stilled above the page, hovering over *res ipsa loquitur,* as if I might underline my way out of this. "Um. Sure. It'll be nice to reconnect."

"When was the last time you heard from him?"

I swallowed. My throat felt dry, papery. "I don't know. A few years ago. We kind of . . . lost touch."

"Maybe he wants to fix that."

"Yeah," I whispered, almost to myself. "Maybe."

On the other end, Amy drifted, already somewhere else. "I gotta go. They charge an arm and a leg for long distance, and Ben's trying to pick daffodils for our centerpieces. Let me know how it goes!"

The line clicked dead. I stayed where I was, with the phone pressed warm to my ear, wishing Amy had shared more.

Finally, I set the receiver back on the hook. The room carried the scent of ink and paper, and the faint sweetness of Giorgio Beverly Hills, which someone had spritzed near the door that morning. My textbooks waited—torts, contracts, outlines clipped together like small traps—but my mind wasn't on elements or holdings anymore.

It was on Jake.

I didn't know how I'd pass the hours until he called.

Jake
Washington, DC
September 1992

The pay phones lined the back wall of the conference center, catching the gleam of harsh fluorescent lights. Beneath them, industrial carpet held the day's grind—spilled coffee, ground-in road grime, stray bottle caps. The whole place smelled like overworked air-conditioning, mingling with the papery tang of fresh programs being stapled and handed out at the registration desk.

Jake stood in the alcove just off the flow, shoulders tight, a slip of paper folded and unfolded in his palm until the edges went soft. The ink had smudged where his thumb kept pressing. Amy's handwriting in neat loops—the number itself carefully written. Under it was a name, *Kelly.* Reading it took him back to Eagle River and their laughter skipping across the lake. He could feel the warmth of the hood of his car against his back. He could hear the melody of an unfinished song he'd strummed for her.

He fed quarters into the slot. Each coin made that hollow, metallic clink as it dropped. The receiver was cold against his ear. He pressed the buttons again, carefully. One ring. Two. He could almost see her crossing the room to answer, almost hear the quick catch of breath right before she said his name—

"We're sorry. This phone has been disconnected. No further information is available."

Flat. Mechanical. Final.

For an instant, he didn't move. He braced a palm against the scratched side panel—felt the tiny burrs of vandal-etched initials under his skin—and made himself breathe.

Then he put the receiver back harder than he meant to. He stared at the mouthpiece as if it might take the words back. All the anticipation and nervous hope he hadn't let himself feel in years—snuffed by a mechanical voice.

Jake exhaled slowly. The slip of paper balled in his fist, and then he smoothed it again. Amy's neat numbers didn't waver. Kelly's name didn't change. He slid the note into his shirt pocket.

Outside the alcove, a crowd of people moved to exit the building. A woman laughed too loudly. The PA cracked alive— "Panel on Franchising begins in five minutes"—and died with a pop.

Jake pulled the conference schedule from his back pocket. Blue ink circles he barely remembered making clustered around sessions he suddenly couldn't imagine sitting through. He folded the paper, slid it back where it came from, and stepped out of the alcove. The chill of the overworked air-conditioning slid under his collar. Bodies jostled around him, and he let the crowd lead him across the carpet toward whatever came next.

✦ ✦ ✦

Kelly
Washington, DC
1992

I sat rigid on the edge of my bed, arms crossed so tightly they might've left marks. The beige rotary phone on my desk kept quiet, its coiled cord curved like a smirk.

The hallway outside pulsed with life. Laughter burst from another apartment. The orange glow of sunset slipped through the blinds. Dust drifted through the bars of color, catching fire as it floated, and suspended like it had nowhere else to go.

I grabbed a pillow and hugged it hard to my ribs, telling myself I didn't care. I didn't need him to call. I wasn't waiting. I wasn't holding my breath for the sound of his voice.

My body betrayed me anyway. My pulse thumped high in my throat. My lips still tasted faintly of the cherry ChapStick I'd swiped on an hour ago—because what if he did call?

The apartment had been silent all evening, except for the hum of the refrigerator and the ticking of the clock. I'd been the only one home, curled on the couch with a pillow clutched to my chest, ears straining for a sound that never came.

When the door slammed, I jolted upright. Trish stormed in, her hair damp from drizzle, cheeks flushed with something other than weather. I had joked about joining her at law school so much that it eventually became my plan, and here we were as roommates again.

"You are not going to believe this," she fumed, tossing her gym bag onto the rug. "Jule blew our phone money at the mall."

The words hit me like ice water. I scrambled to my feet and crossed to the phone. My hand shook as I lifted the receiver and pressed it to my ear. Silence. Not even a crackle.

My jaw dropped. "The line's dead."

Trish froze, guilt flickering across her face. "Oh man. I should've told you sooner."

My hands clenched at my sides, the receiver still in my grip. "She did what? . . . It's been dead all night?"

"All day," Trish admitted, her voice shrinking. "Didn't you notice that neither of us was calling anyone? Man, I should have said something earlier."

My jaw locked. Heat flashed behind my eyes, hot and blinding. I'd been waiting. All this evening, I'd sat still, counting the ticks of the clock, listening for a ring that never came.

And what if Jake had tried? What if he'd called and thought I just didn't answer?

The thought hollowed me out. My stomach dropped, breath shallow. I slammed the receiver down, the sound echoing like a crack of thunder through the small apartment.

"Kelly—" Trish started, but I didn't let her finish.

Amy had said Jake was in town for some kind of convention. The convention center was less than a mile away. Close enough to get there. Close enough to try.

I kicked off my boots and shoved my feet into tennis shoes, yanking the laces tight. My pulse hammered, my breath ragged, urgency swallowing me whole.

If I ran, maybe—just maybe—I could still find him.

Jake
Washington, DC
1992

The phone booth's glass walls streaked with frantic rivulets until the street beyond blurred into smears of pink and blue neon. The sign across the way buzzed like a trapped insect. Inside the booth, it smelled like rusted metal and the stale tang of cigarette smoke. The receiver was cold against his palm.

He hunched over the phone again, a small bouquet of forget-me-nots clenched in his free hand. Cool petals brushed his knuckles whenever he shifted. Pollen dusted his skin where he'd held them too tightly.

He slid in his last quarters. Each coin fell with a hollow, metallic clink that sounded too final. He dialed carefully, fingertip finding each sunken button. One more chance.

The line clicked. Jake held his breath.

"We're sorry. This phone has been disconnected. No further information is available."

He closed his eyes and bowed his head into the tug of the cord. He put the handset back harder than he meant to. The clatter rattled through the booth and into the wet night. Thankfully, this phone released the coins since the call hadn't gone through.

He set the bouquet on the tiny aluminum shelf and smoothed the wrinkled paper beside it. Then he punched another number. He tried for Amy, but the phone just rang. He wanted to scream at the phone and tell her to pick up. Finally, after a dozen rings, Jake hung up.

A sharp knock rattled the booth. A man in a damp coat hovered just outside, water dripping from his hair, impatience etched across his face. Jake lifted one finger. One minute.

He tried Kelly's number again, but it was the same robotic

message. Then Amy's again. Nothing. Disappointment settled as heavy as a stone in his chest.

Jake hung up. The final click echoed too loudly. He looked at the bouquet. It was fragile, hopeful, foolish.

With a breath he couldn't steady, he crumpled the note and dropped it into the overflowing bin below the shelf. It landed among candy wrappers and soggy cigarette packages. He palmed the booth's handle and stepped out into the rain.

Drizzle tapped his face. Somewhere down the block, a siren bent and faded. The man quickly stepped in and took his place.

Jake walked. At the end of the block, a church tolled the hour. His jacket clung heavily to his shoulders, and rain trickled down from his hair into the collar of his shirt. In his hand, the bouquet had begun to sag—stems bent, petals collapsing beneath the weather. Jake walked over to the closest bench and laid it down. Then he turned back toward his hotel, empty hands, empty heart.

Kelly
Georgetown Law School, Washington, DC
September 1992

THE COLD NIGHT AIR WAS SHARP

as it filled my lungs. Each inhale burned before it turned to steam that drifted in front of me and then vanished. My tennis shoes slapped the slick pavement, rubber squeaking when I hit a painted crosswalk. Cars hissed past on wet asphalt. Somewhere a bus exhaled, brakes sighing. A distant siren bent and faded.

I tipped my head back as I ran, ponytail tugging loose at the base of my neck, damp strands sticking to my collar. I searched the sky for the North Star, but all I saw was gray clouds.

The memory rose before I could stop it: Jake and I hanging out by the lake. Crickets filled the silence between our words. We spoke of knights and forget-me-nots. My heart ached because I knew he'd be leaving soon. I realized that in following our dreams we'd miss moments like this.

On the sidewalk now, my breath hitched. The ache was the same, only edged with years. The stars felt cruel for promising to align again, reminding me of what I'd once been brave enough to hope for.

"Really?" I muttered, eyes stinging. "Not funny."

Calves burning. Lungs protesting. Water splashed up my shins from a pothole I didn't see. I pushed harder, as if I could outrun the missed opportunity. Outrun the memory. I approached the convention center, but it was empty. The doors were locked, and the lights were off. Whatever event had been there had cleared out. Not willing to give up, I walked toward the closest hotel, which stood by a church with a tall steeple. As I strode on, the steeple guided the way.

There was no sign of Jake outside the hotel. A guard stood at the door, and I knew that even if I tried to walk inside, there was no way they'd be able to connect me with one of their guests. This was Washington, DC, after all. And who knew if this was even his hotel. There were dozens in every direction.

I slowed near the church. The bells had only just faded. Their echo still hung in the damp air. The stone steps glistened. Water ran in tiny threads along the curb. That's when I saw it. A flash of blue against gray, petals scattered and wet next to a sidewalk bench.

I stopped and bent, rain dripping from the edge of my hood, gathering on my lashes. My fingers were numb when I reached for it. A bouquet. Stems bent. Blossoms pressed flat by the storm. Forget-me-nots.

My throat tightened. The fragile petals clung to my fingertips, silky and flimsy as tissue. Their color was stubbornly bright even in ruin. A dusting of pollen smudged onto my skin. I lifted them to my chest and breathed in the faint sweetness.

Who left them? A stranger with a story I'd never know? A couple who'd argued and made up and forgotten their bouquet in the drizzle? Or—my heart thudded at the thought—could it have been Jake? Had he walked this very block minutes before me, laying these down with the same hands that once tuned his guitar on the hood of that car?

It felt impossible. To be so close . . .

I pressed the broken bouquet closer. The petals were cool against my wrist, and the stems slick beneath my thumb. Rain pattered beside me in soft percussion. All I could think was how close I might have been.

I turned onto the next block. The bells' echo finally faded, but the ache did not.

Jake
Washington, DC
1992

Jake kept walking long after the church bells gave way to the hiss of tires on wet pavement. His steps fell into rhythm with the city, a slow 4/4 that matched the metronome in his chest, and without thinking, he started to hum.

It was a half-finished melody. For him, songs always came from pain. They sprouted through cracks his resolve couldn't seal. Minor third leaning into the open G. The notes came easily. Not a song for the radio. The type of song you sing alone, so the ache has somewhere to go.

What had gone wrong? Disconnected? Just when he'd been so close.

Jake ran a hand down his cheek, and a quick anger rose up. He wasn't mad at Kelly, but at himself. His mind flashed through all the moments when he'd had the chance to tell her how he felt. The hope in her eyes had been evident. More than once, she'd lifted her face toward his, and she'd parted her lips just slightly, as if waiting for a kiss. Yet he'd hesitated. Why hadn't he just taken that one step forward toward her? One step could have changed everything.

Deep down, he knew why. Kelly was incredible, and he had a nagging feeling that if he let her get close, she'd find out the truth. He wasn't good enough for her.

Sure, he seemed like a good catch up there in Alaska. To be truthful, there weren't many guys to choose from. Kelly hadn't wanted to move there in the first place. She'd often talked about going back to the "real world" and her friends. And now that she'd left Alaska, there had to be many more opportunities.

He drew a long breath that fogged in front of him. Maybe Kelly's silence wasn't punishment—maybe it was mercy. Perhaps the disconnected line was God cutting him loose from a story that had already come to an end. Maybe this was the chorus turning.

His only peace was the quiet knowledge that even a sad song is still a song.

God, if you're out there and you care, help me to get past this. Show me this new future—whatever it may be. As much as I can't imagine a future without Kelly, please help me see a light of hope in all these shades of gray that surround me now.

Then Jake's mind turned in another direction. Back in Colorado there was a music studio with a cheerful receptionist behind the front desk. He'd gone there a few times with a friend. He pictured the beautiful woman he'd met there just a few days ago.

Jake pulled his jacket collar tighter around his neck, gripping it with one fist at his throat. Next, he quickened his pace. He'd walk this road and face the storm.

Back in Colorado a few days later, Jake's footsteps echoed on the floor as he entered the studio. A single cone of lamplight pooled over the console table. Cables lay coiled like sleeping snakes across the floor. Gaffer tape scarred the rug where a mic stand had chewed through the weave. An "ON AIR" light over the door had burned out the N.

Jake sat on a battered stool, an old Martin balanced on his knee. The strings bit clean under his calluses. His right thumb worked a slow, stubborn rhythm while his fingers picked out a melody he hadn't intended to write. The pain from a few nights ago had waned. He let an E minor deepen into something darker and then eased it toward a C that didn't resolve, and the unresolved part felt honest. His boot kept time against the rug, a quiet thud the click track didn't need.

Jake wasn't thinking about words. Not yet. He was thinking about breathing and about the way a room changes when a song starts to decide it wants to live.

The latch clicked. A breath of cool air swished in with Nicole. No showy dress. Jeans. Clean sneakers. Hair clipped back in a way that let it keep escaping in soft flyaways at her temples. She didn't try to be anything other than herself.

"You're early," he said, voice rough from days with little sleep. It came out more grateful than he meant it to.

"I wanted to hear you before anyone else." She eased a hip

against the soundboard without touching anything she shouldn't. Her eyes went straight to his hands, not his face. "You sound different when you don't think anyone's listening."

His fingers hesitated on the strings. Most people wanted polish—radio gloss on a finished track. Nicole listened to the fray, to the part that unraveled and told the truth.

Her pen tapped time against a small notebook, not pushing, just keeping pace with the room. "You write like it hurts."

"That's because it does."

She didn't flinch. Didn't fill the space with nervous praise. Instead, she drew a slow breath, tilted her head—listening—and then hummed, barely above the strings.

He followed her instinctively, dropping the tempo a hair, letting the melody settle. He slid a finger up to catch a suspended second and left it there, hanging, so her line could thread beneath.

The air changed. When the last note thinned and disappeared, Nicole smiled. Her smile started in her eyes and then moved to her mouth.

"There. That's something. That's real. You've got more in you than heartache, Jake. You've got hope, too. You just try to bury it under the minor chords."

He studied her. He liked the way she didn't stare straight through him to some version of him from a radio chart. The way she didn't measure him against his past and find him less. Nicole looked at him like he still had a future. Kelly had once looked at him that way. But Kelly hadn't answered. Kelly wasn't here.

Nicole was.

He set the guitar aside and rubbed his jaw. The stubble rasped under his palm like sandpaper. Maybe this was the plan. Maybe the girl with the forget-me-nots belonged to another verse, another life. Maybe the chorus waiting ahead had a different name.

He reached for the tuning keys and nudged the B string up until it sang true against the open E. The pitch wavered, found home, and then settled.

"Again?" Nicole asked.

"Again," he said, and this time the song came faster, as if it had been waiting in the hallway and only needed to be invited in.

Jake
Boise, Idaho

THE MIDDAY SUN SPILLED ACROSS

the cracked sidewalk, warming the ivy that crawled up the side of Kelly's bungalow. Jake shifted his weight, bouquet in hand—tiny blue blossoms of forget-me-nots.

He'd debated for hours if flowers were too much, if they sent the wrong message. But when he saw them at the market that morning, the decision had been made for him. Jake knocked, his heartbeat thudding harder than it should have.

The door swung open, and there she was—Kelly, hair soft around her shoulders, sunlight catching in her eyes. She looked at the flowers, startled.

"What's this?" she asked, her voice cautious but curious.

Jake lifted the bouquet slightly, his smile easy. "Every woman should get flowers now and then."

Her gaze softened, the corners of her lips curving as she reached out to touch one of the delicate petals. "You remembered I like forget-me-nots?"

"I remember everything about you," he said quietly, more truth than he meant to reveal.

The words hung between them, fragile and charged. Her breath hitched just slightly. Their gazes lingered, caught in that familiar pull neither of them had figured out how to resist.

He handed her the flowers, and she put them in water as

he watched from the door. When she approached again, Jake cleared his throat. "You ready to have some fun?"

Kelly's lips curved into a smile that told him she was. She stepped back, letting the door swing wider. "Lead the way."

✦ ✦ ✦

Kelly
Boise, Idaho

It wasn't Jake's SUV waiting. Instead, it was an older truck that had seen better days. As we took off, the opening synths burst through the truck's speakers like sunlight cracking through clouds. Billy Ocean, "Get Outta My Dreams, Get into My Car." I laughed out loud before I could stop myself, the sound whipped away by the wind rushing in through Jake's rolled-down windows.

The Boise air smelled alive. Bright and sharp with the crisp autumn breeze. Coffee drifting from the open doors of corner cafés. It tasted like possibility. The kind you didn't plan for but stumbled into.

Jake tapped the steering wheel in time with the beat, the pads of his fingers keeping a steady rhythm as though he'd been waiting for this exact song, this exact moment. Sunlight caught on his forearms where he'd rolled up his sleeves, and I had to look away before I stared too long.

I leaned into the wind, let it catch strands of my hair and send them dancing against my cheeks. I reached up to tuck them back, but they quickly slipped out again. I let them. Some things were meant to fly free. I sang a line under my breath—half shy, half sassy—and when I dared glance sideways, Jake was smiling straight ahead, taking it all in.

"Billy Ocean?" I asked, tilting my face toward him, my voice lifted over the chorus. "Going retro today?"

"Hey, I found the greatest-hits playlist, and I refuse to apologize." He drummed the wheel harder, grinning. "Besides, this is perfect driving music."

"Only if you're cruising down the coast in a convertible, not this," I teased.

His laugh warmed the space, deep and easy. "This truck is a classic. And you're not allowed to insult it while that smile is on your face. House rules."

I bit the inside of my cheek, trying—and failing—to smother the smile. The wind shoved more hair across my lips.

We braked at a crosswalk, letting a couple stroll across hand in hand. A kid in a red hoodie skateboarded past, wheels clicking over concrete seams. Downtown rose ahead—brick and glass pressed shoulder to shoulder, old buildings stubbornly clinging beside the sleek new ones.

I could feel it then: Jake's secret humming beneath the surface. He kept checking the time, his blinker flicking as he merged closer to the heart of the city. I wondered if he'd spill it now. But instead of blurting it out, he let the music fill the silence between us.

When we started again, I caught him watching a golden retriever leaning out of a Jeep, his ears flapping. When I laughed, Jake laughed with me.

Then I had a profound thought: *Sometimes rushing ruins the gift.*

"Okay," I said, scooting forward, giving him mock seriousness. "I do approve of the sunshine, the playlist, and the windows down. Ten out of ten. You can return the dad truck to the rental agency now."

"First of all, this truck is mine. Second, we're making a quick stop."

"A stop?" I arched a brow, suspicion feigned.

"Trust me," he said lightly, turning right. His eyes glimmered the way they had when he was seventeen—reckless and certain all at once. "I repeat . . . You ready to have some fun?"

I gave him the look I'd perfected as both a lawyer and a mother—half defense, half curiosity. "Define fun."

"You'll know when you see it."

The truck eased to a stop in front of a boutique. Gold-leaf letters shimmered across the window. Three mannequins stood inside, clothed in the colors of fall. Rust-colored long floral cardigan, black tee, olive pants, suede boots. Cozy knit dresses were displayed like falling leaves, and a woman at the register bent over a ribbon and box, her hands moving with care and unhurried precision.

I blinked at the storefront, then at Jake, as the last notes of Billy Ocean rippled away. "What's this?" The words came out too sharp, my defense against hope.

"You said you like to go shopping." He killed the engine, already climbing out. "You said it used to make you feel like yourself."

I stayed still, my hands locked in my lap. "I also said I'm not spending any money on myself right now. I'm not exactly in my 'treat yourself' era."

Jake rounded the truck and opened my door anyway. "Today's on me," he said, his voice low, steady. An invitation, not a demand. He must have seen the bristle rise in me—the one that resisted charity, pity, anything I couldn't afford to accept. But then he added, softer, "This isn't about money. It's about you. About giving you a day where somebody else thinks about what would make you smile."

The words caught me off guard, peeling back my practiced resistance. My heart thudded once, heavy, as I stared up at him. His eyes were steady enough to reflect the whole street.

And I heard something deeper in his words, something I hadn't let myself hear in years. A reminder: God Himself often uses the people we least expect to whisper, *"You are seen. You are worth it."*

I took his arm, rolling my eyes because humor was always safer than vulnerability. "Fine. But I'm keeping score."

He grinned as we stepped toward the boutique, sunlight glinting in his hair. "Please. Like you don't already keep score for a living."

And maybe it was the music still pulsing in my veins, or the faith threading through the day like an unseen current—but for the first time in a very long time, I suddenly didn't feel like keeping score.

The little bell above the door chimed, a delicate sound that seemed to hang in the air as if it had been waiting for me. A soft wash of music—Maggie Rogers, maybe Ingrid Michaelson—drifted through the boutique, warm and low, like sunlight turned into melody. The air smelled faintly of sandalwood, tinged with a citrus brightness that made me want to close my eyes and breathe it in, until I remembered where I was.

Inside, racks fanned out with warm fabrics in creams and golds, like a harvest field. Two women near the fitting rooms laughed and bickered over whether blush pink was their color. Their laughter spilled across the space like it belonged here, like it was stitched into the seams.

The woman behind the counter called, "Good afternoon!" while tying a ribbon around a white box with a flourish. Her bangles clinked as she lifted her hand, silver catching the light. "Welcome to Fern & Finch. Let me know if you're searching for anything special."

Jake's gaze cut toward me. "We are," he said smoothly. "A little bit of 'you, but happy,' and a little bit of 'you, but having fun.'"

I shot him a look—half warning, half disbelief—but my hand was still looped through his arm, and I didn't move it. Something in me didn't want to. His words burned in the quiet places I tried to keep sealed.

The woman laughed like she'd heard stranger requests. "I can work with that."

And just like that, I was swept into something I didn't ask for but secretly craved.

We started slow. A cream sweater so soft it nearly slid from the hanger when I touched it. A blue wrap dress—hydrangea blue—that made my heart flutter in ways I didn't want to name. Jeans that claimed miracles on the tag and, heaven help me, might have been telling the truth. Jake pulled items from racks with reckless abandon, not even bothering with sizes, and the saleswoman—bless her for her fairy godmother instincts—trailed after us, swapping in the right ones.

"This one," he said, holding up a muted green blouse with

delicate buttons that looked like something from another time. "And this," he added, plucking a skirt the color of tea with milk. Then he reached for a loose-woven straw hat the color of late-harvest fields, tied with a rust-colored ribbon, and promptly handed it back to me as though *I* was supposed to wear it.

"I can't pull off a hat," I said as I put it on, already bracing for his reply.

"I disagree," he said, his voice steady, eyes softening. "I think you could pull off anything."

Heat rushed to my cheeks, and I tried to cover it by teasing. "Including breaking and entering? Grand theft auto?"

He smirked. "Felonies excluded. But good try, counselor."

I pulled off the hat and started to put it back, but Jake took it and set it aside. He said he knew someone who would absolutely love it.

He gathered an armful, then another, until he could barely see around the pile of fabric he carried. He leaned sideways, trying to catch my smile, and I gave it to him—bright and unguarded. For once, I wasn't the lawyer, the mother, the woman clawing her way through bills and cases and expectations. For once, I was just Kelly.

"Fitting rooms are open," the saleswoman sang out, sweeping aside a curtain like it was a stage. "Whatever you don't love, we'll take back out. Whatever you love, we'll celebrate. There are chocolates by the mirror. Trying on clothes is like testing out versions of yourself—most fall flat, but every so often one feels like the doorway you were meant to walk through."

"Sold," I said, surprising myself. I sounded almost like the girl who used to dare Jake to climb fences and skip rocks past midnight.

I stepped into the fitting room, hung three pieces, and pulled the curtain halfway closed. "No peeking."

"I'm a gentleman," he said, settling into a velvet chair across from the room. "Mostly."

I took the first dress off the hanger. My hands trembled more than they should have. Why was I so nervous? This wasn't a courtroom. It was fabric, light, mirrors, and the gaze of a man who remembered me before the world had worn me thin.

"Okay," I called, tugging the curtain aside with a game-show flourish. "Moment of truth."

Jake's mouth opened, then closed again, as if words had abandoned him.

I wore the hydrangea-blue wrap dress. Simple, soft, with a waist tie that whispered rather than shouted. The fabric caught the light, and in the mirror, I saw my eyes flash a color I'd forgotten they could be—lake water kissed by the sun.

"Well?" I asked, angling my shoulders like I didn't already know. But I did. I felt it, the weight of his gaze, the unspoken prayer tucked in the silence between us.

"Thumbs up," he finally said, his voice rougher than before. "Actually, two thumbs up. Way up! Off the charts. Ten Billy Oceans out of ten."

I laughed, relief rolling down my spine like a release I hadn't known I needed. I smoothed the waist tie, studied my reflection in the mirror, and tilted my chin. "It's . . . pretty."

"You're the girl who never lost her spark," he said softly. "The you who still looks up at the night sky in wonder. The you who whispers wishes to the stars when you think no one's listening."

I froze. My eyes lifted to the mirror, caught his reflection in mine. He meant it. I could feel it in the way the words settled into me—not flattery, but truth. A truth I'd forgotten to believe.

Something stirred in me, deeper than affection, older than nostalgia. A whisper, the kind that sounded like faith. Like God reminding me that He restores what's been lost, even the hidden corners of a woman's heart.

I ducked back behind the curtain with a nervous laugh that was half gratitude, half surrender.

"Good start?" I heard the saleswoman whisper to Jake.

"Great start," he murmured. "Possibly dangerous."

I closed my eyes against the fabric, smiled, and let myself believe in goodness to come. Then I got an idea. Instead of changing, I darted out of the dressing room and moved toward the men's clothing section.

The moment Jake realized what I was up to, his eyes narrowed.

"Oh no," he said, voice low and certain. "Absolutely not."

I grinned and plucked a short-sleeve linen shirt from the rack anyway, a soft gray that I knew would deepen the color of his eyes. "You're not above the law. Fair is fair."

The saleswoman nearly clapped her hands in delight. She swooped in with a pair of tan chinos and a woven belt, brandishing them like treasure she'd rescued from some forgotten corner. "These will pair beautifully. And hats," she added, eyes twinkling. "We have very good hats."

"I don't wear hats," Jake protested—right before she placed a straw fedora in his hands. Navy ribbon, crown perfect.

I rose on tiptoe and set it on his head before he could argue. My fingers brushed his temple, barely a touch, but enough to make me feel it in my own breath. My pulse stumbled. "You do now."

His mouth quirked. "How do I look?"

"Like a man who gives very generous boat tours," I said, tilting my head, pretending to study him. "Or maybe the kind who bottles his own artisanal honey."

He pulled the fedora off with exaggerated care and returned it to the rack. "I am never wearing that again."

I shrugged, a smile playing on my lips. "We'll see."

I pressed the shirt and chinos into his hands before he could object further, and for once, he didn't resist. A few minutes later, he emerged from the men's fitting room. My eyes flicked down, then up again, and my breath hitched. He looked . . . lighter. Not younger. Not someone else entirely. Just less weighed down.

"Well?" he asked, his voice a little too casual.

I let my smile take its time. "Twelve Billy Oceans out of ten."

The corners of his mouth curved, and I realized I'd given something away—how much I liked seeing him this way, unburdened.

We tried more. A navy polo that made him look like a reluctant golfer. A pale blue button-down that made him look like every promise he'd ever kept. Each one became its own joke, its own small memory, until we were both laughing.

Then came another hat. A baseball cap this time, fern logo stitched on the side. He groaned, but I was already up, close enough to tug the brim so it shadowed his eyes. "There," I whispered, quieter than I meant. "Perfect."

For one heartbeat, the whole boutique hushed. His breath slowed. Mine did too.

We moved to accessories. Sunglasses first. Jake chose aviators so absurd they practically required a pilot's license. I picked cat-eyes dramatic enough to make me look like a French film star. We practiced paparazzi faces in the mirror until one of the older women down the row was laughing so hard she had to wipe her eyes.

"Runway," I challenged, grinning. "Loser buys coffee."

Jake accepted it as if it were the Olympics. With the fedora back on his head, he strutted down the aisle, turned with a bow, and the whole fitting room applauded. I nearly cried from laughing. Then it was my turn.

Cat-eyes. A floppy sunhat big enough to double as a patio umbrella. A gauzy scarf in sunrise pink. I walked, not silly, not overdone, but like I wanted—for one sliver of a moment—to believe the air liked me. That maybe God hadn't forgotten the girl He made me to be.

Jake clapped like a fool, and the saleswoman dabbed at her eyes. "You two are my new favorite show." And both of them insisted I wear the blue dress now, along with a new pair of calf-high leather boots to match.

By the time we were done, the pile at the counter was ridiculous: a cream sweater, a black dress, the miracle jeans, the skirt, the green blouse, and the tags for the dress and boots I had on. The pretty straw hat. Jake's linen shirt and chinos too. I reached for my wallet out of habit, but he touched my hand lightly.

"Hey," he said, soft enough for just me. "I meant it. Today's on me."

The defense rose like muscle memory. I wanted to argue, to insist, to keep my balance sheet clean.

Jake's eyes fixed on mine. "This isn't a rescue. It's a gift. A friend giving a friend a good day."

His words caught in my chest.

I exhaled, shoulders easing. "Okay," I whispered. "But next time, coffee's on me."

"Deal."

The saleswoman wrapped everything in tissue that whispered like leaves. Jake carried the bags, ignoring my protests, and when we stepped back onto the sidewalk, the sun had turned golden, brushing the street in honey.

I looked up at him, heart unsteady. "Thank you," I said. And I meant it—not just for the clothes, or the laughter, or the chocolate by the mirror, but for seeing me.

"You're welcome," he said, just as honest.

And then, with that same grin that used to undo me when we were teenagers, he asked, "Ready for stop number two?"

My mouth curved, wary and curious all at once. "There's a stop number two?"

"There might be a stop number three," Jake said, voice casual, as if we were just running errands on a Saturday morning instead of . . . whatever this was becoming. "But only if you ace stop number two."

"I have questions," I told him as I climbed back into the truck, the skirt of my new dress brushing against my knees.

"And I have evasive answers," he shot back, sliding behind the wheel.

The engine hummed to life, and the speakers picked up somewhere mid-chorus on another eighties favorite. I couldn't even place the song because the sound of my own laughter drowned it out. It was an easy, unguarded laugh I hadn't heard from myself in far too long. And by the way Jake glanced over, that laugh did something to him too.

We merged into traffic, weaving past cafés with chalkboard

menus and corner shops spilling with flowers. Boise's sky stretched endless and blue.

"Can I ask you something?" I said, watching a cyclist dart between cars, his red jacket flashing like a cardinal.

"Shoot."

I folded my hands in my lap, tracing a nail over the hem of my skirt. "Why today?" My voice was steady, but my chest beat against the question. I wasn't suspicious. Just . . . curious.

He kept his eyes on the road, but his tone softened. "Because you've been holding everything for so long. And I wanted you to set it down, even if it was just for a minute. Because you kept telling me you were fine, and all I heard was how tired you were. And because—" He cut a glance my way. "Because you deserve good."

The words burrowed deep, reaching the parts of me that still ached from disappointment, from betrayal, from holding up a house on shoulders never meant to carry everything alone.

My eyes blurred, so I turned toward the window, letting the wind dry what it could. A mural bloomed across the brick we passed—wildflowers twisting into constellations.

Jake didn't press, didn't fill the silence.

At the next stoplight, the breeze had scattered my hair across my cheek. He reached up instinctively, then stopped midair, lowering his hand to the console instead.

"Hungry?" he asked when the light turned green.

"Starving," I admitted, pressing my hand to my stomach with mock drama. "I feel like I burned five thousand calories trying on jeans."

"Science confirms," he said solemnly. "Fashion is cardio."

We detoured to a café where the menu was scrawled in chalk, the air thick with the scent of espresso and warm bread. We carried iced coffees, sandwiches, and cookies back to the truck, where we ate with the windows down, elbows bumping as we unwrapped paper.

He stole my pickles without asking. I stole the last of his cookie without shame.

"It's fair," I said, licking sugar from my thumb. "It's a perk of being the one you're spoiling."

He smiled, brushing crumbs off his jeans.

I leaned back into the seat, closing my eyes as the sun brushed warm across my face. And for ten perfect seconds, I let myself rest there. When I opened my eyes again, Jake was watching me. He didn't look away, and neither did I.

I pushed my wrapper away and leaned back in my seat, my new boots pinching just a little at the toes. My dress still smelled faintly of cedar and tissue paper from the boutique.

I laughed softly, shaking my head. "Well, that was very unexpected. I haven't had a day like this in . . . ever. I don't know how to thank you."

Jake leaned on the console, elbows braced, that steady grin tugging at his mouth like he'd been waiting for this moment. "It's not over yet."

I blinked. "What do you mean, *not over*?"

"I told you there might be a stop number three, didn't I?" He pulled out his phone, the screen glowing between us. Two bold words stared back at me, almost unreal in their brightness.

I gasped and snatched the phone out of his hand. "What?! No way!" My heart slammed into my ribs. My fingers shook.

Def Leppard. *Third row. Tonight.*

"You got us tickets?!" I nearly shouted, earning a glance from the couple in the car next to us. "I can't believe this. Jake, Def Leppard is the balm to my pain."

He chuckled, leaning back like a man entirely too pleased with himself. "I guess I made the right call, then."

"The right call?" I stared at him, then back at the glowing screen, unable to stop grinning. "Jake, I've wanted to see them for years. Years."

His smile deepened, warm and steady, and I swear the world narrowed until it was just me and him and this ridiculous gift that was somehow more than a concert—it was being seen, remembered.

I pressed the phone against my chest, unable to wipe the grin off my face. But then my eyes darted back down, scanning the fine print. And that's when my stomach dropped.

"Uh . . . Jake?"

"Yeah?" he asked, leaning forward like he already knew what was coming.

"The concert starts in two hours."

"Yep." His grin widened, cocky and secretive all at once.

"In Vegas."

"Yep."

I froze, blinking at him, waiting for the punchline. "Jake! Vegas is what—seven hours away? Eight? There's no way we're making it."

His eyes sparkled with that boyish mischief I remembered from summers by the lake, the same look he'd given me before daring me to climb the water tower.

"Come on," he said, crumpling his sandwich wrapper and shoving it into the bag before pushing open his door. "I'll show you."

I hesitated, my brows furrowing. Every rational part of my brain shouted that this was insane, impossible, utterly impractical. But maybe I was tired of being rational. His hand was right there, warm and open and waiting.

So I took it.

Kelly
Boise, Idaho

THE SKY WAS MELTING. THAT WAS

the first ridiculous thought that flitted through my head as Jake's truck rolled through the security gate and out onto a stretch of tarmac. The sunset had gone from gold to honey to something close to apricot. The air smelled like hot asphalt and kerosene, and the wind out there was louder, sharper. It rushed past my open window in a way that made the whole world feel like it was leaning forward with us.

We rounded a bend and there it was: a sleek white jet idling by a private hangar, steps already lowered as if it had been waiting its whole life for us to arrive. The sight knocked the air straight out of me. My mouth actually opened. I wasn't a person who stood around gaping at things, but right then, my jaw forgot it had a hinge.

"Jake?" I said. "Is this real?"

He parked, cut the engine, and turned to me with a grin that was half boy, half man-who-had-decided-on-delight. "What can I say?" He hopped out and came around to open my door like it was a regular Saturday errand. "I hate traffic."

I sat there for another heartbeat. A private jet. For a concert. For me.

When I finally slid out of the truck, the heat of the tarmac came up through my new boots. Jake offered his arm without a word, an old-fashioned gesture that would have made me roll my eyes twenty-four hours earlier. That night, I slipped my hand into the crook of his elbow as if it had always been our choreography.

I didn't know if I was allowed to enjoy this. That was the truth humming beneath my ribs. It was too much. Too generous. Too . . . not me. But when the plane's engine flared, something inside me loosened, just a notch.

We climbed the steps. The cabin was small and gleaming with seats the color of toasted almonds. A smiling attendant in a neat ponytail took my tote and offered sparkling water. My brain was still trying to install new software labeled *What Is Your Life Right Now?*

Jake leaned close. "You okay?"

"I don't know," I whispered back, and then laughed because it was true. "Yes. No. Maybe."

"Good," he said, as if indecision was the correct answer. "That means it's an adventure."

We buckled in. The door was sealed. A tremor shivered through the fuselage, and then the jet pressed me into the seat. Soon, runway stripes became a blur, and Boise dropped away.

I didn't know when my hand found his. I only realized it because his fingers tightened gently. I let myself hold on until the plane leveled and the earth became a quiet geometry of patchwork fields and a silver slip of highway.

"You didn't have to do this." I stared straight ahead so I wouldn't drown in the way he was looking at me.

"I know," he said. "I wanted to."

He said it so simply, but still I didn't look at him. Instead, I tilted my head and let the curve of the window fill my vision. The sun sank lower. It caught the wing in a blade of light.

Somewhere over Nevada, the attendant brought us a tray of mixed nuts and two tiny bottles of ginger ale. We clinked them like twelve-year-olds. The whole thing was absurd. It was wonderful. It was both. Maybe that was the point. Seventeen-year-old Kelly never would have believed this.

When we touched down, Vegas lit up the night with electric

signs and glowing promises. The car hired by someone-who-wasn't-me materialized at the curb and whisked us away. We drove down neon canyons, past people in all manner of dress and undress. I felt heat rising to my cheeks as our car approached the arena.

"Ready?" Jake asked as the car slowed.

"Absolutely not," I said, which we both knew meant *yes, but this can't be happening.*

We were ushered through side-door security and down a long hallway. Joan Jett and Poison opened, and the sea of voices rose, joining in with their songs.

We pushed through the mob, pressed into the front, and found our seats—third row center, close enough to feel the wind from the amps. An excellent cover band was up next. When they finished their set, those who weren't already standing surged to their feet. The first chord of Def Leppard hit like a declaration.

I was singing before I realized I'd started, my voice joining ten thousand others. I was clapping, swaying, laughing like I hadn't laughed since before my life began to collapse in tidy, legal increments. I jumped at the end of the chorus, and my new boots joined me for the ride.

Jake sang and clapped beside me. When I dared glance over, I caught the curve of his mouth—astonished, almost—and the look in his eyes. I understood that look. He saw the seventeen-year-old who had scrawled band names in the margins of her notebooks and the fifty-year-old who hadn't let herself be reckless in a very long time. Jake liked them both.

I smiled and sang louder.

Song after song, the night built. At some point, Jake's shoulder brushed mine, and neither of us stepped away. When a ballad started, the lights turned to a field of stars, and I felt tears press behind my eyes. It was ridiculous to cry at a rock concert, but the emotions—all of them—refused to remain safely tucked away.

During a guitar solo, I leaned toward Jake. "Thank you," I shouted.

He cupped his ear like an older man, grinning.

I leaned closer. "Thank you!"

He nodded once. "You're welcome," he mouthed back. And then the chorus broke, and we were swallowed by it again.

By the time the last encore knocked the roof off, my throat was raw. Worse, my feet were a lost cause, and my face ached from smiling.

When the music died down, people stumbled toward the exits. They chatted as if they'd known each other for a decade. For a second, I felt wobbly because the world had gone from song to hallway too fast.

Jake steadied me with a hand at my elbow.

"You okay?"

I laughed too hard to be cool. "Define okay."

He glanced at his phone, then at a badge clipped to his pocket. He lifted one eyebrow, and I wasn't sure why.

Jake didn't say a word. He simply motioned me to follow him. So I did.

We separated from the crowd and found a door down the hall where a security guard was letting people through in small waves.

"One last surprise," he said, waggling his eyebrows with theatrical villainy. He tapped the badge. "Backstage passes. Meet-and-greet. Photos."

I stared at him. "You're kidding." I looked down at my dress as if it could answer for me. The hem was wrinkled from dancing. I was sure my lipstick had left the planet. "Oh my word. Do I look okay?"

"Better than okay."

And soon it was happening. We'd shuffled through like everyone else. We posed, smiled, and had a little banter about how I'd plastered their posters all over my bedroom walls in the eighties. Camera flashes left little ghosts in my vision.

Joe Elliott laughed, Rick Allen gave me a fist bump, and the camera continued to snap like we were cementing proof of a teenage dream finally coming true. But when we walked through the exit, a man in a headset lifted his clipboard and blocked our way down the hall.

"Just a moment. Can you wait here?"

The assistant's tone was polite but carried that unbending edge of authority.

Jake and I joined a small cluster by the wall, waiting. The hallway smelled of concrete, stale beer, and the faint sweetness of someone's lingering perfume. Posters from tours long past were tacked up like relics—screaming fonts and neon colors. My heart was still pounding from the music and from standing shoulder to shoulder with the band I'd once dreamed about instead of prom dates.

Jake's hand brushed mine. "You look like you had the best time," he said. "Which is exactly the point."

I smiled up at him, giddy and a little undone. The truth was, I hadn't felt this light in years.

The bouncer—a man built like a tree trunk—strode over with a clipboard. He looked at Jake first, then at me. Then back to Jake. "Are you with Kelly Richardson?" he asked.

Jake nodded, puzzled. "Yeah."

The bouncer's expression softened into something I couldn't quite read. "She's been invited to their after-party," he said, his gaze flicking toward me. Then, almost apologetically, to Jake: "Not you. Sorry, man."

"Oh." The word slipped out before I could filter it. Before I could tuck it into something composed and professional.

The door opened for a second—just long enough for laughter and bass notes to spill into the hall. The scent of beer and sweat intensified, then cut off again as the door thudded shut.

Beside me, Jake was quiet. Too quiet.

I turned to face him, and in the fluorescent hum of that concrete hallway, I watched a hundred possibilities flicker through his eyes. Would he tell me to go in without him? Brush it off like it didn't sting? Pretend this wasn't one more door that had been closed in his face?

But he didn't say any of that. He just held my gaze, his jaw set tight the way it used to when a ref made a bad call and he swallowed every word because his dad was watching from the stands.

And at that moment, I wanted to tell him—I didn't care about the after-party. I didn't care about the passes or the access. I cared about us, about the way he'd seen me all day, about the way he hadn't let me carry a single bag or a single burden alone.

The band I'd idolized in my youth was behind that door. But the man I couldn't stop thinking about—the one who made me feel seen again—was standing right here.

I swallowed. The door opened again, and this time a woman with a headset leaned out, scanning the small crowd for me.

It was surreal how fast the world could tilt. Fifteen minutes earlier, I had been one voice in a sea of nothing but song. Now people were saying my name, and I was supposed to decide what it meant to be wanted by a room that wasn't mine.

"Come on," the woman said, smiling. "They'd love to spend more time with you."

I looked at Jake. He did an admirable job of arranging his face into neutral. "Go," he said. "Seriously. 'Balm to your pain,' remember?"

Right. I had said that. I had.

His mouth tipped, self-deprecating.

I could have gone in. I could have been flattered and dazzled. I could also have left him in a hallway with the echo of a door in his ears and the taste of old wounds in his mouth.

What I wanted . . . surprised me.

"Thanks," I said to the woman with the headset. "Give me one second?"

She nodded, stepped back in, the door whispering shut behind her.

I turned to Jake. His eyes were steady on mine. He didn't ask, didn't push. He waited.

I stepped close enough that I could see the fleck of gold in his left iris that only showed up in certain light. "Ready?" I said lightly, tipping my head back in the direction of the parking garage.

"What?" His eyebrows jumped. "Don't you want to stay with the 'balm to your pain'?"

"Nah," I said, threading my fingers through his and tugging

him gently down the hallway. "They're not exactly what I'm looking for."

We made it five steps before we stopped, before he planted in place like he'd just remembered how to be stubborn.

"What are you looking for?" he asked quietly.

There was a beat where the world tilted again—this time toward something I recognized. His question hovered like a door cracked open to a room we weren't allowed to enter yet. My heart raced to the threshold and tripped. I gave in to the only sensible impulse I had left: I laughed. It sounded breathless and real.

"Food," I said, and watched the tension break across his face like a wave collapsing into foam.

"Food," he echoed, chuckling. "Best answer."

We left that place and got burgers in a paper bag big enough to serve a small army. We ate as the car drove us back to the airport. Grease ran down my wrist, and I fumbled for a napkin. Jake handed me one without looking, a muscle memory from a thousand years ago.

I stole two of his fries on principle. He pretended to be outraged and then slid the whole bag toward me like he'd planned it.

As we drove, the city was a kaleidoscope behind us. I was grateful that we were heading away from it for the night. I needed time to process all that had happened. The flight home was quiet in a content way.

By the time we reached my place, the moon had risen as an orb in the sky. The ivy on my bungalow looked almost silver in the light. Jake parked, and we carried in the bags from the boutique, along with another one containing extra burgers and fries.

Inside, my living room smelled like laundry detergent and the scented candles scattered around the room. I set the clothes on the arm of the couch. He deposited the food on the coffee table as if it were precious cargo.

I turned to him, unsure of how to say everything I felt. I decided a simple thanks would have to do.

"I don't know how I can ever thank you for today, Jake," I said. "It was . . . magical."

He studied me, as if committing this memory to a mental hard drive. "Good," he said. "You deserve some magic in your life."

We stood there, not quite touching. The air between us was charged with a hundred unsaid things.

As I looked at Jake, I saw it all—first crushes and notes and a kiss—*that kiss*—at the airport. The years we lost because life does what it does when you're not looking.

He stepped closer. "Kelly, I—" he began.

"Whatever you're about to say, Jake," I interrupted, my palm lifting, my voice trembling just enough to betray me. "Don't."

He stopped. Hurt flashed through his expression. Then he shook his head. "Three decades ago, you were mad at me for not speaking up when I should have," he said softly. "Now you're telling me not to talk about what's clearly going on between us?"

The way he said *three decades* took my breath. We weren't children playing forever. We were middle-aged people who knew exactly how expensive it was to be careless with hearts. I wanted to be brave. I wanted to be wise. I wanted both, and that's why I stepped back half a pace.

"This isn't an appropriate conversation," I said, and I hated that it sounded like we were in a courtroom instead of a living room.

"Why not?" His voice was quiet. Not a challenge. A request.

"Because you're my client." I held his gaze.

"I was your friend long before I was your client," he countered gently, echoing my life back to me. "And I'm not going to be your client forever."

"That's not the point," I said, and my throat tightened around the words I'd been swallowing all week. "Right now, you are. And the only thing that kept me going after my divorce—other than my kids—was my dream of making partner. And now I'm this close to making that happen, and you come in here and . . ."

"What?" His voice was barely above a whisper. He stepped in just enough that I could smell the faint cologne he wore and the salt of the fries we'd eaten and something that was just him.

I looked away. My eyes landed on the stack of files on my side table, the neat little life raft I'd built out of diligence and ambition.

"If I let this in—if I let *us* in—before it's time, I could lose both." My voice shook on the last word. Both. The thing I almost had and the thing I almost had again. The judge and jury inside me, ruthless as always, nodded in somber agreement.

"Don't shut me out, Kel," he said, and the nickname undid something small and central in me. "Talk to me."

I should have. I should have cracked the door and let him see the room where I kept the boxes labeled *Fear, Pride*, and *Worthy*. But the day was still inside me—the jet, the music, the hallway where I chose him. I was sweetly, dangerously tired. I didn't trust my yes. I didn't trust my no.

"I can't," I whispered. I made myself look up and say the rest. "You need to go."

"Kelly—"

"Please, Jake." I stepped back, and my shoulder caught the edge of the door. The knob was cool against my palm. "Just go."

The quiet between us wasn't empty. It was full of what he could say and what he couldn't. He watched me for a long heartbeat—eyes full of hurt and hope.

"Okay," he said softly. "Okay."

He turned. The door opened with a small sigh. He stepped outside, then paused, like he might say my name. He didn't. The door closed with the gentlest click I'd ever heard.

I stood there, hand still on the knob, listening like a cliché for the sound of his truck. The moment stretched thin.

After I heard him leave, I leaned my back against the door and slid down until I was a heap of new dress, tired feet, and a heart that was too full and too fragile.

I pressed my palms to my eyes and let the tears come. Not because I was broken. I cried because I was being put back together, and it hurt in all the places I hadn't realized were bruised.

I cried for the girl who believed that being perfect might finally make someone stay, and for the woman who learned she didn't have to earn belonging after all. I cried for the version of me who kept waiting to be chosen—first by Jake, then by Troy—and for the hollow ache of realizing I never truly was. I cried for every quiet compromise I had made just to feel wanted, and for the way I was only now discovering that joy doesn't come from being picked. It comes from being *whole.*

I cried for the way he had looked at me under concert lights and the way I had looked back, knowing exactly what I was saying without saying it. I cried for the line I drew that night and for the way he respected it, even though I could see it cut him.

When the sobs softened to hiccups, I pulled my knees up and rested my forehead on them. The living room was dim. In the quiet, I whispered the only prayer I trusted then, the one that didn't try to tell God how to fix anything: "Help." Just that.

Help me guard what needs guarding and open what could be opened.

Help me keep my word to myself and hear yours when it comes.

Help me know the difference between fear and wisdom.

Help me, please, not to miss the good in front of me because I was too busy protecting myself from the past.

I stood after a while, blowing my nose into a crumpled tissue and reaching for the glass of water I'd abandoned on the counter. Half the glass went down in a swallow, cool and clean. It washed away the tight ache in my throat.

I kicked off my boots, my toes sighing with relief against the cool floor.

The bungalow looked like a storm had passed through—paper bags slouched on chairs, ribbons curling like forgotten party favors, tissue spilling over edges in pale, crumpled waves. I bent to gather one, nudging another bag with my knee, and it toppled.

A small box slipped free, skittering across the hardwood before settling at my feet.

I froze.

The lid was pale, tied with a narrow ribbon. When I picked it up, the faint scent of cedar and paper clung to it, like the boutique itself had followed me home. I loosened the bow with careful fingers and lifted the lid.

Inside, nestled in soft white padding, were earrings—delicate forget-me-nots in silver and blue. I absolutely had not seen him sneak this onto the counter.

My breath caught. I touched one earring with the tip of my finger, and a slight shiver ran through me. My smile broke even as fresh tears welled, blurring the little flowers until they shimmered.

Because love—real love—was careful with the way it gave gifts. And maybe, I thought, just maybe, God was teaching me to be careful with the way I received them too.

I washed my face and stared at myself in the mirror. My eyes were red and my hair looked like it had danced under stadium lights, because it had. I looked like a woman who had lived a day. A whole day. A day that was too much and just enough.

In the bedroom, I sat on the edge of the bed and picked up the letter I'd found the night before—the one where a boy I used to love confessed that my words felt like home. I didn't open it. I didn't have to. I knew the lines by heart, and that night I needed a different kind of reminder.

I set the letter down and crawled under the covers, the big city far away, the hush of my own rooms settling back around me.

Before I switched off the lamp, my phone lit up with a notification. A text from Amy.

How was your day???

I considered sending the whole saga—airplanes, amps, that hallway where I chose loyalty over flattery, and the living room where I asked a good man to leave. Instead, I sent the smallest truth I could manage.

Big. Beautiful. Complicated. I'll call you tomorrow.

When the light clicked off, I closed my eyes—the echo of a chorus humming under my skin—and permitted myself to sleep without solving anything.

I turned onto my side and pulled the sheet up to my chin. The last picture that bloomed behind my eyes was ridiculous and perfect all at once: me in a blue dress under lights, his face lifted to mine, both of us singing a song we used to shout from the back seat of a car that had no business going as fast as it did. A lifetime ago. A breath ago. I smiled in the dark.

Kelly
Boise, Idaho

THE HIGHWAY UNSPOOLED LIKE A

ribbon beneath me, gray, gleaming, and endless. Morning clung to the hills in a watercolor wash of blue and apricot. Even through the vents, the air smelled like dust and pine and the ghost of the coffee I hadn't finished. My hands were steady on the wheel. My jaw wasn't.

I had told myself to sleep in, to let the night settle into its proper boxes: wonder, gratitude, ache. Instead, I'd been up at dawn, folding some outfits into a tote, watering the philodendron, and locking the door with a click that sounded too loud for my little bungalow.

Now Idaho slid past my windows in long, curving breaths. I drove past fences, fields, and the occasional barn painted the color of rust. The part of me that loved a plan tried to make sense of a drive with no destination. But I knew where I was going . . . sort of.

After I put enough miles behind me, I hit the speed dial button on my steering wheel. It rang twice before Janie picked up.

"Morning," she said, and I could hear her pouring coffee. "Why are you up so early? It's Sunday. Why are you calling on Sunday?"

"Janie," I said, too abruptly. "I need you to transfer Jake's case to a senior partner."

"What?" Something clattered—her mug, probably hitting the counter. "Why?"

Because I danced under concert lights with the man who used to be my whole world. Because a private jet can cross state lines, but it can't outrun your heart.

"Conflict of interest," I said, crisp, professional. "Personal and professional lines aren't as clear as they should be."

She was quiet for a beat, but then her words rushed out. "Did he do something? Did someone say something? Kelly, you've worked this case like your life depended on it. Mr. Alden and Mr. Langford are counting on you."

"I know." The road curved around a stand of firs, sunlight breaking through the branches. "I'll draft a transition memo today. I'll walk whoever takes it through everything—strategy, deadlines, quirks. But I can't be point anymore."

"You could," she said gently. "You're choosing not to."

"Yes." The word carried both relief and grief. Both belonged.

"Okay," she said, and the word opened between us like a parachute. "I'll talk to Alden. He's going to ask why a senior partner and not Langford."

"Because the hearing's in less than a week, and it needs someone with authority in the judge's chambers. Langford's brilliant, but optics matter right now. It has to be clean."

"Copy that." I could imagine her taking notes and planning my new reality in a series of emails. "Do you want me to say anything to . . . him?"

My throat closed. The view opened to the valley floor, a cabin's roof, and a silver ribbon of river winding away. "No. I'll reach out when it's appropriate."

"When it's appropriate," she echoed, her voice softer now. "Okay, I suppose I can't argue with that. Where are you, anyway?"

"Driving."

"To where?"

I glanced at the empty passenger seat, at the tote buckled in like a child. "I'll let you know when I find out."

Her laugh was kind, not mocking. "Text me when you stop. And, Kelly?"

"Yeah?"

"I'm proud of you," she said. "For drawing a line before someone else had to draw it for you."

The call clicked off. The road kept going. My chest loosened just enough to pull in a full lung of air.

Hours pressed and unspooled. The sky shifted, and I cycled through the radio, from classic rock to country, and then to a podcast about why we hoard our pain like treasure.

I passed a truck with a dog grinning into the wind. I passed a couple in a convertible holding hands across a console.

By early afternoon, pines thinned out, giving way to sandstone. I took the next exit for gas.

I was standing by the pump when I saw them: a little girl and her dad, hands swinging, her pigtails sloppy and *perfect,* her T-shirt stamped with tiny blue flowers. Forget-me-nots. The same color Jake had pressed into my palm. The same shade I'd worn in a dress while a song made us both teenagers again.

I faltered, barely a stutter-step, but enough to fumble the cap on my water. They didn't notice me. Why would they? The dad opened their van door with an absent pat to her head while she chattered about candy and dogs.

But the flowers . . . simple, five-petaled, a dot of yellow. A heart could mistake them for a sign.

By the time I reached Sedona, the cliffs were rising like cathedrals against a fading sky. I rolled down the window, letting the air—warm with sage and dust—wash over me. Idaho felt far away. So did the corner office—the brass ring I'd been chasing like it held the key to my worth.

In Sedona, nothing was square. Nothing polished. Later, after dropping my tote in the Airbnb, after lacing up sneakers and running a trail that burned my lungs and steadied my soul, I sat on a ridge and looked out over the desert. The sky was streaked with blush and umber, as if God had painted it and then smudged it with His thumb.

When I got back to the rental, I pulled my planner from the tote and drew a line down the middle. Two columns: Fear and Wisdom. I filled them until the words blurred. Then I added one more under Wisdom:

> — When the case is over, talk to
>   Jake. Face-to-face. No drama.
>   No escape routes. Tell him my
>   whole truth. Ask for his.

The page looked braver than I felt. But that's what faith was, wasn't it? Writing your future in bolder ink than your present could hold and then living your way into it.

I whispered a prayer into the dusk, three words I knew God always heard: "Help me, Lord." And then I let the stars have the rest.

Jake
Boise, Idaho

The kitchen was too quiet. The kind of quiet that pressed against a man, reminding him of everything missing. Jake leaned on the counter, phone pressed to his ear, waiting for the ring that always ended the same way—in voicemail.

"Hey, it's me," he said when the tone sounded. His voice was rougher than he meant it to be. "Just checking in . . . again. Call me back when you can, okay?"

He ended the call, set the phone face down on the counter, and stared at it like he could will it to buzz. It didn't. It hadn't for over a full day. It wasn't like Kelly not to answer, especially after the day they had spent together on Saturday.

The floor creaked. He looked up to see Rae and Chris

hovering in the doorway. Their faces mirrored each other—hesitant, concerned, like kids who'd been forced into adulthood too soon.

"Still no answer?" Rae asked gently, her dark hair falling over her shoulder.

Jake shook his head. "No. Not once."

Rae's expression softened. "We're sorry, Dad."

His brows lifted. "Really?"

She nodded and stepped closer. Chris hung back, hands shoved deep into his pockets, shoulders hunched. Rae nudged him with her elbow, urging him on.

Chris exhaled hard, staring at the floor before meeting Jake's eyes. "You were in a dark place for a long time. With Mom. With Grandma. You were . . . just getting through." His voice faltered. He glanced at Rae.

Rae picked it up, steady. "We can't remember the last time we saw you smile like you have lately. If Kelly's the reason for that . . ." She paused, her gaze locked on her father's. "Don't let her go."

Chris nodded, jaw tight. "I agree."

The words landed heavier than they expected. Jake felt his chest tighten, not from sorrow this time, but from something rarer—hope.

He looked between them. "Are you two giving me your blessing?"

Rae's lips curved, small but certain. "We want our dad back."

Chris moved forward, finally, and Jake pulled them both into his arms. His grip was firm, maybe too strong, but neither of them pulled away.

For the first time in too long, the silence in the kitchen wasn't empty. It was full of forgiveness, of loyalty, of something like faith. And maybe, just maybe, it carried the courage he needed to fight for what still mattered.

Jake
Boise, Idaho

THE POLISHED FLOORS OF THE

law firm clicked under Jake's shoes as he strode down the hallway. His reflection created a faint shimmer in the glass walls. He carried the weight of determination in his shoulders, a decision formed over restless nights and unanswered calls. He needed to see Kelly face-to-face. No more voicemails, no more waiting.

He stopped in front of her office door and knocked, his pulse thudding with a hope he didn't want to name.

The door stayed closed.

"Kelly?" he called, pushing down the edge of desperation in his tone.

Instead, Janie appeared from the far end of the hall, a stack of files balanced in her arms. She paused when she saw him, adjusting her grip as her expression shifted between recognition and discomfort.

"Mr. Forester?" she said, her voice polite but guarded.

Jake straightened. "Is Kelly here?"

Janie shifted the files to her other arm, the motion buying her a second before she answered. "No, she's not."

There was something too final about the way she said it. Not just an absence, but a door being shut.

Jake frowned, studying her. "Okay, well . . . can you tell her to call me when she gets back?"

He turned, already resigning himself to waiting, when Janie's voice stopped him.

"Actually, Mr. Forester—" She hesitated. "Didn't you get my email? Your case has been transferred to another attorney in our office."

Jake froze. He turned back slowly, eyes narrowing. "What? Why?"

"Ms. Richardson said there was a conflict of interest." Janie straightened a little, reciting what sounded like words she'd already practiced. "She thought a senior partner would be better suited to take over your custody hearing."

For a moment, Jake just stared at her, the words knocking the breath out of him. Kelly transferred his case without telling him.

Janie shifted again under his gaze, clearly uncomfortable.

"My understanding," she continued carefully, "is that nearly everything's been agreed upon, so it shouldn't drag on much longer?"

Jake blinked, dragging his thoughts back from where they'd gone spinning. "What? Oh, um . . . yeah. Thanks." His voice sounded hollow even to himself.

He turned again, this time more slowly, his feet dragging as if the floor had turned to sand. But behind him, Janie bit her lip harder, torn. And then, in a rush, the words burst out:

"She's not home, if that's where you're heading."

Jake stopped dead. Slowly, he pivoted back to face her, hope flaring through the fog like a match to kindling. His voice came out low, almost demanding.

"Where is she?"

Janie looked at him for a long moment, conflict written all over her face.

And Jake waited, his heart in his throat.

Jake
Boise, Idaho

His feet on the courthouse steps felt heavier than they should have. Jake tugged at his tie, loosening the knot at his throat until he could finally breathe. The late-morning sun glared against the pale stone façade, sharp and unflinching, like it wanted to remind him that nothing about this process had been easy.

His new lawyer—a silver-haired man in his early sixties with a steady handshake and the no-nonsense air of someone who'd seen every custody battle imaginable—clapped him once on the shoulder.

"Congratulations," he said, his voice brisk, final.

Jake nodded. "Thank you."

They exchanged a few more pleasantries before parting ways, the lawyer striding down the sidewalk while Jake lingered on the steps for a breath he didn't realize he'd been holding.

It was over.

Shared custody. Done. The months of tension, the endless paperwork, the depositions, the late nights when he'd wondered if he was doing right by his kids—it all ended here. He should have felt relief. And he did, somewhere deep down. But layered over it was something else, something heavier: the sharp awareness of who wasn't there to share it with him.

Jake slipped his phone from his pocket and scrolled to Amy's number. She picked up on the second ring, her voice warm, familiar.

"Hey, Jake. How'd it go?"

He walked toward the lot, weaving between people in suits and dresses, all of them scattering back into their own lives. "We agreed on shared custody," he said, the words tasting surreal. "It's over."

A pause, then a smile in her tone. "I'm glad to hear it."

Jake stopped by his truck, resting his hand on the roof, his reflection staring back from the glass. "I need to see her, Amy."

The line was quiet for a beat too long. Then Amy sighed. "She's pretty freaked out, Jake."

"I know," he said quickly, pressing his palm against the metal as if the steady weight could keep him grounded. "I know she's in Sedona, but her paralegal won't give me the address. Now—" He swallowed hard, the determination rising like heat from the pavement. "I'll drive through that whole town and knock on every door looking for her if I have to, but I'm hoping you'll help me out here."

Amy didn't answer right away. Jake could picture her, lips pursed, drumming her nails on something close, the way she always did in high school when she was torn.

"Come on, Ames," he pressed, his voice gentler now. "It was your butting in that got us into this mess. One more time can't hurt anything."

She let out another sigh, this one less resigned, more knowing. "I'll drop a pin."

A buzz lit up his phone a second later, the map app pulling up an address, a red dot glowing against the desert background.

Jake's throat tightened. "Thanks, Amy."

Her answer was quiet, but steady. "Go get her, Jake."

The line clicked dead, but her words stayed with him.

He shrugged out of his suit jacket, tossing it into the back seat with a carelessness that would have horrified his lawyer. Right now, none of that mattered. The tie came off next, shoved into his pocket as he scrolled for flights with fingers that shook with something that wasn't nerves—it was resolve.

Sedona.

He wasn't going to wait anymore.

Kelly
Sedona, Arizona

THE NIGHT IN SEDONA IS DARKER

than dark and brighter than bright all at once. Out here, away from the hum of traffic and the choke of city lights, the stars don't just scatter—they blaze. The Milky Way sweeps across the sky like a spilled river of diamonds, and there it is again: the North Star, brighter than ever, steady and unflinching.

I stepped off the porch of the Airbnb, hugging myself even though the air was warm. I took a second to stretch and then headed out for a walk. My lungs expanded like they hadn't all week, breathing in the crisp desert night. My eyes tilted upward, hungry.

And then it happened. The stars seemed to align. The North Star held its post, and the others fell almost perfectly into place around it. Almost.

A lump built in my throat. My chest ached. It felt like the universe was reminding me of something I didn't want to admit. And just like that, I was seventeen again.

Kelly
Eagle River, Alaska
May 1987

The hallway of Eagle River High stretched before me, lockers dented from years of teenage impatience. I clutched my books close to my chest, weaving through the swarm of students changing classes. My gaze lifted and there he was— Jake. Leaning against his locker like he owned the place, hair falling across his forehead in that careless way, grin crooked but true.

For half a second, his eyes met mine. Something flickered there, like he wanted to say something. My heart leapt— ridiculous, hopeful.

But then Bridgette slinked in, all lip gloss and laughter, looping her arm through his and tugging him toward her. He glanced at me again, guilt softening his smile, but it was too late. The moment was gone.

Hurt scorched through me. I looked away and walked faster, the books pressing hard against my ribs as if they could hold me together. Behind me, I knew he was watching. Regret was written in his silence. But regret doesn't erase what's real.

Later that day, I sat in a classroom, near the window, pretending to take notes while the teacher droned on. My pen moved, but the words didn't mean anything.

The bell rang, but I didn't move. Chairs scraped back. Voices rose. Students poured out until the room was empty. Empty, except for me. I was still staring, still lost.

"Kelly?" The teacher's voice cut in, gentle but firm. He was in his thirties, tie crooked, chalk dust smudging his sleeve. "Everything okay?"

I blinked, finally realizing the classroom had cleared. My cheeks burned. Hastily, I swiped at my eyes, gathering my books with clumsy hands. "Sorry. I didn't hear the bell—"

He held up a hand, stopping me. Concern softened his features. "I haven't seen Mr. Forester walking you to class recently. Did something happen between you two?"

I forced a laugh, but it cracked. "More like nothing ever did."

His brow furrowed. "Could've fooled me."

My throat tightened, and I gripped my books like armor. "It doesn't matter now. He's graduating next week and going to college out of state. I'll never see him again."

The teacher leaned back against his desk, considering me with a knowing half-smile. "You never know. People have a way of coming back into our lives when we least expect them."

I shook my head, frustration bubbling with the tears I wouldn't let fall. "But how do you know if they're the right one?"

He paused, eyes kind. "Trust me—you'll know." A beat. "Want my advice?"

I hesitated, then nodded.

"If the timing is right, you'll find your way back to each other."

Kelly
Sedona, Arizona

I blinked hard, dragging myself back to the present, back to this desert night and the stars that seemed to lean closer, as if they'd been listening.

The teacher's words echoed across decades, threading themselves into the ache in my chest: If the timing is right . . .

I wrapped my arms tighter around myself, staring at the North Star until my eyes stung. For so long, I'd been afraid of bad timing, of missed chances, of loving too much or too late.

But standing here, the sky pressing down with its impossible beauty, I couldn't help but wonder:

What if the timing *is* finally right?

I choked on the thought, shoved it down, and forced my legs to move. The run back to the Airbnb felt urgent, as if motion alone could keep the memories from catching me. My feet pounded the dirt path, lungs burning, arms pumping. But no matter how fast I went, my heart was still back there—seventeen again, waiting in the hall for him to speak.

Waiting for Jake.

By the time I reached the cottage, sweat cooled on my skin in the night air, but inside I was trembling. I bent over, hands on my knees, willing my breath to steady. The desert was hushed, save for the distant trill of crickets. Every shadow felt alive. Every memory pressed closer.

I leaned against the porch railing, trying to quiet the storm inside. The silence stretched, long and heavy, until—the crunch of gravel jolted me back.

Headlights swept across the yard, sharp and white against the red earth. My heart seized in my throat. The beam illuminated the edge of the Airbnb.

The car slowed, then stopped.

For a heartbeat, I couldn't move.

And then—him.

Jake stepped out, tall and steady, the years hanging on his frame but not dimming the way the air seemed to shift around him. He stood in the glow of the headlights, a man shaped by storms, by loss, by faith. Familiar. Unmistakable.

"Jake?" My voice cracked, thin and unbelieving. "What are you doing here?"

He looked at me as though time had folded in on itself—like all the years, the hurt, the distance had been nothing but a long road bringing him back to this very place. His eyes were steady, his jaw set, but his voice was rough with something rawer than resolve.

"Thirty-two years ago, I made the mistake of letting you go. I'm not doing that again."

The words cut through me, sharp and tender all at once. My knees wavered. My breath snagged. And then he was moving, crossing the gravel with the sure stride of a man who'd already decided.

When he reached me, his arms came around my shoulders.

I sank into them before my brain could form an objection. The world tilted, and the fight I'd been carrying in my chest dissolved like salt in rain.

And then his mouth found mine. Time stilled.

The kiss wasn't frantic, wasn't desperate. It was steady, claiming, reverent. His lips were warm, softer than memory, firmer than a dream. I felt the faint scrape of stubble against my skin, the heat of his breath mingling with mine, the faint taste of coffee lingering from a day that already felt a lifetime away.

My hands clutched the fabric of his shirt. I felt the beat of his heart there, hammering against my palms, strong and sure and so impossibly alive. His hand cupped the back of my head, fingers threading gently into my hair, holding me like I was both fragile and unbreakable.

The desert pressed in around us. The air smelled of juniper and dust. My whole body shook—not from fear, but from the enormity of it. From the way a single kiss could unravel decades of silence and stitch it all back together in one breath.

When we finally broke apart, my forehead rested against his, both of us gasping like swimmers who had waited too long to surface. My chest heaved. My eyes stung. His thumb brushed away a tear I hadn't even felt fall.

"Jake, I can't—"

"Why not?" His gaze searched mine, fierce and soft in the same moment. "I'm not married anymore. The divorce is final. And you're not my lawyer anymore either."

"That's not the problem," I whispered.

"Then what is?"

I stepped away from him and the dam inside me gave way. Words I'd held behind my careful smile rushed out, unfiltered, raw.

"You broke my heart, Jake. Long before my ex-husband did—and in much smaller, sharper pieces. I've never loved anyone the way I loved you. That night, when I saw you kissing Bridgette—"

His face crumpled, regret etching deep lines into him. His voice cut in, low and urgent.

"I was an idiot back then. I didn't know what I wanted. And when I finally figured it out, I didn't know how to say it. So when I saw you with Troy, I got jealous and did something stupid. The worst kind of stupid."

I shook my head, swallowing hard. "Jake. It's okay. You and me . . . maybe we just weren't meant to be."

But he stepped closer, eyes burning with something I couldn't turn away from. "What if we are? What if we just didn't realize it back then? What if this—" his hand swept between us, as if trying to catch the air itself—"is our second chance?"

Hope glimmered in his eyes, so bright it nearly undid me. I turned away, arms hugging myself, a fortress against his nearness. "But what if it's not?"

Gravel crunched under his boots as he came closer. "Why not? Things are different now. We're different now."

I whirled, anger spilling out of the ache. "Exactly! If it didn't work then—when we were young and free of all this baggage— how is it going to work now? With ten kids between us, with ex-spouses, with entire lives lived apart?"

He didn't flinch. His eyes held steady. "I don't know," he said quietly. "But isn't that part of the adventure?"

The word caught in me. Adventure. Once, long ago, that was what we'd promised each other without even saying it aloud.

Jake reached for my hand, wrapping it firmly in his. His voice softened, sure and trembling all at once.

"I've never felt so much peace in my life as I have these months with you, Kel. You're it for me. You always have been." He lifted our joined hands toward the sky. The stars burned like fire scattered across velvet, the North Star gleaming steady and true. "Everything points to you," he whispered.

My heart fractured and healed in the same breath. I wanted to resist, but the storm inside me met the calm in him and couldn't hold. He pressed his forehead to mine, eyes closed, steady as prayer.

"Let me love you again," he said. "Start this new life with me."

The last of my walls gave way. I wrapped my arms around him, clutching him like the years had been nothing but a pause. Our lips found each other again—slower now, but no less certain.

As the stars shimmered above, I knew this wasn't chance.

And in that quiet, I also realized I wasn't seventeen anymore. I wasn't a girl waiting in a hallway for a boy's words. I was a woman—worn, scarred, but still capable of being seen, still capable of being loved.

And for the first time in a long time, I let myself believe that maybe—just maybe—God had brought him back not to undo the past, but to redeem it.

Jake
Sedona, Arizona

The night stretched on like ribbon, hours unspooling in quiet grace. Jake couldn't help but smile as he and Kelly lay side by side on the narrow cottage bed, their heads sharing a single pillow. No barricades. No excuses. Just two souls who had circled each other for decades, finally allowed to rest in the same space.

Their shoes were abandoned near the door. The quilt was tangled around their legs, a nest of warmth and comfort. They were fully clothed, but it didn't matter. In fact, it was just right. The sound of her laughter—unguarded, bubbling into the dark— was more intimate than anything he'd known in years.

They talked until the small hours, voices low, weaving old memories with new confessions. She teased him about his devotion to Springsteen. He countered with her borderline obsession with Def Leppard. They laughed over high school pranks gone wrong—their favorite was when Troy spray- painted the mascot and Jake took the blame. And then, softer, they marveled at what time had stolen and what it had given— children, scars, a hard-won wisdom that only came with living long enough to feel regret and offer forgiveness.

At one point, Kelly laughed so hard she pressed her hand

to her chest, tears streaking down her face. Jake's heart caught. It was pure, unfiltered joy. He thought then, with an ache that humbled him, that if God never gave him another gift, hearing her laugh like that again would be enough.

Eventually, words drifted into silence. Not the kind that separated, but the kind that stitched people closer. Jake could feel the rhythm of her breathing, steady and sure, grounding him in ways he hadn't realized he still needed. For the first time in years, maybe decades, he felt at peace.

They fell asleep like that—faces close, hearts steady. Friends, yes. But with something more flickering at the edges, fragile as a candle flame waiting for air.

Morning arrived slowly, slipping through the thin curtains in pale ribbons of gold. Jake stirred first. For a while, he stayed still, drinking in the hush of the room, the faint birdsong outside, the unfamiliar sweetness of waking without weight pressing on his chest. Then he turned—and saw her.

Kelly had curled toward him in her sleep, her hair spilled across the pillow they shared. Her lips parted slightly, her face softened, unburdened. She looked younger like this, untouched by the heaviness she carried in the daylight. Jake's chest ached, not with longing but with reverence. He'd seen her fierce, seen her broken, seen her carry the world with nothing but grit. But this—watching her breathe in the quiet of morning—felt like the rarest gift.

Her lashes fluttered. Slowly, she stirred, eyes opening to find him already watching. For a heartbeat, they just looked at each other. Then her lips curved into a sleepy, breathtaking smile.

"Good morning," she whispered, voice husky from sleep.

Jake couldn't help the grin that spread across his face. He brushed his fingers lightly against hers, reverent, as though even this slight touch might scare the moment away. "Good morning, beautiful. Still planning on loading up the car and driving back with me in a few days? Or maybe it's me driving back with you?"

Her smile widened, soft and certain. "From now on, I plan on going everywhere with you, Forester."

The words sank deep, untying something knotted inside him. Relief, joy, maybe even redemption. He leaned in and kissed her softly, tenderly. Not hunger. Not urgency. Just promise. A vow written in touch.

When they parted, he reached to tuck a strand of hair behind her ear. His hand lingered, memorizing the shape of her, before he finally spoke, his voice low and gentle. "Before we go, there's someone here in Sedona I have to see."

Kelly tilted her head, curiosity glinting through the sleepy warmth of her gaze. "Really? Who?"

Jake hesitated. The answer pressed against his chest, heavy but certain. He couldn't keep it from her anymore, not after this.

He let out a slow breath, the weight and the hope tangling together. Then, with quiet resolve, he whispered the name.

✦ ✦ ✦

Kelly
Sedona, Arizona

The late sun poured over the parking lot in molten strokes, gilding even the cracked asphalt with grace. Jake pulled into a space near the edge, cut the engine, and let his hands rest heavy on the wheel. The low stucco walls and red-tile roof of the nursing home rose ahead of us, glowing under the Arizona sky.

I clutched the gift bag tighter, the tissue paper rustling like nerves in my hands. It wasn't just a visit. We both knew it. The air between us was weighted with something larger, something holy.

Jake's voice broke the stillness. "You ready?"

I turned, meeting his eyes. His shoulders looked steady, but I could feel the quake beneath, like the tremor of an unseen fault line. "Are you?"

The corner of his mouth tugged into something like a smile—wry and brave all at once. He opened his door. "Let's find out."

Inside, the halls smelled of antiseptic threaded with lavender lotion. Strange, but not unpleasant. Nurses moved in soft currents, their shoes squeaking faintly against polished floors, their voices hushed. An older man in a cardigan shuffled past with a walker; a young nurse bent low to hear him, smiling with the kind of patience that felt like love.

Jake strode with purpose, but I felt his pulse beating in the air between us, a rhythm I couldn't ignore. I matched his steps until we reached a corner room. He knocked once, then pushed open the door.

"Mom," Jake said, his voice reverent, almost boyish. "There's someone I'd like you to meet. Or re-meet." He glanced at me, his smile curving slow.

The sight stole my breath.

It was her. Propped against crisp pillows lay the woman I remembered—but altered.

The bag nearly slipped from my hand.

Time had drawn its map across her face, carving valleys where smoothness once lived. Her hair, pale silver, fanned softly over her shoulders. Her lips were faded, her body thinner, frailer. And yet—I still saw her. The way she'd once stood behind a beauty counter, perfectly put together, every detail deliberate. Immaculate. Confident. Magnetic.

And still—her smile. I'd seen that smile more recently too. *It was her.*

The same smile that had found me years ago when I was unraveling, when divorce still clung to me like a scarlet letter. She had stopped me then, lifted my chin, and told me I was worth fighting for. I'd pushed her wheelchair into the shade, and even then she'd carried herself with quiet dignity.

Now she looked fragile. But her presence filled the room.

The woman whose approval I had wanted all those years ago. The one whose words had carried me through more dark nights than I could count.

Jake's mother studied me, her eyes cloudy but searching. For a moment, I feared she wouldn't place me. Then recognition bloomed—fragile but certain. She lifted her hand, slow and trembling, but sure.

"Of course I remember," she whispered, her voice thin yet warm as woven thread. "How are you, dear?"

I moved closer, my heart pounding, my hand trembling as it closed around hers. "It's so good to see you again, Mrs. Forester." My voice cracked, betraying how much this moment meant.

Jake's gaze was on us, his chest rising like he could finally breathe.

"Mom," he said, voice thick. "You wanted to see me happy. Well . . . here it is." He looked at me then, eyes fierce and tender all at once. "You're seeing it."

Her lips curved. She squeezed my hand with surprising strength.

"My sweet girl," she said softly, her gaze shifting between us. "Are things making sense now?"

I nodded.

"It always seems to work that way with love."

The words landed like a blessing, like a benediction. My throat closed with tears. Jake swallowed hard, his shoulders trembling with unspoken gratitude.

I placed the gift bag on her lap and peeled back the tissue paper to reveal the pretty straw hat Jake had bought when we were at the boutique—wide-brimmed, its rust-colored ribbon fluttering as we pulled it out of the bag.

Her eyes lit. She pressed it against her head, girlish delight spilling from her lips. "Oh, it's beautiful. Just perfect for the garden."

Jake laughed, rough and tender, the sound of a man surprised by joy. I sat at her side, listening as her laughter blended with mine, threads of sound weaving something steady, something whole.

Through the window, Sedona's rocks glowed under the falling sun, gold burning into red. And in that room—in the weight of her blessing, in the fragile joy of her smile—I felt it at last.

Peace. Peace settled into my bones like it had been waiting all along.

The late sun slanted through the blinds, laying stripes of gold across the bed. Mrs. Forester tilted the hat on her head, ribbon sliding against her shoulders, and for a moment, she looked almost girlish again. Then her eyes softened, settling on me with something heavier.

"Kelly," she said, her voice catching. "I owe you an apology."

My throat tightened. "An apology?"

She nodded slowly, her frail hand still curled around mine. "Back then, the closer it came to Jake leaving home, the harder I was on you. I told myself I was protecting him. But the truth is—I was afraid."

Jake shifted beside me, his head bent as if he, too, had been waiting years for these words.

Mrs. Forester's gaze flicked toward him, then returned to me. "I've always been able to keep everything in order. My house. My work. My appearance. But I couldn't keep him under my thumb." Her voice broke on the words, but she pressed on, strong in her frailty. "At the time, I thought his love for you was pulling him away from me. That you were the reason he wanted to spread his wings."

Her eyes glistened. "But now I see—it wasn't you pushing him away. It was life calling him forward. Growing pains. Wings ready to fly. God made children that way, you know. He makes them love deeply and leave when it's time. I see that now."

The tears I'd been holding spilled over, sliding hot down my cheeks. Jake's hand came to rest lightly on my back, steady as a promise.

The room was quiet except for the hum of the air unit and the sound of my pulse in my ears. I bent, pressing her cool hand to my cheek. "I forgive you," I whispered.

Something softened in her face, a peace that made her look younger than she had a moment before. "Thank you," she breathed. "That means more than you'll ever know."

Jake exhaled, as though he'd been holding his breath since we walked through the door. He leaned down and kissed his mother's forehead. "We love you, Mom."

She smiled, her eyes closing for a moment under the weight of blessing fulfilled. "And I love you both. More than I ever managed to say."

Through the window, Sedona's cliffs burned with the last

fire of the day, shadows lengthening across the red earth. Inside that little room, surrounded by the scent of lavender lotion and the faint rustle of ribbon on a straw hat, something long broken had been made whole.

Jake
Sedona, Arizona

Jake slipped his arm beneath his mother's, steadying her as she shifted to the edge of the bed. She was lighter than he remembered, her bones fragile beneath his hand, but there was still a spark in her eyes, a determination that belonged to the woman who had raised him.

"Mom," he said gently, "how about some fresh air?"

She looked down at the wide-brimmed hat in her lap, her fingers brushing the ribbon with a quiet joy. "Yes," she whispered. "Let's take her out for a proper debut."

Kelly's eyes met his, soft and shining, and together they helped her rise. Slowly, carefully, Jake guided her into the wheelchair parked near the window. Kelly knelt to smooth the blanket over her lap, tucking it neatly around her legs before lifting the hat and setting it lightly on her head.

"There," Kelly said with a smile, adjusting the brim so it framed her face. "Perfect."

Mrs. Forester caught Kelly's hand in hers. "Thank you, dear. Not just for this—for everything." Her voice broke, but her smile didn't falter. "You've given me back my son."

The words nearly undid Jake, but he swallowed hard and bent to kiss her temple. "Come on, Mom," he said, his voice thick with emotion. "Let's show that garden what elegance looks like."

They wheeled her outside, into the courtyard where desert flowers stretched in bursts of crimson and gold. The air was cooler now, dusk settling its lavender hand over Sedona, the cliffs glowing like embers.

Mrs. Forester tilted her chin to the sky, the ribbon fluttering against her cheek. "Isn't it lovely?" she murmured, her face lifted toward the light.

Jake stood on one side. Kelly stood on the other. Their hands brushing against the chair, against each other. In that moment, with his mother smiling beneath the hat and the desert painted in evening fire, Jake felt something steady root deep inside him.

The cottage was quiet when they returned, the kind of quiet that felt like a blanket rather than an absence. Jake set his keys on the counter and let the hush sink in, the echo of his mother's words still stirring in his chest. Kelly trailed in behind him, setting her bag down with care, her face thoughtful.

For a while, neither of them spoke. The night pressed soft against the windows, and the scent of desert air clung to them— juniper, dust, and the faint sweetness of his mom's lavender lotion still on his hands. Jake leaned against the counter, arms folded, watching Kelly tuck a strand of hair behind her ear.

Kelly's eyes glistened. "That was beautiful, Jake. She gave us her blessing."

The word blessing filled the air like incense. Jake pushed away from the counter, moved closer until he could see the reflection of the lamplight in her eyes. "You know," he said, his voice roughened by honesty, "I think that's the first time in a long while I've felt . . . free. Like maybe it's not too late to build something new."

Her lips parted as if to speak, but no words came. Instead, Jake reached for her hand, careful, slow—like he was asking, not assuming. She let him take it. Their fingers laced naturally, like the years apart hadn't happened at all.

"Friends," she whispered, though the word trembled. "We're still just friends."

Jake smiled softly, pressing his thumb against her knuckle. "Friends. With the promise of more, when the time is right."

Kelly's shoulders eased, and for the first time all day, Jake heard her really laugh—a light, uncertain sound that melted into the quiet. They sank onto the couch side by side, her head resting against his shoulder, his hand still holding hers as the clock ticked gently in the background.

It wasn't fireworks. It wasn't a grand declaration. It was something simpler. Sweeter. The steady kind of beginning that grows roots before it blooms.

And as Jake sat there with her, the desert stars wheeling silently outside, he thought: Maybe this is what second chances really look like. Not the rush, not the blaze—but the quiet certainty of being where you're meant to be.

Kelly
Sedona, Arizona

"WE ARE GATHERED HERE TODAY

to join this man and this woman in holy matrimony."

The minister's voice floated into the September Sedona air, soft as silk against the red cliffs that rose around us, against a sky so wide and blue it felt borrowed from heaven itself.

I tried to focus, to listen line by line, but my eyes kept drifting to Jake. There he was, standing under an arch woven with forget-me-nots. The tiny blue blossoms gleamed like the stars we once traced with our fingers—his hand over mine, guiding me to constellations and promises we were too young to name. Cream linens rippled across the tables, napkins pinned with North Star holders that winked like they'd been waiting for this part of the story all along.

But the real beauty wasn't in the details. It was in Jake's smile—steadfast, tender, the kind of smile that said, "You're home now." And somehow, in the same breath, it made me feel seventeen again, dizzy with hope.

The rows of guests blurred into a watercolor backdrop—Ben and Amy whispering and laughing, Janie leaning toward Mr. Alden and making him chuckle with something she said, Jake's children lined up imperfectly but proudly.

Lauren sat near the aisle, dabbing her eyes, while Braxton and Alex flanked her like bookends. My boys were steady, protective, and already teasing her about crying before the ceremony had even started.

Lauren's husband Mike was missing from the row, but only because he'd promised to keep the kids happy at the hotel pool until the reception.

In the very front, a chair sat draped in tribute—Jake's mother's wheelchair, her pretty straw hat perched on top. The sight tugged tears to my eyes before I could stop them. It was as if she were with us, blessing this day the way only a mother could.

"Do you, Kelly, take Jake to be your lawfully wedded husband?"

Jake grinned at me, and for one suspended moment, time folded—the boy who once let me slip away, and the man who fought to find me again were one and the same. I grinned back, and it felt like forgiveness, like grace, like every fracture in me had been mended into something stronger.

And when I said, "I do," I meant it with my whole life—every scar, every healed place, every stitch of second chances God had woven into me.

The moment hung suspended, sacred, until the sharp pop of champagne broke the spell. Corks soared into the sky, laughter followed, and bubbles fizzed like joy released into the desert air.

* * *

Amy
Sedona, Arizona

Weddings make people weird. That was Amy's conclusion.

Because while Kelly stood up there glowing like she was on the cover of *Brides* magazine—all luminous and starry-eyed, with Jake looking at her like she'd just invented oxygen—she was trying very hard not to laugh-snort in the middle of holy matrimony.

Ben leaned close, muttering under his breath. "If he cries before the vows, I owe you twenty bucks."

"He's already misty," she whispered back. "Pay up."

Sure enough, Jake blinked furiously, pretending it was just desert dust and not emotions leaking out of his eyeballs. Amy pressed her lips together, trying not to giggle, but a little squeak slipped out anyway. Kelly shot her one of her patented I-heard-that looks from under her veil. Oops.

The minister's silky voice talked about covenant and forever, and all I could think was how surreal it was. Jake—the same Jake who had strummed his guitar near an Alaskan lake—was up here promising eternal devotion. And Kelly—her fierce, unflappable friend who once swore she'd rather cross-examine tax law than fall in love again—was looking at him like he hung the actual North Star.

Amy sighed, partly from sentiment, partly because her Spanx were cutting off circulation.

Then came the kiss. Oh, the kiss. It wasn't the demure, church-lady-approved kind. Nope. Jake dipped her like he'd been practicing for months, and Kelly's bouquet nearly went flying into the minister's face. The crowd erupted, cheering, clapping, whooping like it was a rock concert. Honestly, with all the Def Leppard songs queued for later, it basically was.

Ben leaned in again. "Think they'll notice if I sneak out for more champagne before the reception officially starts?"

"Yes," Amy hissed. "And also no—you should bring me one too."

When the recessional music kicked in, guests spilled into the aisle. Amy caught Kelly's eye as she walked past, her hand clasped in Jake's, their smiles blinding. And at that moment, she stopped teasing.

Because for all the jokes and the whispered bets, this was the real deal. Her best friend had found her way back to the boy who once made her heart cartwheel—and now, decades later, he was still making it flip.

Later, of course, she would corner her on the dance floor and demand all the details, probably while belting "Pour Some Sugar on Me" into a plastic flute of champagne.

But right then, as Sedona's cliffs burned gold in the late sun, Amy just clapped and cheered like everyone else. Because love, apparently, wasn't just for fairy tales. Sometimes it was for a girl from Eagle River who'd waited a very long time for her happy ending.

And she couldn't be any happier for her best friend.

Kelly
Sedona, Arizona

By the time the sun dipped low, the celebration had spilled into full bloom. Music blared—loud, shameless, pure '80s nostalgia—choruses shouted half in tune, glass after glass clinking. Jake caught my hand and spun me across the dance floor as if he'd been waiting over three decades to do it. My dress flared, his laughter tumbled into mine, and for one dazzling heartbeat, it felt like the cliffs themselves were clapping along— Sedona blazing gold behind us, love blazing brighter still.

I was catching my breath, sipping champagne, when a tap landed on my shoulder.

"Richardson," Mr. Alden said, sharp as ever in his suit, though flushed with warmth and wine. His eyes twinkled. "It was a beautiful wedding. Though I wouldn't expect anything less from you."

"Thank you for coming, Mr. Alden," I said.

He pressed an envelope into my hand. "A little something from me and Langford."

I blinked. "Thank you."

His gaze softened. "We were impressed with how you handled Jake's case. It takes integrity to know when to step away."

Warmth rushed to my cheeks. "That means a lot."

"That corner office still has your name on it," he said, voice deliberate. "But we'll talk after the honeymoon."

I almost laughed, breathless with surprise. "I . . . I don't know what to say."

"Say nothing. Just enjoy this night."

He disappeared into the crowd, leaving me reeling. Before I could even tuck the envelope away, Jake swept me off my feet, spinning me until I squealed.

"What was that about?" he asked, laughter tangled in his voice.

I held up the envelope. "A future."

He kissed me, quickly and sure. "You already are mine."

Later, when the music slowed and the stars began to pierce the sky, I noticed Rae sitting alone at a table. Her chin rested on her hand, her expression shadowed. Something tugged at me, gentle but insistent.

I slipped from Jake's arm and crossed to her. "Rae? Is everything all right?"

She shrugged, eyes down.

I pulled out the chair beside her. "Did something happen with your boyfriend?"

She shook her head. "No, it's not him."

"Then what?" I asked softly.

She hesitated, then whispered, "You like fancy things—shopping, makeup. And I don't. I'm scared we don't have anything in common. That you won't like me."

My heart cracked. I reached for her hand. "Oh, Rae. I've been scared too."

Her eyes lifted, startled. "You have?"

I nodded. "I keep wondering—what if you all don't like me?"

Her frown deepened, uncertainty swimming there.

I squeezed her hand. "But here's what I know: love is stronger than fear. I love your father very much. And I want to love all of you too—if you'll let me."

Her eyes brimmed, and when she nodded, we hugged—real, tight, no hesitation.

"There are two of my favorite girls."

Jake's voice wrapped around us. We looked up to find him grinning, hands on his hips.

"Mind if I steal the bride?"

Rae smiled, cheeks flushed. "Go for it, Dad."

I slipped back into his arms, my heart full. And as we swayed beneath the desert sky, stars flickering awake one by one, I knew fear would come again. But so would love. And love—always—would be stronger.

Kelly
Sedona, Arizona

The desert stretched endlessly before me, the sky a velvet canvas so black and so vast that it felt like it had been turned inside out, shaken until every star in the Northern Hemisphere tumbled loose.

I sat in the back of Jake's red pickup truck, skirts spilling around me like a tide of tulle, the hem of my wedding dress brushing the dusty tailgate. My shoes had been abandoned hours ago. My toes curled against the cool metal bed, the earth's pulse humming beneath me.

A bonfire crackled nearby, its flames throwing amber light across the sand, across the curve of Jake's jaw, across the fragile edges of everything we'd nearly lost.

He sat beside me, jacket tossed away, sleeves rolled to his forearms, guitar balanced against his knee. His fingers moved steady and sure, coaxing a melody I'd only heard in fragments until tonight. But here, under a cathedral of stars, the song was whole.

Not written for a stage. Not meant for radio. Written for me. For us.

The music wound itself around me, soft as a vow, strong as a tide. I closed my eyes and let it carry me—every note like water smoothing stone, every word like a thread stitching me back together.

> *I will.*
> *When everything else falls away, I will.*
> *When the years weigh heavily, when the*
> *nights feel long, when the world says*
> *it's too late—*
> *I will.*

When I opened my eyes, he was watching me. Steady. Tender. Sure.

The guitar fell quiet, but the song lingered, pulsing in the stillness between us.

I smiled through the ache in my chest. "You wrote me a promise."

He shrugged lightly, though his eyes gave him away—eyes that had been carrying this truth longer than either of us wanted to admit. "I wrote what I should've said a long time ago."

I leaned closer, my veil brushing his arm, and kissed him. A kiss that tasted of shadow and starlight, tears and laughter, heartbreak and healing. A kiss that gathered up all the years, all the ache, all the hope.

And in that moment, I knew. With every scar. With every healed fracture. With every second chance stitched into me—this was home.

Time slipped sideways. The desert blurred, and suddenly we weren't the bride and groom in the back of a pickup truck anymore. We were two kids in Eagle River again, hovering in that sacred breath before the one kiss that had to last us three decades. We hadn't known the wait would carve whole lifetimes into us . . . or that today proved it had all been worth it.

The years fell away. All that was left was the truth.

I had been finding my way back to him all along.

Above us, the stars burned infinite, eternal. And there, brighter than the rest, the North Star glowed—steady as a vow, constant as breath.

I pressed my forehead to his, whispering against the smile I couldn't hold back. "Turns out, there really is a design. A purpose to all of it."

He pulled me closer, his voice rough, reverent. "Yeah. It led me back to you."

The world dissolved into black, but love—as sure as the stars, as certain as breath—sang on.

Kelly
Boise, Idaho

BOXES LINED THE HALLWAY LIKE

a cardboard maze, each one labeled in my messy scrawl: Kitchen, Books, Garage, Kids' Room. Sunlight slanted through the big picture window, making stripes of gold across the hardwood floor—real hardwood, worn enough to feel like history but still sturdy enough for the future we were building.

The house still smelled like fresh paint and packing tape, but underneath that, there was something older, something warm. It didn't feel like my house or Jake's house. It felt like ours.

Somewhere down the hall, Sadie and Becca were arguing over whose room had the better closet. Laughter floated from the backyard where the younger ones had discovered the tire swing. It was chaos. Beautiful, noisy, ordinary chaos.

I crouched near a half-unpacked box in the living room, tugging out folded blankets. My hair was in a messy knot, leggings streaked with dust. The hem of my sweatshirt brushed the floor when I leaned forward to stack another pile.

Behind me, I heard Jake's low chuckle. "This box says *Miscellaneous*," he teased, lifting one off the stack. "Which is basically code for 'I gave up.'"

I grinned over my shoulder. "Don't judge me. We've moved a small army."

He set the box on the coffee table, the sleeves of his T-shirt hugging the muscles in his arms as he cut through the tape. "Then let's see what mysterious treasures we've got in here."

He dug past some dish towels, a set of wind chimes, and a stack of mismatched mugs before his fingers stilled. Slowly, he drew out a small velvet box, scuffed with time but still elegant.

I froze, breath catching. "What's that?"

He opened it with careful fingers. Inside lay his old class ring—the gold dulled with years, the engraving softened but still legible.

"I thought I lost this," he murmured. The sound of his voice was softer than the room, almost boyish in tone. "Guess it followed me here."

He turned toward me then, still crouched on the floor, the box balanced in his palm.

My throat tightened. "Jake . . ."

He shifted to sit cross-legged beside me, the kids' laughter still drifting in through the open back door. He held out the ring. "I know you're my wife now. I know we've already said our vows. But this—" He tapped the ring lightly. "This is where it should have started. I want you to have it."

I took it from him, my fingers brushing his. The gold was warm from his hand, but heavier than it should have been. Years lived. Years lost. Years found again.

Outside, one of the kids yelled for him, and his face lit up like sunlight through clouds. He squeezed my hand, pressing his forehead briefly to mine. "We're building something real, Kel. Something messy and beautiful. And I'm here forever."

I looked around at the boxes, the scattered shoes, the swing creaking in the yard. It wasn't a perfect house. But it was ours. It was home.

I held up the ring, catching the light from the window. "Looks like we both carried each other longer than we knew."

Jake's smile deepened. "Looks like."

Outside, the kids burst into laughter again, and for the first time, the sound didn't feel like an interruption. It felt like a soundtrack.

He reached over, brushing a stray curl from my cheek. "Come on," he said softly. "Let's get a little more unpacking done before the pizza shows up."

I laughed, wiping at my eyes. "Okay."

And right there, with boxes still stacked and the future still unwritten, we began. Not with a grand gesture. Not with a perfect picture. But with two rings, a house full of kids, and two people finally, completely home.

The LORD directs the steps of the godly. He delights in every detail of their lives.
Psalm 37:23 NLT

THE END

ACKNOWLEDGMENTS

Every book is a constellation of people whose talents, vision, and encouragement light the way. *As Sure As the Stars* would not exist without an extraordinary team behind it, and we are deeply grateful.

To Andrea Doering and Robyn Mulder—your editorial wisdom shaped this story with clarity, compassion, and depth. Thank you for your steady, thoughtful guidance.

To Nova McBee and Chelsea Bobulski—your remarkable screenplay work breathed cinematic life into this project long before the book was finished. Your storytelling instincts influenced every chapter.

To our producers, Guy and Amber Lia—your creative passion and unwavering belief in this story pushed it from possibility into reality. Thank you for dreaming boldly with us and championing every step.

To Epic PR—thank you for amplifying our message, connecting us with new audiences, and helping this story shine beyond the page.

To Colossal—your strategic guidance, branding insight, and behind-the-scenes expertise helped shape how this story meets the world. We are grateful for your partnership.

To America's Favorite Couple—your support, enthusiasm, and shared platform brought energy and visibility to this project. Thank you for celebrating love stories—especially those that get a second chance.

To Jonathan Shuerger—your publishing expertise steadied the ship and made complicated decisions feel simple. Thank you for your clarity and commitment.

To Roseanna White—your stunning cover design captured the heart of this story before a single page was turned. What a gift your artistry is.

To James Rubart and Mackenzie Koppa—your audiobook

performances brought warmth and authenticity to these characters. Hearing this story through you is a joy.

To Karen Lewis—thank you for shaping our website and social media presence with creativity, clarity, and excellence. You make everything look effortlessly beautiful.

To Janet Grant, Tricia's longtime agent and steady champion—thank you for your wisdom, encouragement, and belief. Your guidance behind the scenes made this journey possible.

A special thank-you to those whose real lives and relationships shaped the heart of this book:

To Cindy, Bryan's mom, whose love and influence helped form the man at the center of this story. You did a fantastic job raising the boy whom I could never forget.

To Debbie and Jerry, whose friendship, timing, and gentle nudges played a quiet but pivotal role in bringing two old hearts back into each other's orbit. Your presence helped this story come full circle.

To our husbands and families—thank you for the late-night brainstorming sessions, for grace during deadlines, and for believing in this story right alongside us. Your love gave us the space to create.

To our early readers, prayer partners, and the friends who simply asked, "How's the book coming?"—your encouragement carried us further than you know.

And finally, to *you*, the reader—thank you for stepping into this journey. Stories come alive when they find a heart to receive them, and we're deeply honored yours is one of them.